Brock,

DANGEROUS KISSES, GRUESOME BITES

ROBIN GOLDBLUM

keep away from wendigos!

Robin Goldblum

ISBN: 978-1-951191-00-9
Published by Of Ink & Pearls Publishing Co

Editor: Lindsey Teske
Interior Design: Lyubomyr Yatsyk
Author Headshot: Ann Beth Goldblum
Cover Designer: JD Cover Designs
Cover Photography: Straylight Photography
Cover Models: Sugey Cruz and Josh Kradz
Map Illustration: Danijel Vujanović

DEDICATION

I must thank Collinda Verhagen for planting the idea of a zombie-western story in my head. I was never much of a western fan, but it helped having influences like Brisco County, Jr, The Walking Dead, 28 Days Later and Cowboys and Aliens. I loved the similarities between the Native American cannibalistic Wendigo and the more modern zombie, so I figured they are probably different versions of the same monster.

Additional thanks go to my beta readers, Robyn Green, Jennifer Maniscola, Linda Roth, Gracie Bryan and all the others (you know who you are!) Thank you to Tiffany Cortese for holding both a drawing and video contest in her class for my book promotions. This book wouldn't have been nearly as good or promoted so well without my editor, Lindsey Teske. And, of course, thank you to my wonderful husband, Jeremy Burton, who supported me through the 5-year creation of this book despite working long hours, long driving commutes and three babies in three years (twins!)

MAP OF MORELY

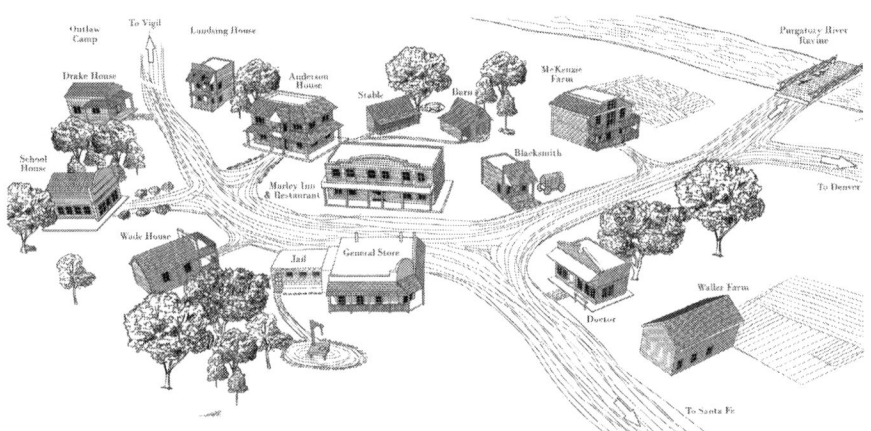

PROLOGUE

The farmhand opened his mouth to scream, but all that emerged were wet, hacking coughs. His chest tightened as fluid filled his lungs, and he passed in and out of consciousness as he gasped for air. A feverish fire burned through him. Thrashing around on his narrow bed, he knew he was going to die.

He hadn't told anyone he was sick, that he'd been bitten a few days earlier. Each day, the sickness got progressively worse. Now pain pulsed at the back of his head in sync with his thudding heart. Bile roiled in his stomach, and he'd snuck away to his space in the back of the barn. He regretted the stupid choice. He needed a doctor, not sleep.

The dog had been rabid. It was the only explanation. But did rabies come on this fast?

He'd been out in the back fields, gathering sheep that had strayed when the damned dog took off. In spite of her training, shouting did nothing to bring her back. She'd been hot on the trail of something in the wilderness. The boss had been angry when he'd broken the news about her loss, demanding he find her.

She'd come back the next day, limping on back leg and wounds covering much of her body. Dried blood matted the fur around her mouth. He'd started walking towards her as soon as she limped through the field, elated at her return. When she saw him, she laid down and whined.

Landing on his knees beside her, he'd hesitated to touch her. Her wounds appeared more severe than when he'd initially spotted her. Her

1

back leg wasn't just injured, it was mangled. The wounds on her abdomen looked like claw marks, one slit opening into her abdomen. Chunks of missing flesh lined her back.

His heart had broken at her pain. She'd basically been his dog in all but name, sharing his dinner and enjoying belly scratches every evening. Never had she suffered this terribly, even when he'd had to pull thorns from her paws or bind her broken ribs after the bull kicked her. As gently as possible, he'd attempted to slide his arms underneath her body to carry her back to the farm. She'd only groaned slightly at the movement.

As he'd tried to lift her, she'd screamed, high-pitched and horrible. She'd flailed, and he'd lost his grip on her. Her body crashed to the ground. The scream had changed into a savage growl, her head whipping back at him with teeth bared.

Instinct took over as he'd grabbed for his gun, knowing she was too far gone to save. Before he'd been able to shoot, her sharp canines had punctured through his thick pants and into the flesh of his calf.

He pulled the trigger. Blood seeped down his leg, mingling with hers as it soaked into the ground at his feet. Tears had welled in his eyes as he'd crumbled to the ground, running his hands through her thick fur, the life now deserted from her body.

He'd kept the entire episode a secret, burying her beyond the grazing fields. The punctures on his bruised calf bled some, but no one seemed to notice his limp. Unfortunately, the wound worsened, red lines spreading up and down his leg.

The farm he lived and worked on was nestled in the remote western territory of Colorado, miles away from the nearest settlement. The closest doctor lived in Morley, almost a day's journey there and back. For him, the distance to the farmhouse may as well have been as far away as the ocean.

He needed help. With an enormous effort, he heaved his body off the bed. Too weak from sickness, his legs couldn't support his weight, and he crashed to the floor. His chest spasmed, and coughs stole his breath. But this was his only chance for survival. Painfully, he crawled

2

out of the barn. The penned animals crowded along the wall as far from him as possible, as if sensing his impending doom.

Out in the night, he paused, a tiny bit of joy swelling his heart. The farmhouse lay ahead, just up the path. If he could just get close, he could wake someone up. Digging his nails into the dirt, he moved a little further.

A clawing pain raked through his chest. Blood-tinged fluid spurted out of his mouth as coughs exploded from his lungs. He tried to turn over onto his back but collapsed, trembling from the effort, his face flat in the dirt. Dark, thick blood flowed out of his nose. A seizure gripped him, and his body jerked and spasmed involuntarily. As the shaking slowed, so did his heart. He gasped for air one last time, and his eyes popped open, staring at nothing.

Dawn crept up on the horizon, and a rooster crowed to the morning sun. The body twitched, a jolt of electricity firing through the brain. The invader inside took control, sending tendrils of power through the dead nervous system. A door slammed nearby as the farmer's son stepped out, still yawning as he headed toward the barn for his morning chores. With an uncanny awareness of approaching life, the dead farmhand jerked up and stumbled on two unsteady legs towards the boy. His screams woke the entire house, bringing more victims to the monster.

HAPTER 1

Sheriff Bill Anderson stepped out of the sheriff's building. He breathed in the fresh morning air, running fingers through his curly, brown hair. His lanky frame stood tall and confident. The sun shone brightly on his clean-shaven face, and he smiled at all the signs of spring in full bloom surrounding him. Birds chirped as they flitted through town and pecked at the dirt road, and flowers blossomed on the trees. Despite heading into middle age, days like this made Bill feel giddy like a kid.

The building behind the sheriff served as the center of law enforcement for Morley, a small farming town in the southern Colorado territory. In a town as small and remote as Morley, they rarely needed law enforcement. Some might think it a boring job, but Bill preferred to think of it as keeping a happy peace.

Bill pulled open the door to the general store, which also served as the town's post office. The sheriff smiled as Isaac Smith bustled around the store, which contained everything from food to cloth to tools to seeds.

"Good morning, Sheriff! Hope you and the family are well." The gray-haired man plopped a sack of sugar onto a growing pile of items on the counter. He pulled a pencil from behind his ear and marked off a number in his registry pad. "Just got a huge shipment of provisions yesterday. We should be well stocked for the next couple months until the next supply wagon rolls through. I've got mail for you, if you don't mind waiting for me to finish sorting this order."

"Sure thing, Isaac. Mind if I help myself to your coffee?" Bill gestured to the coffee pot past the counter.

"It's the good stuff. Not like the swill the girls call coffee over at the inn." Isaac paused then asked, "Have you heard any news that they're sending more troops to deal with the Indian unrest?"

Bill shook his head as he reached for the coffee pot.

Isaac sighed. "I got a letter from my sister in Ohio. My nephew stayed in the Army after Lincoln's War ended five years ago and he's been sent West. She's so afraid he's going to be scalped."

Bill sipped his coffee, the welcome burn sliding down his throat. "Yes, I've seen some reports of fighting with the Indians, although mostly in Utah."

"It seems so far away from Morley, but I would hate for our trading agreement with the Apache to be put in jeopardy." Isaac shook his head, then checked the list. "Daniel, got a delivery for you to the McKenzie farm!"

The stock boy stuck his head through the doorway. "Oh, hi Sheriff! Didn't see you there." The slim young man, tiny next to Bill, came into the room pushing a wheelbarrow. He began loading the supplies, a wide smile on his face.

Isaac handed Bill a stack of papers. "Those are the new Wanted posters."

Bill flipped through them, glancing at the pictures and reward amounts. Cattle rustlers, bank robbers, fraud. Half of them were the same troublemakers he'd heard about with the last supply wagon. None of them came near Morley it seemed.

He stopped when he came upon a new set of pictures. Big letters advertised MURDER. Two hand-drawn faces looked back at him, names underneath. Jimmy Blythe's broad nose and scruffy beard sat atop a thick chest and thicker waist. Warren Olson's mean eyes were out of place with his boyish good looks. The paper went on to report that these men had murdered a cattle rancher and his wife just north of the town of Vigil and were thought to have kidnapped or killed the son, Alexander. A thousand-dollar reward hung over their heads. Along the bottom large letters stated, "DEAD OR ALIVE."

He would have to make sure Deputy Wade reviewed this. Vigil was not far from Morley, only a day's ride. Absentmindedly, Bill took the envelopes Isaac offered and shuffled towards the door, studying the faces on the poster.

"Hey Sheriff, one more thing." Isaac brought him back to reality. The older man licked his lips and blurted out, "I may have a problem with the Lansing farm. Zeke's tab is dangerously in the red. He never settled up for last year's seeds when harvest time came around, and now he's looking to add more credit since the supply wagon's come in. Jane's been giving me as much money as she can from teaching, which is the only reason I haven't cut them off yet. They haven't even replaced that horse they lost over the winter. But if I keep seeing him gambling away in the inn every night, I'm going to be forced to do it."

Frowning, Bill nodded. Ezekiel Lansing was becoming a real problem. Lucy Rodgers over at the inn had already complained about him causing issues with other patrons. The man was an angry drunk. It was also a badly kept secret that he often laid hands on his wife. "Thanks for the warning. Let me know before you close his tab." Bill waved and headed out the door.

Across the street, Lucy swept the wooden planks of the inn's porch. Her curly red hair was cut short and she wore baggy brown pants. Being the tough-as-nails inn owner, she refused to give the place up to any man or turn it into a brothel after her father died in a brawl. Most of the town accepted her running the business and her particular clothing choices because she had good food and drink. There were a few who still bullied her, but she could hold her own in any fight. The petite woman smiled as he strolled over.

"Good morning," he greeted her. "Any guests? Other than Roy, I mean."

"Actually, we do have a new one!" Lucy reported cheerfully. "A reporter from New York City doing a story on settlement life in the territories. His guide abandoned him when they got here, so he might be here longer than expected. He'll want to interview you and probably Deputy Wade, too. Maybe Jane about education out here."

6

"Sounds interesting." Bill had never been interviewed before and wasn't sure how interesting the readers in New York City would find Morley. He hoped nothing too intriguing happened while the reporter was visiting. "What's his name?"

"Mr. Harold Belmont."

A window on the second floor opened and a strawberry-blond head appeared. "Hi Sheriff!" Eighteen-year-old Abigail Rodgers didn't have quite the rebellious personality of her older sister, but she made up for it with biting sarcasm.

"Good day, Miss Rodgers."

Lucy squinted in the sun as she glared up at her sister. "Have you finished changing those sheets yet?"

Abigail rolled her eyes. "Working on it."

Bill grinned as she disappeared back inside.

After checking in at the other stores composing the main street of Morley, Bill went back to his building. He dropped the wanted posters and mail on the desk then put his feet up for a moment of relaxation before cleaning the guns and inventorying the ammunition.

The door slammed open and a short black man ran in, panting heavily. "Sheriff, help!"

Bill was out of the seat in the blink of an eye. "What's happened, Frank?"

"A body! There's a dead body in my field!"

Bill's eyebrows shot up. "Go wake Deputy Wade! I'll meet you out there!"

Frank nodded and ran around back while Bill headed to the farm. Frank Waller owned the pig farm on the eastern side of town. The farm generated a good profit, but some people didn't like having a black man producing more than them.

Frank's wife sat on her front porch. Esther Waller had chocolate brown skin and slanted eyes, making her look almost Egyptian. She appeared distressed. She had good reason.

"Is your boy in school?" Bill asked as he neared.

"Yes, sir."

"Good. Go inside until we make sure it's safe."

Bill drew his gun, prepared for anything as he walked carefully into the waist-high wheat field. About halfway across, the stench of rotting flesh struck his nose like a punch and he rocked back a step. He was fairly certain that the body had once been a man, but that was just guessing. It had been chewed up, ripped apart. Blood soaked into the ground and bones showed through patches of ragged tissue. Flies buzzed noisily around it.

Victor and Frank ran up behind him.

"What in tarnation happened?" Victor spat out as he covered his mouth and nose. Stubble covered the deputy's face and his thick black hair lay in a tangled mess. Victor Wade worked the night shift, but this warranted his attention, especially considering the annoying grumblings the man made about how boring Morley was. A dead body sure wasn't boring. "Where the hell's his head?"

"Over there." Bill pointed at a mangled mass a couple of yards away.

"Was it coyotes?" Frank asked.

Bill examined a large pack over to the side, a dismembered arm still attached to it. "Not sure. There are still some provisions here. I'd have thought coyotes would've finished those off, too. If this guy was able to carry around a pack this size, he probably wasn't old or sick. Coyotes don't usually bother healthy people who can fight back. Not unless they're rabid."

"Buzzards might've got to him," Frank offered.

"But they wouldn't have killed him," Bill countered.

"Then what would've done something like this?" Victor shot back.

Bill had no answer.

CHAPTER 2

Calvin Drake easily maneuvered his horse over the rocky ridge and into the expansive valley below. Three men on horseback waited patiently in the valley, plains grass waving gently around the horses' legs.

Calvin sat upon Sky, his Quarter horse. She wasn't young, almost sixteen years old, but he'd gotten her for a good price. He'd changed her name from Sassy to Sky because there was nothing sassy about this good-natured mare. Steady on long-distance travels, she could still gallop when needed. Completely devoted to Calvin, the horse seemed to enjoy his long periods of silence and never caused him grief.

The Jicarilla Apache men slid off their horses as Calvin approached. Nantan, the lead man with angular features, wore a plain band of cloth tied behind his head. The other two were younger and had no headbands. Calvin had learned when this arrangement first started that he wasn't dealing with the head of the tribe but one of his favored warriors. The younger ones were there as protection and pack mules.

Nantan greeted Sky first. With a smile on his face, he rubbed the long bridge of her nose and scratched behind her ears. She snorted happily and nudged at his hand. He chuckled, palming some sweet clover, which she munched greedily. Nantan patted Sky firmly on the neck, straightened, and turned to Calvin. The smile had disappeared, but merriment remained in his eyes.

Calvin never minded that Nantan always greeted the horse first. He didn't really care about social niceties. He'd always lived on the outskirts of society anyway. He had a feeling Sky was part of the reason the Apache had even allowed him to start trading with them. Her sweet, open personality won over the initially stoic men. However, it wasn't the only thing that opened trading.

Nantan gestured towards Calvin's pouch. Calvin nodded, knowing exactly what he wanted. Carefully, he pulled out the bottle of moonshine. It was his brother Martin's own brew. Calvin had slipped it in with the other goods at the beginning of their trading experience and the tribe had clamored for more. Nantan examined the bottle carefully, slipping off the lid and smelling the contents. Then he nodded to Calvin, signaling they were ready to commence with the rest of trading. Calvin pulled out another bag of goods.

The large sack contained a generous amount of coffee beans, a small bag of tobacco leaves and a ream of paper. After careful inspection of these goods, the Indians showed off their items for trade. An extremely large buffalo pelt, which must have come off a full-grown bull, had been tanned to a buttery softness, it's fur swaying as the breeze tickled it. A few pounds of buffalo meat were included, and Calvin's mouth watered at the thought of steak for Martin and himself that night. Several intricately designed baskets rounded out the offerings. They were very popular back east with people who clamored for hand-worked art from the western wilderness,

Calvin nodded, accepting the offered wares. He carefully rolled the pelt and secured that and the sack onto the back of his saddle. As he moved to mount Sky, a voice stopped him.

"Hold," Nantan said.

Calvin turned back. It was rare that they ever actually spoke. Luckily, Calvin was practically an expert at communicating with body language. When they first started, Nantan did reveal that he had a grasp of the English language, but it seemed like he didn't like using it.

"Warning. Wendigo invading land." His arm swept out in front of him, conveying all the lands around them.

"Wendigo?" Calvin didn't know this word.

Nantan looked down, trying to think of the appropriate English.

Then he looked back at Calvin and said, "Demons. Eat man flesh. Dangerous."

Calvin frowned. "There are demons that eat people invadin' our lands?"

"Yes. Like Big Owl, but small."

Calvin wasn't sure what to make of that, but he wasn't about to dismiss it off-handedly. Even though the native peoples tended to be superstitious, for them to actively warn him seemed greatly important.

"Thanks for the warnin'," Calvin said sincerely.

"Warn others," Nantan stressed.

"I will."

All four of them climbed back on to their respective horses, nodded farewell and Calvin turned in the opposite direction. As he rode back to town, his mind wandered back to the unexpected warning. While he didn't necessarily believe it, a shiver ran up his spine and the hair on the back of his neck stood up.

These thoughts lingered as he rode into town, tying Sky up outside the general store. Isaac, his partner and the man who sold the Indian goods to the supply wagons, was very pleased with the Apache goods, especially the huge buffalo pelt. He felt sure it would pull in a great price. Isaac handed over Calvin's share from the recent supply wagon, which Calvin pocketed without counting. The gray-haired old man was trustworthy.

Before he left, Calvin asked Isaac about the warning, feeling stupid for even bringing it up. "You ever hear of a Wendigo or Big Owl?"

Isaac shook his head. "Can't say I have, son. What are they?"

"The Indians said they were demons that eat human flesh. Said they were invading our land." Calvin wished he hadn't even mentioned it when Isaac's face registered surprise. "Probably just superstition," he mumbled, bolting out of the store.

As he rode to the run-down little house he shared with Martin, he counted his profits. It was a nice sum. An age-old daydream popped into his head. He imagined his house fixed up, a new pot in front of a blazing hearth, delicious smells drifting through the air as a woman with her back to him stirs delectable meal. The woman's hair used to be blond, like his mother's, but lately had shifted to brunette. He shook his head. It would take a lot more trading to achieve that dream.

He never let his brother know just how much he made from that arrangement but paid him generously for the moonshine. Calvin considered treating them both to supper down at the inn one of these nights. Lucy made a mean beef stew that tasted so good compared to their usual squirrel and rabbit meals. However, tonight they would feast on the two buffalo steaks he'd stashed away for them.

After putting Sky back in her pen and giving her a fresh carrot for her trouble, he headed to the Lansing farm. He wanted to find Martin and make sure the man was doing his job. It wasn't like there were so many jobs in this town, and Martin had already lost one job since they'd moved to Morley a three years ago. Calvin was sick of moving.

Calvin checked the fields and the chicken coop, but no Martin. He knew Martin wouldn't be up at the house, considering he avoided Zeke Lansing as much as possible. Even though Zeke was the boss, neither Drake brother could stand being around the arrogant sod. As he peeked at the chicken coop, he let out a breath of exasperation seeing the birds hadn't been fed yet. Incompetent fool. Calvin grabbed the feed and threw generous handfuls to the hungry birds.

Sticking his head into the barn, Calvin spat Martin's name in a harsh whisper. He hoped Zeke wasn't in there, but there was no way to know with that man's erratic behavior. A lot of the time Zeke would be passed out in one of his fields by this time of the day. Calvin listened but no sound came to him. Luckily no Zeke, but where the hell was Martin?

He tried again, louder this time. "Martin!"

A loud snort came from the loft, and Calvin stepped all the way into the barn. After a second, snoring could be heard clearly from above. Calvin rolled his eyes and made his way up the ladder.

Martin, soundly sleeping, lay curled in the fluffy hay. His mouth hung open and arms rested comfortably on his chest. There was a definite resemblance between the brothers but also noticeable differences. Compared to Calvin's lithe figure, Martin was built like a bulldog, right down to his underbite. Calvin also kept his blond hair somewhat shaggy, whereas Martin cut his very short. In contrast, a full beard graced Martin's face, but Calvin couldn't stand the itch of growing out his beard, so he shaved every few days.

Calvin kicked him in the shin.

Martin shot up. "I'm just checking the hay!"

Calvin glared at him, disgusted at his laziness.

"Damn it, little brother! I thought you was Zeke." Martin heaved himself off the floor, off-balance for a moment before settling into a solid stance.

"What the hell you doin' sleepin'? Don't you know you need this job? I am not movin' again!" Calvin resisted the urge to grab his brother and toss him from the hay loft.

"Calm down. Ya know Zeke don't really care what I do so long as I get everything done. 'Sides, I was getting up anyway. Bout time to milk old Bessie." He gave Calvin an infuriating smile as he climbed down the ladder.

Calvin gritted his teeth and followed.

"Oh yeah, forgot that you gotta fix the water pump over at the schoolhouse. Jane asked if you could come by today or tomorrow for it," Martin mentioned over his shoulder.

Calvin's stomach clenched at the mention of Jane Lansing's name. He didn't know why, but Zeke's wife twisted him into knots. He couldn't even talk to her. He knew the bastard treated her like dirt, and it made him want to punch the man repeatedly.

"Okay," Calvin acknowledged, giving no indication of his discomfort. Then he remembered the warning. "Hey, Martin, you ever hear of a wendigo?"

"Nope. What is that? An ugly whore?" Martin laughed at his own joke.

"It's a demon that eats human flesh. The Indians told me they're invadin' our lands."

"Well, shoot. That don't sound like a fun way to go."

13

CHAPTER 3

Deputy Victor Wade sat at the large desk in the sheriff's post, writing his notes about the mangled body found that morning on Frank Waller's farm. Bill would write a report to send to Denver, the nearest city with a large courthouse. Victor didn't do much writing, so he struggled with finding the right words.

Victor resented that there was only one desk. Even though it was technically supposed to be a communal desk, the entire atmosphere around it screamed Bill. He felt like a bystander, and it pissed him off. Bad enough that this crappy little town was usually so dull, but he didn't even merit enough to get his own desk.

He had to admit seeing that body was exciting. Nobody had any idea what would have done something like that. Probably really had been coyotes, even if they left behind the rations in the pack. He wished a person had done it, an outlaw that he could string up on the gallows outside of town. There hadn't been a hanging in Morley for more than a decade, not since those cattle rustlers murdered Connor McKenzie's farmhand. Victor had been a teenager then, but watching the former sheriff sentence those men and carry out their execution had been inspiring.

It irked him to no end when Bill had been made sheriff over him. They'd both been deputies under the former sheriff, and when the old man stepped down, the townsfolk had voted for Bill to succeed him. True, Bill was older, more level-headed and truly did give a damn for the people in this settlement. But, damn it, he wanted to be the one with the power of life and death.

His eyes went to the wanted posters hanging on the wall. If he were in charge, there'd be a lot more active pursuit of those lawbreakers in his territory. His eyes caught on the two murderers who'd raped that young girl. If he were in charge, they would pay with their lives.

The door squeaked open. He hoped it wasn't Bill because he sure as hell wasn't giving up the desk yet. His head jerked up, and he beheld a beautiful sight.

Martha Anderson pushed a baby carriage through the doorway. She adjusted the blanket around the sleeping baby and walked up to the edge of the desk. Her long brown hair, pulled up by an ivory clip with stylish curls spilling down, looked so silky. Her dress had a tight bodice buttoned up to her neck and a full skirt, as well as fancy lace around the neckline and wrists. Its bright-pink color contrasted sharply with the drab dresses typically worn around this town.

"Good day, Victor. Is my husband here?" Martha smiled sweetly.

At her pleasant voice, warmth flared in his body. "Sorry, he's still investigating that dead body over at the Waller farm. I think they were taking it over to Doc Silverstein's." He stood up from the desk.

"A horrible tragedy! The whole town is whispering about it. Was it someone we knew?" She fingered the lace at her collar.

Victor couldn't take his eyes off her long, graceful fingers manipulating the fine material. He licked his lips. "No, just a drifter. Had a large pack with him." He took two large steps toward her.

She backed up, and her eyes widened but kept her voice light. "I heard coyotes might've done it. Should we be worried about the children?"

He followed her as she backed into the wall. "Tommy should be all right. He's fifteen and always seems to be with the McKenzie youngsters. And I'm sure a good mother like you doesn't let baby Harry out of your sight. But I think you may want to keep a close eye on Simon. He and his friend Emily do tend to go exploring on their own a lot, don't they?" His hand came up and captured hers, stopping her from fiddling with the lace.

She inhaled sharply, and they stared at each other, their faces close together. Blinking, she looked away. "Victor, think of your wife… and my husband."

His fingers gripped her chin, pulling her eyes back to his. "Tell me you don't feel this…" he paused, finding the right words. "This connection between us." He moved closer, his body barely touching hers. "Kiss me," he commanded.

Her eyes widened as her lips pressed thin. In his mind, she wanted him, only resisting out of loyalty for Bill. He rubbed his thumb along her jaw, and her breath caught. He leaned in and held, waiting.

She trembled. Then the mounting tension broke as she hungrily kissed him. Her lips enchanted him, the taste of her intoxicating. Her hands slid up his chest, twisting in his shirt but, just as fast, firmly pushed him away.

"I can't!" Martha squirmed away from him. Baby Harry awoke from the sudden noise and cried out. She turned quickly, grabbed the baby carriage, and flew out the door. It banged shut behind her.

Victor touched his lips, relishing the memory of her passionate betrayal of Bill. He smiled, a chuckle escaping him. It bloomed into a full laugh, and he couldn't stop himself. Collapsing into the desk chair, great peals of laughter exploded from him, full of maliciousness.

Bill's desk and Bill's job weren't all Victor wanted to take.

CHAPTER 4

The afternoon slipped away as Calvin walked to the schoolhouse with his tools slung over his shoulder. A quaint building, just one room, that Jane Lansing made look friendly and inviting by keeping the white walls and red shutters freshly painted. She'd even painted little flowers on a twirling vine around the front door.

Calvin paused across the yard as the door opened and children ran out. Emily, Jane's daughter waved to him. He tentatively raised his hand back. The Simon, the sheriff's boy, grabbed her hand and they ran off.

He walked around the side of the school to the water pump. It had had problems before with the handle getting stuck, so Calvin tested it. Yep, same issue. He stood up and reached for his tools, but movement from the window caught his eye.

Jane. She hadn't yet seen him as she straightened up the desks, and he couldn't help but stare. Her brown hair was tied up in a severe bun, and freckles contrasted against her pale skin. Her plain dress didn't show a lot of skin, but was modest, an orange color with a cameo necklace around her neck. To him, it was perfect. It fit her in a way that hinted at her curves. She moved away from the students' desks and sat down at the teacher's desk in front to read something, concentrating hard. He watched, mesmerized, as she bit her bottom lip, pulling it into her mouth with her teeth. She must have read something amusing because a small smile slipped across her lips.

He realized he'd stood staring at her like an idiot for several minutes and mentally slapped himself. What the hell was wrong with him? This was his brother's boss's wife! He'd never been like this with a woman before. He pulled out his tools and got to work on the water pump handle.

Once the cool, clean well water flowed out, he washed his grimy hands and face. Running his fingers through his unkempt blond hair, he walked to the door of the schoolhouse. Pausing, he briefly pondered doing this job for free. Then he could avoid the awkwardness of seeing her. He all but turned into a mute around her, despite her being so nice and respectful to him. No, he resolved. Knowing her, she'd seek him out to pay him the money he was owed. Taking a deep breath, he pushed through the door.

She looked up and smiled brightly as he came in. "Water pump give you any trouble?"

He shook his head, his eyes darting around nervously.

"Good. Let me get you something. I have some nice eggs."

He nodded jerkily. As she turned away, his eyes flitted over a stack of books on a table beside him. Usually he wasn't interested in books since he couldn't read them. However, the top book had a picture of an Indian in full headdress on the cover. It looked a lot like Nantan, and he wondered if it mentioned anything about the wendigo. He opened the front cover, hoping for pictures inside.

"It's a book about Indian myths and legends."

He startled, not realizing she had come up so close to him.

"The kids love it, lots of stories from all the different tribes. You can borrow it if you want," she offered.

He closed the cover, stepping away from it and shaking his head.

"It's really okay. You can just bring it back whenever you're finished with it." She picked the book up and held it out.

He took another step away from her. His eyes went to her face for a brief second then became glued to the floor.

"Can you read, Calvin?" she questioned gently.

His cheeks burned, and he prayed he wasn't blushing. Forget the eggs. He glanced over his shoulder at the door, calculating how quickly he could bolt.

"I could teach you," she proposed.

He shook his head vigorously. Just thinking about stumbling over words, sounding like a fool in front of her, was more than he could bear.

"Okay. How about if I read it to you? You could come tomorrow after class ends," she suggested instead.

Whether it was the thought of spending time listening to her nice voice or the prospect of hearing stories from the Indians that so intrigued him, he was never sure. It didn't matter, because the word came out of him before he fully realized what he was doing. "Okay."

She blinked and her eyebrows rose. He wondered if she realized it was the first word he'd ever actually spoken to her.

Then her smile returned full force, brown eyes sparkling above her freckled nose. "Okay then."

CHAPTER 5

Lucy Rodgers strode to the schoolhouse at an easy pace, her boots digging into the dirt. Other than her sister Abigail, Jane was her closest friend and confidant. She enjoyed talking with Jane about all sorts of things, because the woman could be funny one moment, intuitive the next, and a great listener whenever she needed it. She also knew Jane always felt better unloading her difficulties with Zeke that she couldn't tell anyone else. Today, Lucy had a specific purpose for seeking out her friend.

The door to the schoolhouse opened. Lucy stopped, thinking Jane might be leaving earlier than normal. Calvin Drake rushed out in a hurry, his head down. He jumped a little as she neared him but nodded as he walked past her. Lucy turned and watched him follow the road toward his place.

Entering the building, she found Jane sitting at her desk, flipping through a large book. "Was that Calvin Drake I saw leaving?"

"Yes. The water pump handle was stuck again, so he fixed it," Jane said off-handedly.

"You gotta admit he is one fine-looking man. Especially when you watch him walking away." Lucy turned to the door, as if she was still able to watch him.

"Lucy!" Jane's mouth gapped open before giggling.

Lucy joined in. "Come on, admit it." She sat on the edge of the desk.

"Okay, I admit it. I doubt any woman wouldn't admit he's good looking, at least in a rough kind of way." Jane sobered and narrowed her eyes. "You know, you're both unattached. Maybe you could set your cap for him."

Lucy caught a brief frown flicker across Jane's face after the comment, but she decided to ignore it, laughing harder. "Oh, I wish! After he moved here, I used every feminine wile knew on him. I even put on a dress! He turned bright red, mumbled that he had to go feed his horse, and ran away. That man does not have eyes for me, not that many do. At least now that I've stopped trying to entice him, he can talk to me in full sentences."

"You're lucky. He won't talk to me at all. I mean, he just said his first word to me today. He acts like I'm trapping him in a corner. I don't think he likes me. I wonder if Zeke said something nasty to him." Jane sighed and leaned back, her shoulders drooping.

"I highly doubt anything your idiot husband could say would scare Calvin Drake off. Maybe he's infatuated with you." Lucy winked at her, hoping to bring her friend out of her sour thoughts.

Jane burst out laughing and shook her head. "You're kidding! Why would anyone ever have an infatuation with me? Especially a man like him who could have a pretty woman like you."

Lucy leaned over and rested her hand on Jane's arm. "I don't exactly dress and act like the kind of woman most men want. And I don't want to hear that kind of talk from you. Maybe your husband doesn't see it, but I know how beautiful you are, and maybe Calvin does, too."

"You're forgetting he won't even talk to me. Besides, Zeke would kill me if he ever thought there was another man."

Both of them looked away. Lucy grappled with her anger. It was likely Jane's statement was not an exaggeration.

Lucy spoke up. "How's it been with him lately?"

Jane sighed and rubbed her shoulder. "Worse than ever. He keeps grumbling about the planting not getting done, but I don't know what he's been doing out there in the fields all day! When I asked, he…lost his temper."

Lucy winced at the thought of the wicked bruise likely under Jane's dress. "You should leave him. Come stay with me. I always have more than enough rooms open for you and Emily."

"I know. I want to. I've fantasized about running away for so long. Did I ever tell you I tried once? Emily was a baby, crying through the night. He told me to shut her up or he'd shut her up. I got so scared, I scooped her up and left the house. I only made it as far as the schoolhouse when I realized I couldn't go. Outside of Morley, I had nothing, no one. I hung my head and went home.

"With his outbursts worsening of late, I've started preparing for it. But I couldn't stay with you. I couldn't stay in Morley. I'd have to run, because if he ever found me, he'd kill me. He's already made that promise." Jane's voice had dropped to a whisper, her hands clenched into fists in her lap.

"Bastard." Lucy gritted her teeth. "One day he's going to get what's coming to him, and you'll be free."

"I hope I'm alive to see that day."

"You will be." Lucy hoped she was right. She shifted her body and changed the topic. "Actually, there was a reason I came other than just gossiping about Calvin Drake."

"Yes?"

"I have a guest at the inn. A reporter from New York City, and he's writing a story about life out here in the territories. He even mentioned if he has a good enough story, he may write a book."

"It'll probably be a short book if it's just about Morley," Jane laughed.

Lucy swatted her on the shoulder. "Don't make fun. The man is a complete city boy, and I'm amazed he survived traveling from the train in Denver. He told me had the most awful guide and the man abandoned him here in Morley! So refined, but he's got spunk and dedication I admire. Since you're the schoolteacher here, he wants to interview you about education in Morley. What do you think?"

Jane sat up straighter, smiling at first but then frowning. "I'd like to, I just don't think Zeke would let me. I'm sorry. I think he's envious of me being a schoolteacher. Like it makes him look stupid or something. He's always threatening to burn down the schoolhouse, but we need the money to survive."

As Jane's face crumpled and tears welled in her eyes, Lucy's heart clenched. "I think I might be able to arrange it for you to have this interview with Zeke's permission. I'll give you both free dinner and, even though I'll probably regret it, two free beers as payment. There's no way he'll pass that up, especially since he's going to drink both beers anyway. That'll loosen him up enough."

Jane grinned, the sparkle returning to her eyes. "You're right. I'll do it!"

CHAPTER 6

The door to the sheriff's building opened and Deputy Victor Wade stepped outside. He blinked at the afternoon sun and yawned. Usually he'd be just getting up to take over in the evening. However, after all the excitement of the day and being off his normal routine, he decided to catch a few more hours of sleep. He licked his lips, the stolen moments with Bill's wife permeating his thoughts.

He whistled as he walked around the building and across the narrow path to his house. It had been built as the original sheriff's house, but had come to him when Bill married Martha, whose father had constructed them a huge house down the road. He briefly pondered the rich bastards who'd settled Morley. Jealousy stabbed him when comparing them to his poor parents. Only Connor MacKenzie remained of the originals, still rich. Martha's parents with her seven younger brothers and sisters had moved back east, disgusted with the limits of frontier living. He'd heard her older brother had settled in California. Jane's parents both died. Her father withered away after Jane's older brother had fallen to his death off the Purgatory River bridge, but her mother died in the dysentery outbreak. It left the farm to her idiot husband, Zeke. He'd spent most of the assets, leaving them worth almost nothing.

Unfortunately, his good mood didn't last past his front door. The furniture in the main room had been pulled out from the wall, scattered haphazardly through the middle of the room. A vase that sat on a side table was tipped over, a puddle of water on the floor, and the flowers ripped apart. Petals and leaves littered the sofa, chair and table.

Victor leaned over and picked up a frame that lay upside down on the floor. Shards of glass fell out as he turned over the only photograph he had of his parents; the cost had been too exorbitant for them to afford more than one when the traveling photographer had come through Morley. Both of them were dead now. Rage flowed through him as he stared at the large gash in the picture, running right through his mother's face. A growl rumbled in his throat as he smashed the photograph against the fireplace mantle it used to sit upon, breaking the frame. Yet, he didn't let go of it as he stomped to the kitchen on the other side of the room. Luckily, that area appeared to have been spared.

"Cora!" he bellowed.

The floorboards creaked from his left, in the bedroom. He knew exactly where she was.

"Cora!" he howled as he flung open the closed door. "You'd better get your ass out here and explain yourself!"

The bedroom was even worse than the main room. The mattress, flipped off the bed, lay lopsided against the frame. Every drawer of the small dresser hung open, clothing dangling out and scattered about the room. The heavy curtains he used to keep the sun out when he slept during the day lay crumpled on the floor. But no Cora.

Victor stalked over to the closet and yanked it open. A timid, blonde woman crouched in the corner of the small space, covered with winter clothes. She refused to look up at the man towering over her but kept her face buried in his thick winter coat. She shivered as he leaned down toward her.

"What did you do?" he hissed. Before Cora could give an answer, he grabbed her by the arm and hauled her out of the closet.

Tears filled Cora's red-rimmed blue eyes, which widened when Victor held the ripped picture in front of her.

"Did you do that? Can you replace that?" he screamed. He threw the picture across the room. "Why?" He slammed her hard into the wall.

Cora's voice rasped out in a whisper. "There were bugs."

Victor pursed his lips, analyzing that response.

Words rushed out of Cora. "I swear, there were bugs everywhere! Crawling through the furniture, on the walls, even in our clothes. They were trying to bite me, and I had to kill them all!"

Victor glanced around. There were no live or dead bugs to be seen anywhere. Sighing, he released his hold on her.

She fell to the floor and immediately began rummaging through the piles of clothing. "I swear it, Victor! I'll find those bugs I killed."

He watched as she frantically tried to find imaginary bug bodies. At one time, he'd been so madly in love with her, dazzled by her beautiful blond hair and her enchanting laugh. A few people had tried to warn him there was something off about her, but her parents were only too happy to marry her off to the young lawman-in-training. Her unusualness had been subtle in the beginning. Then came the joyful birth of their daughter, followed quickly by her devastating death from the cholera epidemic. Cora's condition worsened drastically after that.

As Cora continued rummaging around, Victor proceeded to replace the mattress on the bed. He straightened the disheveled sheets then stepped around his wife into the closet. He grabbed a box from the highest shelf, where she couldn't reach.

The lid came off and Cora became aware of him. Gasping, she leapt to her feet and tried to run for the door, but Victor caught her by the wrist and flung her onto the bed. Using his bulk to hold her thrashing body still, he removed the leather straps from the box and tied her down.

"Please, Victor, no! Don't bleed me again! I promise I'll be good! No, no, no!" She writhed and pulled at the restraints, tears pouring from her eyes.

"Shut up! You're not going anywhere 'til the Doc gets here."

She sobbed, blubbering spit all over herself.

As Victor looked down at his sniveling wife, the last little bit of sympathy he had for her flickered out.

CHAPTER 7

The sun slowly sank beyond the horizon, ending the long day in Morley. Stars winked into existence as Doctor Israel Silverstein trudged past the inn, smiling a little at the happy sound of someone winning at the card table. He strode past the seamstress's place and a little way down the road to his office. He glanced across the street at the smithy. The faint glow of the embers in the forge caught his eye, before stepping through his own front door. He inhaled, the faintest charred smell permeating his office was almost invisible to him.

Israel dropped his doctor's bag in the little office downstairs and trudged up the stairs to his apartment. He'd spent the day trying to bring the fever down on the Bauer baby and calm the anxious parents. Then Victor Wade had demanded he do another bleeding session on his wife. Not a pleasant way to end a rough day for either of them.

Victor had been the one initially to bring up the bloodletting. Israel resisted, seeing the practice as outdated and barbaric. But Victor pushed for it, demanding something be done as she became more unstable. Drugs being too expensive and hard to come by in the territories, Israel had relented. Cora had lain there quietly, determined to endure it, and Victor had been exuberant for weeks afterwards when it seemed like her symptoms had supposedly resolved. Israel suspected it was more from weakness than real correction.

This time had not been so agreeable. Cora's explosive episode floored Israel. The little house had been in shambles. Victor had tied her down, but she still struggled and screamed obscenities at him.

Victor kept apologizing, but it was no use. The whole experience weighed on Israel's soul.

He slumped down in his favorite chair and grabbed the most recent copy of The American Journal of the Medical Sciences, which had just come in on the supply wagon. Not long into his reading, the words blurred in front of his eyes and he slipped into sleep.

The nightmare was the same as always. At ten years old, he stood in the freezing Russian cold, watching his house burn down. His mother clutched him, weeping. When the roof collapsed, she'd fainted, but he still waited, still hoped his father would rush back out of the house with Israel's brother in his arms. Neither of them ever emerged.

A weak knock at his door downstairs startled him awake. He groaned as he lifted himself out of the chair, his joints stiff from falling asleep sitting up. "Oy gevalt, when did I get so old?" he asked himself, his Russian accent thicker with exhaustion. He smoothed his bushy mustache and headed downstairs.

He opened the door, expecting to see one of the townsfolk, either sick or anxious to get him to an ailing loved one. Yet, his porch was empty.

Confused, he stuck his head out and looked around. A bloody handprint painted his door. Squinting, he examined it. The blood wasn't fresh, although it was still damp. He wouldn't have missed it when he'd come home earlier, despite his exhaustion. The print was newly made.

Another soft noise whispered from the woods. Israel stepped off the porch and peered into the darkness. A figure moved away from him. He opened his mouth to call out, to let the person know he was available if they needed medical help, but something inside stopped him. The way the figure moved was wrong. In a matter of seconds, it disappeared into the woods.

Israel closed his mouth, and for several minutes, he scrutinized the handprint on his door. A ghastly sense of foreboding gripped him.

CHAPTER 8

The full moon hung in the night sky over Morley, the air crisp and silent. At the McKenzie farm, the monster slipped out of the field behind the main house. If someone looked from a distance, it would appear to be a Native American man, wearing buckskin pants and vest with shoulder-length black hair. Once closer, it would be obvious this was far from a normal man. It shuffled along in a most uncomfortable manner, its top half bent at an impossible angle, as if its spine had been broken. A hole in its back oozed clotted blood and its white eyes darted back and forth.

At first, it meandered aimlessly. The farm dog, who would have alerted the family, had slipped into the house and was fast asleep under the housekeeper's bed. The monster had free rein. One of the chickens in the coop flapped her wings and resettled in her nest, making a fatal mistake. The monster latched onto the noise and stumbled into the fencing around the chicken coop.

It pushed determinedly against the barrier, grunting in anticipation of catching prey. The chickens flapped around more. The monster was now in a frenzy. It pushed harder on the chicken wire, which cut into its skin. The damage went unnoticed with its next meal almost at hand.

Finally, one of the nails securing the wire gave way, and the monster fell forward into the chicken enclosure. The chickens squawked as it reached out hungrily for them, capturing one poor chicken in its hands. As it ripped into the bird, several others fled out of the fence that had just collapsed. A stubborn old hen bit the creature's thumb when it grabbed her, but it consumed her along with the piece of its own flesh she's taken.

It moved on, gorging itself on more chickens. The rooster ran past the creature's feet, desperate to escape its clutches, but gaining its full attention instead. Clumsily the wendigo swiped a hand at the rooster. The bird ducked out of reach, screeching loudly. Lurching forward, the monster pursued the fleeing rooster back through the field and disappearing out into the countryside.

Lights flared on in the farmhouse and the farmhands' bunkhouse. Farmer McKenzie ran out of the house, his rifle clutched firmly in his hands. His three children, Duncan, Rebecca and Clara, followed close behind. Clara was the first to spot the chicken coop, and her hysterical screams mingled with the frightened sounds of the surviving chickens.

CHAPTER 9

The news of the mutilated body at the Waller farm and the chicken massacre at the McKenzie farm spread through Morley like wildfire. Jane learned the dreadful news from parents who brought their children to the schoolhouse. Understandably, both Clara McKenzie and Nate Waller were absent. She went ahead with her planned lessons, but a surreal quality permeated the whole day, especially without Clara's help with the younger students.

As the school day ended, rather than run and play, most of the children talked and whispered amongst themselves as they headed home. "Emily! Simon!" she called before they got to the door. "You both know what went on today. I want you to stay together at all times unless you're with someone you know. Don't play in the woods today, and don't talk to strangers." Jane thought a moment. "Actually, why don't you both go over Simon's house? I'm sure Simon's mother will make you a snack."

Simon shoved his hands in his pockets and shifted from foot to foot. "What if my ma isn't home? A lot of days she isn't. Sometimes visits Mrs. Smith above the general store or gets our food from the McKenzie's farm."

"Well, if she isn't home, then go to our farm. Emily, you'll check in with your father or Martin. I want an adult to know where you are." As little as Jane wanted Emily exposed to Zeke, she'd rather the girl deal with his temper than be found ripped apart.

Emily nodded and grabbed Simon's hand, and the two of them headed out the door.

"Remember, no playing in the woods today!" Jane shook her head and returned to work, although her thoughts strayed.

The town of Morley had always felt so safe. People never locked their doors, children played happily without supervision, and no one thought twice about walking down the street alone at night. Now everything had changed.

Jane walked through the room, straightening up. She glanced at the book of Indian myths and legends on her desk, and butterflies came to life in her stomach at the thought that Calvin might actually come to hear her read to him. He might not show up, and she was trying to steal herself against the disappointment. Something about this man who refused to talk to her intrigued her.

Jane had almost given up on him as she finished her lesson plans for next week when a soft knock brought her head up. He stood in the open doorway. Even though she had noticed his good looks before, she re-examined him after her little talk with Lucy yesterday. His blond hair lay boyishly mussed above his eyes, which darted around the room, looking everywhere but at her. His clenched jaw mirrored the tension in his body, and he fidgeted with the bottom corner of his shirt.

"Hi." Jane smiled. "I wasn't sure you would have time to listen to me read, but I'm glad you're here." She stood and fetched a chair from against the wall.

He moved stiffly and, following her lead, lowered himself onto the edge of the chair, ready to jump off and run at any second.

She flipped to a chapter she'd marked earlier that day. "Martin told me you're trading with the Apache nearby. I figured you'd like to start off with one of their legends. Is that okay?"

He nodded and sat back just a little.

"This one's about how the earth was made safe by killing the four monsters who preyed on humans." She took a deep breath and started reading, focusing on each word of the story.

When she reached the end, she glanced up from the book. "What did you think?"

"I liked it." His voice was gruff and he leaned forward slightly. "Are there any stories about the Wendigo or Big Owl?"

"Um, let me see." Surprised he'd made a request, she flipped through the pages. "Here, Big Owl. No story, but it does state that this is a dangerous Apache monster, often portrayed as a giant, man-eating ogre." She scanned further through the entries. "The Wendigo Spirit Demon." When she'd found it she rotated the book so he could see the picture.

He moved in closer, squinting at the artist's rendering. The picture resembled a man, but the differences were disturbing. The creature had no pupils, its eyes completely white. There were areas on the neck and shoulders with no skin covering the muscles underneath. Yet, the most distressing aspect of the drawing was the mouth. It looked like the lips had been drawn back impossibly far, the teeth unnaturally prominent.

Calvin's eyes came up and met hers for a moment. She wasn't sure, but it seemed like there was fear in them. Then his gaze fell away and he sat back in the chair. Nodding, he indicated she should continue.

Jane turned the book toward herself again. "This particular tale of the wendigo was translated from a French fur trader, who was associating with the Algonquian people near the Great Lakes at the turn of the century. It notes there are variations on this mythical creature spreading up through Canada, but it's usually associated with cannibalism." Jane frowned at the thought.

She began to read aloud:

It was our last trading mission before the great snows. The entire group was looking forward to reaping the benefits of their hard work. As my men finished piling the lush furs on the backs of the horses, the Indians made approving gestures at the guns we'd offered.

The leader of the Indians was named Keme. As I was about to bid him farewell, one of his hunters approached in haste. Keme listened and smiled. He turned to me and gestured toward a massive elk skin atop one of the horses. They were going to hunt a great elk.

Despite the threatening clouds, I was determined to see a great elk brought down by the Indians. My men were anxious to get back to camp, and I allowed them to go ahead. Only my best man, Bernard, remained by my side as we joined the three Indians.

As we tracked the beast into the forest, the snow began to fall. At first only tiny wisps of white, it soon became a great avalanche. The snow blocked our view. Keme halted, forcing us to go back. My disappointment was high at the bad fortune of the weather.

Through the falling snow, we saw the figure of a man approach. Keme called out to him, but he did not answer. Instead he moved closer, and we saw he did not move like a normal person but like an elderly man who should never have been this deep in the forest. A sense of foreboding came upon me.

Keme spoke a word and his hunters produced their various weapons. Not fully understanding, Bernard and I raised our guns. When the figure reached us, I saw it was no man but a demon! Its skin had frozen gray and its rotting teeth were huge in its gaping mouth. Even with no eyes, it was able see us.

It attacked Bernard, biting deep into his arm. Outraged, I fired at the demon. My bullet went through its blank eye. It fell dead into the gathering snow.

Bernard cried, gripping his bleeding arm. Keme, his largest hunter, and I carried him back to our camp while the fastest hunter ran for the medicine woman.

Despite the chilling temperature, Bernard burned with fever, delirious from the pain.

His cousin, Edwin, met us on the edge of camp. In my own tent, we attempted to bandage the wound but could not stop the hemorrhaging. We all feared his death was imminent.

The medicine woman arrived just as he took his last breath. Bernard was beyond her assistance. Some of my men, wary of her being a witch who would steal his departing soul, tried to push her away. However, I did not subscribe to such superstition, and allowed her in the tent to examine the body. My men and the Indians remained outside by the fire.

"Wendigo," was the only word she stated upon seeing his wound. Without warning, she drew a long blade from under her cloak, and lunged at my dead man!

I held her back, but she was relentless. Crying for help, both my men and the Indians rushed into the tent. Keme spoke to her, but when she repeated that same word, he paled and gestured to me that she must be allowed to continue. As we argued, me with words and him with motions, Edwin sat by Bernard's dead body protectively.

Then the body stirred, and I thought we had all made a terrible mistake. Bernard's eyes snapped open, but they were now completely white. The demon had possessed him! He attacked his cousin sitting by his side, biting into his neck. As Edwin flailed away, red blood flowed freely between his fingers as he pressed on his wound.

The deafening sound of a gun blast reverberated through the tent. The bullet hit the possessed body's chest. It should have been a killing blow, but it didn't stop the demon. Other men fired, but still he came at us.

Finally, with a defiant shriek, the medicine woman plunged her knife into Bernard's forehead. The demon inside must have been destroyed, for he fell, truly dead now.

Our stunned attention shifted to Edwin as the medicine woman pointed to him. He was slumped on the ground in the corner, dead as well. "Wendigo." She shook her head sadly. Then she and the Indians walked out of the tent and out of our camp.

Understanding, I drew my gun and put him to rest with one shot to the head. He was able to rest in peace.

Jane closed the book, and they both sat there for a moment. Somewhat disturbed, she contemplated the meaning of the French trader's account.

Calvin cleared his throat and stood. "Thanks."

Jane jumped up. "You're welcome." She figuring he'd gotten what he needed with that myth and walked behind him to the door.

He hesitated, nervously running his fingers through his hair. "C-can I come back again? For...for this?" He stared at his shoes, mumbling.

She gently touched his hand. "I'd like that," she told him honestly.

His eyes widened slightly, but he didn't jerk away.

CHAPTER 10

The door to the Anderson's house swung open as Simon ran in. Even the sheriff of Morley didn't lock his door, confident in the safety of his town. Emily followed close behind him, admiring the large house. Someday Emily hoped to live in a house like the Anderson's. Not that her house was small, she even got her own room, but this house was much nicer. It had a parlor to greet guests, running water inside and Mrs. Anderson even had her very own sewing room.

"Mother! I'm home!" Simon yelled out at the top of his lungs. There was no answer. Simon tried again. "Tommy! You here?" Nothing. Simon shrugged. "I bet they're helping at the McKenzie farm after what happened last night. You know my brother's sweet on Clara."

"Want to stay here?" Emily asked. "I bet I could make us a snack without your mother."

"Nah, my house is boring. Let's go to yours," answered Simon.

The two children skipped down the road to the Lansing farm, tragedy not dampening their playful mood at the moment.

At the front steps, Emily paused. "I'm supposed to check in with my father." Her voice was troubled. Usually she tried to steer clear of the angry man. Rarely did he pay any mind to his daughter, usually only when he was annoyed or angry with her. Emily wasn't a stupid child; she knew what her father did to her mother behind closed doors. Lately, those incidents of her father's temper were getting louder and more frequent.

She tentatively opened the door, and they both slipped inside. Loud snoring assaulted their ears, and Zeke lay splayed out on the sofa, passed out. A large whiskey bottle with only about a quarter of liquid left was still clutched in his meaty hand.

"Should I wake him?" Emily whispered, inching a little farther into the room.

Simon silently shook his head no.

An extra loud snore burst from the drunken man, and he rolled onto his side. The kids jumped back and ran into the kitchen. Emily grabbed two apples and they left out the back door. The tension of being close to her father released as soon as she got back into the sunshine.

She tossed Simon an apple. "Better check in with Martin then. He won't watch us, but at least he'll know we're here if Mama comes home." Emily munched her apple.

They found him in the barn, sharpening and oiling the tools. He carefully worked on the pitchfork prongs.

"Hi Martin!" She waved, running up to him. She knew he liked to act tough and grumpy but underneath it, he'd been kind to her. Whenever she ran from her father to the barn, Martin would find her and comforted her in his no-nonsense, curse-filled way. He always made her feel better.

Simon eyed him warily, but then both of them leapt into Bessie the cow's straw bin, burying themselves inside.

The cow mooed at them, nosing Emily.

"Get yer asses outta there before ya mess her food up!" Martin waved the pitchfork at them.

The kids jumped out, but Emily couldn't keep the smile off her face.

"You hear about what happened at the McKenzie farm?" Emily asked, hoping to pass on the gossip.

"Yep, nasty stuff. The Scot and I may not be close, but I feel bad his little girl had to find that mess."

Emily's mouth turned down in a frown. "Yeah, those poor chickens!"

"What do you think did it?" Simon spoke up.

Martin looked thoughtful. "Woulda said a fox or a coyote but he had some sturdy fencing 'round that coop. Musta been something huge to break through."

"Mountain lion?" Simon pressed.

"Maybe."

"Anyway, Simon and I are going to go play. Mama told us to check in with an adult because of everything happening. Okay?" Emily pulled hay from her hair and tossed back in the bin.

"Not sure if I qualify as an adult," Martin smirked. Then he tilted his head. "Don't ya have some chores? Like collectin' the eggs?"

Emily rolled her eyes. "I'll do it later."

Martin shrugged. "Ain't no skin off my teeth."

Emily grabbed Simon's shirt, pulling him out of the barn with her.

From behind, Martin shouted, his voice taking on a serious note. "Stay where I can hear ya! You see anything, just shout!"

"Okay!"

Simon slowed down as they neared the woods. "Maybe we should play in the back of the barn instead." Usually he loved playing in the woods, but Emily noticed him squinting at the shadows from the waving trees.

"Nah, Bessie the cow gets annoyed when we run around her too much. Come on, we'll stay within sight of the farm."

Simon accepted this answer, and they stepped through the tree line.

"What do you want to play?" Emily questioned him.

"Let's play tag!" Simon yelled excitedly. "I'm older so you're it!"

Emily huffed. "So you're eleven now. My eleventh birthday is only a couple months away."

"Doesn't matter. I picked the game and those are the rules."

"No, you got to pick the game so you're it!" She giggled, pecked a kiss on his cheek, then took off into the woods.

Simon swiped his cheek and chased after her. He caught up with her when she stopped short, running into her back. They almost tumbled together to the forest floor but caught themselves in time to stay upright.

Emily could feel Simon push away from her, but she couldn't move. Her eyes were glued to the scene before her. The blood drained out of her face and her heart pounded in her chest. She heard Simon's feet shift on the dead leaves as he moved around her, then he gasped loudly. His body froze beside hers.

Blood covered everything, and the stench of rot wafted at them with the breeze. A huge black bear carcass lay curled on the ground, partially dismembered and covered with bloody wounds ripped into its hide. A woman's body lay draped over the bear, facing away from them, her once-pretty bonnet and frilly white dress covered with blood.

Emily couldn't tell what blood came from the woman and what came from the bear. Her left leg had been ripped off at the knee and flung against a nearby tree. Her left hand had also been amputated and rested next to the dead beast's mouth.

Her breath rushed out in a whimper of terror with it when the woman's head unexpectedly swung around to face them. Fresh bear blood covered her face, and she continued to chew entrails as her blank, white eyes examined them.

Opening her mouth wide, the entrails fell out, forgotten. A gasping, gurgling noise emerged, and the large teeth snapped shut with a click. They opened and closed repeatedly as the one-handed, one-legged dead woman slowly slithered toward the children.

With a scream, Simon grabbed Emily's hand, and they raced back to the farm. Martin had already abandoned the barn, making his way towards the woods with the pitchfork in hand.

"Martin, Martin!" she cried. "There's a dead woman in the forest!" She bent forward, gulping down air in an attempt to keep her stomach's contents from boiling up.

"No, she's not dead! She was eating a bear!" Simon interjected.

Martin glared at them with his eyes narrowed and his lips pursed. "Show me," he ordered.

Emily reached for Simon's hand, gaining strength when his fingers curled into hers as they headed back the way they'd come. Before they quite reached the grisly scene, the sounds of moaning and dragging echoed through the trees. Martin held out his hand to stop the other two, his finger on his lips to indicate quiet and gestured for them to stay put. The he crept forward with the pitchfork held securely up.

The monster dragged herself along with one hand and pushed off the ground with one foot and a bloody knee. Emily held her breath, fearful for Martin as the creature moved faster at the sight of him. Smelling like death, the dead woman snapped her jaws open and closed, swaying her head back and forth.

Emily watched as sweat trickled down Martin's neck. He gripped the handle of the pitchfork with white-knuckled hands. Driving the freshly sharpened points through the monster's neck, Martin flipped her on her's back. He wrenched the pitchfork out and slammed it back through the monster's chest, into the heart.

Letting go of the pitchfork's handle and turning back to the children, Martin shook his head. "If that ain't one of them wendigo demons ma brother talked about, then nothin' is."

Emily's eyes widened. Her finger pointed behind him.

Martin whirled around and gasped to see the dead woman pawing at the pitchfork embedded in her chest. With a new sense of urgency, he grabbed the handle again and stabbed the creature over and over.

Jaws snapped open and closed as she slowly crawled toward him again, ignoring Martin's efforts.

In a panic, Martin raised the pitchfork as high as his arms would stretch. With all his strength, he thrust the pitchfork through the dirty bonnet. Black blood spurted out, and the thing collapsed to the ground.

CHAPTER 11

The Lansing farm seemed strangely quiet to Martin as he herded the children into the house. He couldn't push the image of the rotting woman with the snapping jaws out of his mind.

"Get upstairs and stay there," he commanded.

They nodded solemnly and scampered away, slamming the bedroom door shut.

Martin strode into the living room and looked down at his drunken boss with disgust. Sure, there'd been many a day where Martin had indulged to the point of passing out. But he didn't beat on women and children like this asshole. Martin got a little satisfaction in forcefully poking Zeke in the chest.

"Wake up."

Zeke snorted loudly as his body jerked awake from the minor assault. Squinting at Martin through half open eyes, he settled back down.

"Get out of my fucking house or I'll fire you." Zeke mumbled at him.

Martin smiled, deciding to push his limits. "You ain't gonna fire me. I'm your only farm hand. You need to get your ass up. We got a problem."

Zeke came awake fully. "What problem?"

"I'll show ya." Martin walked towards the back door.

Zeke sat up and groaned loudly, clutching his head. Martin chuckled under his breath, loving to see his boss suffering from his hangover.

Zeke staggered up, caught himself on the door jamb and breathed deeply, his breath horrible, a mix of rancid food and stale alcohol. He steadied himself and walked behind Martin out the door.

When they came upon the dead woman, Zeke just stared at her. Martin could practically see the wheels starting to turn in his dull brain, trying to figure out what the hell he was looking at. Then the temper came, as it always did when Zeke didn't understand something.

"What in tarnation did you do, you sick bastard? Kill some woman on my land? Mutilated her too!" Zeke waved his arms at the bloody scene, spittle flying out of his mouth with each word.

Martin circled the body. "Bollocks to that! I didn't kill her!" He paused, thinking. "Well, I kinda did. The kids found her eating a bear, and she went after them. Had to stop her. Come see this." Martin nodded his head past the mangled body.

They crossed several yards to reach the bear's carcass, and Martin flinched when Zeke stopped to heave his whiskey lunch into the bushes before stumbling the last few steps to stare slack-jawed at the ripped-open abdomen and partially eaten organs.

Martin nudged the woman's torn leg with his foot before slowly backing away from the bloody scene.

"We gotta get the sheriff."

Zeke nodded silently and staggered back to the house, where he lay back on the sofa, huddled as if to hide from what they'd witnessed.

Martin clenched his fist. The scoundrel never even asked about his kid, who had seen the horrific sight first. Martin glanced toward the stairs, knowing the girl was smart enough to keep Simon safely up in her room. Someone had to fetch the sheriff.

As he stalked down the road, he caught sight of Calvin walking next to Jane, practically shoulder-to-shoulder. Martin had never seen his skittish baby brother this close to a woman willingly. Neither of them seemed to notice him observing them.

"Hey, brother!" Martin took wicked satisfaction when his brother jumped away from Jane. A blush crept its way up Calvin's face, and even Jane seemed to have a guilty look. Just what was going on between the two of them?

"Hi Martin," Jane said sweetly, recovering first. "We just ran into each other on the road."

Martin took off his hat, an uncharacteristic gesture, and nodded to Jane. "Something's happened at the farm. I'm gettin' the sheriff."

Jane's hand fluttered to her throat, and she went pale. "Oh no! What's happened? Emily?"

"Emily's fine. I put her upstairs in her room with Simon. Why don't you head to the house while my brother and I get the law?"

Jane took off without another word.

"What happened?" Calvin eyed him, frowning.

Martin let the words spill out, describing everything. He finished saying, "It was one of them demon wendigo things you told me about! Cussed thing was comin' for the kids. I took her out with a pitchfork to the head."

Calvin's eyes opened wide, his eyebrows going up. "How'd you know stabbin' it in the head would kill it?"

"Doesn't a stabbin' in the head kill just about anythin'? 'Sides, stabbin' it anywhere else didn't seem ta work. Come on, were losin' the light, little brother."

CHAPTER 12

Sheriff Bill's head pounded, threatening to explode. Never had anything like this happened in Morley. He usually had to deal with claims of theft, scuffles between neighbors, or public drunkenness. Now he had two dead bodies and several mutilated animals. To make matters worse, the story he'd gotten so far about this incident with the woman and the bear didn't make any sense.

He'd already helped load the woman's dead, disfigured body, including her amputated leg and hand, onto a cart the Doc's assistant drove. Now he stood with Doctor Israel Silverstein, who also served as undertaker for Morley, as they both stared down at the large body of the black bear. The sickening stench hung heavy in the evening air, and Bill wanted nothing more than to get clear of the reek.

"What should we do with the bear's body?" The thought of trying to bury it was not an appealing one.

"Just leave it herrre. The scavengers vill take care of it," Israel directed him in his faint Russian accent. The aging doctor twirled his massive, bushy mustache. "This whole thing is meshuganah."

Bill glanced at him. "Using those strange words again?"

Israel chuckled. "It means crrrazy. Seemed appropriate."

Bill nodded in agreement.

Deputy Victor Wade walked up behind them, groaned, and covered his nose. "Got the statements from Martin Drake and the kids. Martha and Jane are with them. You want to go over this?"

Bill turned and they started walking back to the house. "Yeah. So what'd they say? Did the bear kill the woman or did the woman kill the bear? Because it sure looked like they killed each other."

"Well, unfortunately we still don't have an answer to that question. Your son and the Lansing girl thought both of them were dead when they came upon the scene. Then your son told me the dead woman was actually eating the bear. When she saw them, he said she looked like she wanted to eat them too." Victor sighed. "He is just a kid. He could be making that up."

Bill pushed his hat up, trying to work out his son's words in his head. "Nah, I don't think he would make something up about this. I believe that's what he saw, even if it doesn't make any sense."

"The Drake brothers also offered up a theory. It sounds like a bunch of Indian bullshit but it might fit the scenario here." Victor rolled his eyes. "Called it a Wen-di-go. Some kind of demon that possesses dead people and makes them eat people. Although this was a bear and not a person. And we're talking about the backward Drake brothers."

Bill pointed his finger at his deputy. "None of that. Those two are members of this community and will be treated as such."

Victor narrowed his eyes at Bill before looking away. More and more lately, Bill had gotten the impression that Victor didn't like when Bill exercised his authority, and it made him less certain about placing his life into his deputy's hands.

Brushing it off, Bill said, "I'm going back with the Doc to examine the dead woman. I'll try to get more information on what happened here, maybe even figure out who she is. We know she isn't from Morley, and the next closest town is Vigil. Not exactly around the corner. I want you to take Martha and Simon home and go door-to-door and alert people. We don't want to cause a panic, but make sure people are aware of their surroundings. Encourage everyone to carry a weapon and, if possible, not to be out alone."

Victor didn't meet his eyes but nodded as he went back in the house. Bill watched him, the hairs standing up on the back of his neck. Then he and Israel climbed on the cart and headed for the Doc's place on the other side of town.

CHAPTER 13

Martha quietly walked home with Victor and Simon, little Harry cooing in her arms. Her thoughts wandered back to the kiss she'd shared with Victor a few days earlier. She loved her husband, but Bill had been so distant lately. They were hardly ever intimate. Half the time they were together, they fought about stupid things.

It didn't help that Victor had turned his attentions to her. He was very handsome and so sure of himself, almost to the point of being cocky. She found herself drawn to that attitude. Martha and Victor's wife, Cora, had been friends years earlier but had grown apart as Cora became more difficult to deal with. Victor needed a real woman, someone to take care of him and give him children like a wife should.

Victor gave her another alluring smile as they neared the house, which she ignored by looking up at the clouds. Simon seemed not to notice as he ran for the door, all of them following.

"I'm gonna go write this all down on my slate. I don't want to forget anything! It'll be like my report for Papa and maybe it'll help him solve the crime." Simon jumped up and down. "Right, Victor?"

"That's right, partner. You make sure you get every little detail in there for us."

Simon took off up the stairs.

"You can write that until your father gets home, but then you have to do your figures for school tomorrow." Martha yelled up the stairs.

"Tommy here?" Victor glanced through the doorway into the living room.

"No, he's with Clara. She's still shaken up from all the killed chickens." She laid Harry in the bassinet in the living room for a nap. He closed his eyes without protest. "Thanks so much for walking us home." She smiled, motioned to the door and walked toward the kitchen down the hall. Her children were in the house and she didn't want any awkwardness like the other day.

Victor didn't take the hint. He followed her, watching as she started to chop vegetables for dinner.

She eyed him warily. "You don't have to stay until Bill gets back. I'll lock the doors."

Without a word, he moved behind her. His body pressed against hers, and one hand slid across her hip. She tensed as his other hand gently moved her stylish curls off her neck. Her breath caught as his lips softly pressed a kiss to her skin. Her heart fluttered, rapidly creating a music that pounded in her ears. It felt good, his kisses on her neck. Her head fell back, and her body softened as she forgot herself for a moment.

"Stop!" She spun away from him, unconsciously waving the knife still in her hand at him, trying to ward him off.

Victor smiled and looked down at the knife. "You gonna use that on me?"

Martha brought the blade down, willing her confusion away. "We can't do this, Victor. Bill is your boss and he's my husband. I love him. Maybe if he wasn't, it would be different."

"So if Bill wasn't here, we could be together?" Victor pressed her.

Martha sighed, weary from the emotional turmoil. "I don't know. Maybe in a different life. But we can't do this. Bill's an important part of both our lives, and that won't change. You've got to think of Cora, too. She's sick. Do you understand?"

"I understand." Victor abruptly strode out of the house without another word.

CHAPTER 14

The sun lazily drifted down to the western horizon. A few clouds drifting across the sky threatened rain. On the northern road, three men on horseback stopped at a crudely written sign.

Morley — 2 miles

Warren glanced back at his overweight companion. "Jimmy, you ever heard of Morley?"

The fat, bearded Jimmy scratched his head. "Nope. But we need more supplies. Almost outta food."

Warren snorted in disgust. "You're a fat pig, Jimmy. Told you not to eat so much." Warren pushed his Stetson up, regarding the sign again. "I think Morley sounds like a place deserving of our attention."

"Can we please stay in town, Warren? It'd be so nice to sleep in a real bed instead of on the goddamn ground," whined Jimmy.

"Shut yer trap. Too dangerous, and it's gonna be dark soon. We'll set up camp off the road for tonight. Tomorrow we'll scope this place out, maybe find a whorehouse. Can have our fun, then take everything we need. 'Sides, what the hell would we do with our prize there?" Warren tilted his head toward the third horse.

A young man's frightened eyes looked back at him above the gag in his mouth. Rope securely tied his wrists and stretched to wrap around Warren's saddle horn. Dried blood streaked down the side of his face from a wound that had stopped bleeding long ago, and his right eye was swollen shut.

"You ever hear of this town, boy?" Warren jerked on the rope roughly.

The young man shook his head no.

"You better not give us any trouble, or else you and the fine people of Morley are going to pay for it. Got it?" A malicious gleam twinkled in Warren's eye.

The traumatized young man nodded.

CHAPTER 15

The morning dawned bright in Morley. The clouds threatening rain had moved off across the prairie, leaving the day cool but fresh. Martin rolled over, knowing he should already be at the farm, but he didn't care. It wasn't like Zeke got up early to check on him anyway.

He stretched lazily and climbed out of bed. Pulling on his clothes, he made his way into the main room of the tiny house. He stopped short. His brother sat at the table drinking a mug of coffee.

Calvin usually woke up at the crack of dawn to go hunting. He did this every morning religiously, and it kept them well-stocked with meat. Often, Calvin would trade his kills for other goods and food. Martin believed Calvin really enjoyed his early morning hunts, and it was a rare day that Calvin didn't go out.

"You want some of these eggs I made?" Calvin pushed a plate of scrambled eggs across the table.

Martin nodded, taking the seat across from him. He dug into the eggs. "You got a job or something this mornin'? Why ain't you out huntin'?" Martin questioned him around bites of egg.

"We got plenty of meat," Calvin retorted.

Martin ignored the fact that this would never have stopped Calvin before. He finished his eggs and pulled on his boots.

Calvin got up as well and followed Martin to the door.

Martin looked back at him, unsure what to make of his brother's behavior. "Where you goin'?"

"I'm goin' down to the farm with ya. I wanna make sure there ain't any more of those things lurkin' around."

Martin's smirked. "Awww, is my baby brother gonna walk me to work to make sure the big, bad wendigo doesn't eat me?" he cooed then ruffled Calvin's hair harshly.

"Horseshit! You wasn't so happy about that wendigo you killed yesterday."

Martin conceded to this point. That moving dead woman had scared the hell out of him. Together, they walked down the road to the Lansing farm. Calvin was mostly quiet, like always, while Martin complained. "There's a lack of available women in Morley."

"What about one of those two down at the inn? They're pretty, even that one that wears trousers." They turned down the road to the farm, the main house just ahead of them.

"Nah, neither of them seems to be too interested in the good stuff I got to offer. I might have to go to Santa Fe just to find a woman." Martin eyed his brother. "What'd bout you? You bed either of them?" Martin knew Calvin hadn't, but he got a sick thrill watching his brother's face turn red.

Before either of them could say another word, the door to the house flew open, and Zeke marched out. It didn't appear he saw them, or else he just ignored them as he slammed the door closed and headed out to the fields. Martin was glad not be acknowledged, because he never was sure when his boss's temper would turn on him.

"Wonder what bug crawled up that bastard's ass?" Martin commented.

Calvin didn't respond. Martin glanced at his silent brother to find his eyes on the house. Following his brother's line of sight, Martin saw just what had captivated Calvin's attention. The memory of yesterday flooded back to him.

"Holy shit!" Martin punched Calvin's arm hard.

"What the hell, Martin!" Calvin gave him an angry look as he rubbed his arm.

Martin ignored him, watching Jane moving around behind the window Calvin had been focused on. "You didn't come here for me. You came here for her! Are you bedding her?"

"What? No!" Calvin shook his head vigorously.

"Then what in tarnation was that yesterday with the two of you walking so close together down the road? And skippin' hunting to come down here this morning?" Martin pressed him.

"It ain't like that. She's a nice lady with a nice kid and an asshole husband."

"Yeah, that's all true. But she still ain't none of your business."

Calvin didn't respond, his lips pressed together as he stared down at the ground.

Martin laughed obnoxiously at Calvin's expense. "Goddamn, little brother! Here you are tellin' me I got to do good and keep this job. All the while you've been sweet on the boss's wife. Don't get into a tangle with that bastard, he's one mean son of a bitch," Martin warned him as he walked off to the barn.

Calvin's eyebrows rose at his retreating form.

CHAPTER 16

Jane was very surprised when Calvin asked if he could walk with her and Emily into town. She hadn't even known he was there. He just kind of appeared as she came out of the house. Like usual, he hardly talked at all, only answering a few questions from Emily about trading with the Indians.

Jane no longer got the impression that Calvin didn't like her. Did he feel like he had to escort them to protect them against the danger that had come to Morley? She wondered if he pitied her because her husband didn't give a damn about their safety. She knew a lot of people in town felt sorry for her and the heat of shame warmed her cheeks. Calvin didn't seem like that kind of person though. In fact, she'd felt bad for both the brothers when they'd moved in a few years ago. They hadn't had a good reputation, especially Martin. Jane had ignored the mean comments of others and had accepted them into the community before most. Now she wasn't sure what to make of Calvin's actions, if he was doing the same for her. No matter his motive, she was glad for the security of having him along. There were other feelings that seemed to well up in her when he was around, but she desperately tried pushing them away. Those feelings would only cause trouble.

When they got to the schoolhouse, Jane waved good-bye, and he nodded his head to her before heading farther into town. She opened the schoolhouse, letting the fresh air in.

Emily skipped over to Simon, who was walking up with his brother, Tommy. Martha pushed the baby carriage behind them.

"Good morning. Seems like it's too beautiful out after all the scariness yesterday, doesn't it?" Jane made small talk.

"Yeah, Simon told us all about the living dead woman eating the bear and dragging herself after them," Tommy blurted out, his words fast.

Martha's smile didn't hide the exhausted slump of her shoulders. "Yes, it was very awful yesterday. I hope that's all the excitement we have in Morley for a while."

"Me too," Jane agreed before changing the topic. "I was wondering if I could ask a favor?"

Martha nodded, her hands absently rocking the carriage as baby Harry whined softly.

"A reporter wishes to interview me at the inn this evening. I was wondering, could Emily could stay with Simon at your house? Zeke and I could pick her up on the way home. Or, if we're running late, she could stay overnight. Would that be okay?"

Emily's head whipped up. "No! I'm old enough to stay home alone! You've let me do it at least twice before!" She crossed her arms over her chest.

Jane placed a hand on her hip. "I know you have but you're not staying alone after what happened in the woods yesterday. Who knows what could have happened if that thing made it to the house?"

Martha knelt down in front of Emily, which left Jane speechless. The sheriff's wife was never rude, but Jane got the impression that she only tolerated Emily because of Simon's fondness for her daughter. Martha smiled. "You know, I've been needing some help with baby Harry lately. Maybe you could be his nanny. What do you think?"

"Really?" Emily's frown lightened some.

"Yes. And you and Simon could have a sleepover."

Simon answered for her. "Yes, yes, yes!"

"Aww, your little girlfriend's going to sleep over?" Tommy smacked Simon on the back.

"Shut up, Tom! You wish Clara could sleep over so you can kiss her some more. I heard you were kissing her over at the old bridge," he retorted.

Tommy's face turned bright red, and he glared daggers at his brother.

Martha shot back to her feet and grabbed her eldest son's arm. "Thomas Robert Anderson, I don't want you going anywhere near that Purgatory River bridge! Kids have died falling off it!" Martha's jaw snapped shut and her shoulders hunched as she turned to Jane. "I'm so sorry, Jane. I didn't mean to bring that up."

The blood rushed out of Jane's face at the mention of that bridge, but she pasted a smile on her lips. The memories of her older brother's deadly plunge off the Purgatory River Bridge eighteen years earlier threatened to overwhelm her. With a firm resolve, she shoved those thoughts to the back of her mind. "Don't trouble yourself over it."

Martha turned back to Emily. "I'd need help changing his diapers, bathing him and feeding him. Do you want to be Harry's nanny?"

That was enough for Emily. "Yes!" she agreed. The two children ran into the schoolhouse as some of the other children arrived.

"Thank you," Jane told Martha sincerely.

"It's not a problem. Bill's being interviewed as well. I'll pick up the kids from school this afternoon," Martha said as she wheeled the carriage away.

CHAPTER 17

Jimmy snored loudly in his sleep. Warren would occasionally kick the bastard when the noise became too much of a roar. Their hostage lay a few feet nearby, tied firmly to a stake in the ground with his mouth still gagged. Alexander was happier away from the two criminals as their unappealing body odor was cloying. Not once since he was kidnapped had they stopped to bathe.

He had slipped in and out of sleep through the night, never quite reaching a truly restful state. Nightmare images of his parents shot dead and Warren raping his sister assaulted his dreams. He figured they'd taken him hostage to demand a ransom from his elder brother, who stood to inherit their farm.

Once awake, Alexander tried every night to wriggle out of his bindings. Raw wounds now circled his wrists, and he'd never once been able to budge the knots. As stupid and uncoordinated Jimmy was, he knew how to tie a good knot.

He snapped out of his thoughts as Warren rolled over, pushing his blankets off. The man stretched, spit, and wandered off, most likely to relieve himself. Jimmy snored on happily. The fire had died down during the night to almost nothing, letting the chill morning wrap Alexander in it's cold grasp, a small annoyance compared to everything he'd been through already.

Warren rushed back into the camp, and a spark of hope flamed in Alexander that someone had discovered them. Hoping to not attract unwanted attention, he pretended to be asleep.

Warren nudged Jimmy. "Get up."

Jimmy groaned. "It's barely daylight," he complained and rolled over.

Warren growled, kicking Jimmy hard in the back. "Get up!"

Jimmy yelped and scrambled to his feet. Alexander thought he saw a flash of fear in the big man's eyes.

Warren grabbed a rope. "Found something." He strolled over to Alexander. The young man knew he wasn't going to get out of this unscathed.

Warren leaned over him and slapped Alexander across the face. Even though he was prepared, it stung. He sat up with a grimace. Warren removed his mouth gag. "Wakey, wakey. Time to earn your keep."

They followed Warren away from the camp to the body of a large deer. The doe still breathed despite gross wounds around the head and neck. Long gashes marred the skin at the shoulders. She twitched her legs slightly as they stood over her.

Warren grinned. "The flank meat is still good." He pulled out his knife and finished the doe off.

"What'dya think done this, Warren?" Jimmy peered at the mutilated face. His nose wrinkled and his brow furrowed.

Warren shrugged. "How should I know? Maybe a wolf pack." He started tying the rope around the legs.

Jimmy looked around with caution. "Wolf pack? Ya think there's wolves around here? Why do ya think they woulda left it still alive?"

"I don't know! Maybe they got scared off or something. Stop asking stupid questions and help me!" Warren waved a meaty fist at him.

Jimmy, Warren, and Alexander managed to drag the large animal back to the camp, even though the two outlaws refused to untie their hostage's hands. Jimmy got the fire going while Warren butchered the good meat off, and soon the delicious aroma of roasting venison wafted through the air. Alexander's mouth watered as Warren sliced up pieces of the cooked meat. The two men ate with gusto and Alexander almost cried with hunger as he watched, forgotten.

Finally, Warren looked over at him. "You want some breakfast?"

Alexander only nodded, not daring to speak.

With an evil grin, Warren dug out three travel biscuits and threw them at Alexander. "Enjoy."

CHAPTER 18

The school day went by fairly fast. The children all wanted to talk about what happened in town. Jane tried to explain it the best she could without causing too much fear. Yet, she wanted to convey how important it was right now to stay aware of their surroundings and never be out alone.

Even the parents seemed to understood the severity of the situation, showing up to walk the children home. Martha came for Emily and Simon, who practically jumped for joy at the prospect of baking a pie and staying up late for stargazing. Tommy couldn't seem to get away to the McKenzie farm fast enough.

Jane started straightening the desks, which always seemed to get shoved around when the children bolted for the outside. That was when he appeared in her doorway, silent as a ghost.

"Hi!" She worried it might have been a little too bubbly of a greeting for him and was relieved when his mouth quirked up in a half smile. "Here for another story?"

He nodded.

They settled in the same spots as last time, her at the desk and him in the chair. She flipped open the book, then stopped at a marked page.

"This is a tale from the Cherokee tribe about how we got sunshine on our side of the world." She read to him about how several animals tried to take the sun from the other side of the world but failed. Only Grandmother Spider succeeded, also bringing fire to the Cherokee. Then she closed the book and laid it back on the table. "Did you like that one? I thought it was kind of cute."

He nodded, his eyes holding hers for just a moment before darting off. "Got time for another one?" he asked quietly.

She gave him an apologetic smile. "Sorry. I'm being interviewed tonight at the inn. A reporter from New York is apparently interested in education out here in the territories. Not sure what I'm going to say. I doubt anything I do here will be very exciting to him."

"He'll love talkin' to ya. I mean, the kids here all love ya," Calvin offered as they moved towards the door.

"Thanks, I appreciate that. Hope I don't make too much of a fool of myself in front of him." She laughed a little.

"Doubt you could do that." His voice was just barely above a whisper as she waved good-bye.

CHAPTER 19

Jane strolled slightly behind her husband as they made their way to the inn. He occasionally spoke, usually a negative comment about whatever they passed, but he basically talked to himself, not expecting a response. As they passed the Anderson's house, she ignored his envious comments over their grand house and his comparison to their own house falling into disrepair. Jane just hoped Emily was having fun inside.

The sun touched the horizon, and lanterns burned around the entrance to the inn. Music floated out the open door, along with the bustle of people inside. Zeke pushed through the door like he owned the place. He was there practically every night, but Jane rarely joined him. With all the darkness surrounding them lately, people gathered together for comfort. She smiled at her fellow townsfolk enjoying a good time with each other.

Lucy smiled brightly at Jane as their eyes meet. She noticed Lucy wearing a blue gingham dress, an odd occurrence for her friend. Jane wondered if it was a special occasion. Lucy scooped out a large plate of beef stew, whispered something to George behind her, and brought the one plate over to them.

"Good evening, Zeke and Jane." She nodded at them. "Zeke, why don't I set you up right here?" She indicated the last stool at the counter and laid the heaping plate down along with a fork.

George brought over a tall mug of beer, and Zeke sat down approvingly. The hulking black man, an ex-slave, frowned as Zeke gulped down the beer. Zeke failed to notice the disapproval.

"You don't mind if I take Jane upstairs now, do you?" Lucy asked him sweetly.

Zeke just dug into his plate, waving a dismissive hand at his wife as he shoved delicious meat into his mouth.

Without another word, Lucy took Jane's wrist and led her up the stairs in the back of the inn. When they got to the top, they both stopped and giggled, feeling giddy that they'd gotten away from Zeke so easily.

"Are you ready?" Lucy paused before one of the guest rooms.

Jane nodded, swallowing heavily and smoothed out the non-existent wrinkles from her dress.

Lucy knocked on the door and a quiet response granted them entrance. Jane saw a tall man with round-framed glasses perched on his nose and dressed in a smart, three-piece suit. He stood up from the rickety desk with a small smile on his face.

"Mr. Belmont, this is Jane Lansing. She's the local schoolteacher in Morley. Jane, this is Harold Belmont, the reporter from New York City who has come out to do a piece on life in the territories," Lucy introduced them.

They shook hands warmly.

"Thank you so much for participating in this project, Mrs. Lansing." The reporter pushed his glasses up.

"I'm excited to be a part of all this. Will this be printed in the newspaper?"

"Oh yes. I'm mailing back articles to my editor as I'm going along this trip. Although, Morley is very remote, so I probably won't be able to mail back the articles I write about here until I get to Santa Fe. If you'd like, I can make sure a copy of the newspaper gets sent to you in a few months," he offered.

"That would be wonderful!" The prospect of her name and words being printed in the newspaper was like a dream come true. Jane would be so proud to show it to Emily and her students. Of course, she would have to keep it hidden from Zeke. He wouldn't be so happy of her getting so much attention.

"I'm actually hoping to have enough articles to compile into a book." Harold's smile widened at the idea.

Jane smiled encouragingly at him.

"Well, I'm just going to sit by the door so I can listen in case any chaos breaks out downstairs. You won't even know I'm here, but nobody will be able to say you weren't chaperoned." Lucy pulled a chair into the doorway.

Harold took a step towards Lucy. "Thank you so much, Ms. Rodgers." His voice quivered slightly. "Your help has been invaluable."

Lucy grinned at him and laid her hand against his arm. "Good. Now you two get to work."

A hint of pink brushed across Harold's face as Lucy sat by the door, facing away. Jane beamed inwardly, sensing something brewing there. Perhaps Harold was the reason for the dress?

Getting back to business, Harold guided her to a seat next to the little desk. It was covered with papers. He pulled out his fountain pen and opened a worn, leather-bound journal. He asked several questions about how she ran the schoolhouse, the school supplies she had available, the number of students, and if there were a lot of children in Morley that didn't attend school. Then he asked what subjects she taught, and if it included current events, like the newest scientific discoveries and exciting inventions.

Jane tried to answer all his questions, and he seemed to take a lot of notes. She hoped this meant she was thorough and engaging. When he moved the ledger aside, she figured he was finishing up the meeting. However, he grabbed a different piece of paper already half covered with writing.

"Could you speak briefly about the incident that happened in the forest on your property yesterday? The whole town is talking about it, along with the findings at the Waller and McKenzie farms. It's most unusual."

Jane glanced at Lucy, who had turned her head to listen.

Words failed her. She searched her mind for an appropriate answer, but none seemed to come. Then she nodded. It was better for people to know what was happening than to keep quiet. She told him everything Emily had related to her. Then, almost as an afterthought, she mentioned the story she had read to Calvin.

"I know this is going to sound so silly, but I have this book of Indian myths and legends. I had read a story about the wendigo, a demon that possesses the dead and makes them rise again. These demon-possessed people crave flesh, especially human. It just seemed like this was what Emily and Simon were talking about when they described the 'dead' woman coming after them." Warmth spread across her cheeks as she felt Lucy's eyes boring into her, but she squared her shoulders in an effort not to appear too foolish. "Sorry, you probably don't want to hear about ridiculous stories about monsters from the native peoples."

"No, that was fascinating. I'll look further into this myth in relation to the incidents in Morley." She saw him write the word 'wendigo' and underline it twice. "Do you mind if I look at that book some time?"

Jane nodded and they all stood up.

Harold smiled at Jane. "Thank you so much for your help. I'm excited to work on my notes now."

Jane thanked him for the opportunity to be in the paper and wished him luck with his book. As she left, Lucy grabbed Jane's arm and pulled into her apartment at the end of the hall, excitement bubbling in her eyes.

CHAPTER 20

"Here, you must be starving!" Lucy drew her over to the table, which held a steaming plate of beef stew and a piece of bread beside it. "What do you think of him?"

Jane placed the small napkin in her lap and inhaled the aromas. Her mouth watered as her stomach rumbled. She talked between bites. "I've never been to a big city like New York, but when I think of someone coming from there, he is the exact picture of what enters my mind. Refined and soft-spoken, but not afraid to ask difficult questions. I admit I was surprised when he asked me about the strange going-ons."

"He's genuinely interested in the territory life, the reason he traveled out here. But there was a spark of excitement that lit up in his eyes when you told him about the wendigo myth. My breath caught seeing his mind working."

Jane tilted her head. "He's very different from all the other men, isn't he?"

Lucy looked down, picking at her skirt. "I've never met a man like him. He's so smart and educated along with being so polite. I guess I'm so used to the rough men that come in here, and I have to act tough and dress like them to get their respect. I think I really like Harold and how he treats me like a lady."

Jane put her fork down and reached to take Lucy's hand. "I think he likes you, too."

Lucy's head shot up, her eyes wide. "You think so? He's so nice to everyone that I couldn't tell if there was…something."

"Oh, there is. I saw it. When you touched his arm earlier, I caught him smiling. I bet he finds you fascinating. A strong woman out here in the territories, running her own inn. He's probably never met anyone like you either."

Lucy changed the subject. "Guess who's downstairs right now."

Jane rolled her eyes. "My idiot husband? I already knew that."

"Well, yes. But someone else, too. George told me when he brought your plate up."

"Come on. Half the town is down there. Just tell me," Jane said, exasperated.

"Calvin Drake."

Jane's insides came alive with butterflies. Just seeing him thrilled her. She quickly squashed that thought, keeping her face neutral. "Not sure why you think I need to know that."

"Come on, there's something going on with you two, isn't there? I know he's been coming to the schoolhouse in the afternoons," Lucy pressed.

"Who told you that?!" Jane knew Calvin would be upset if people found out he couldn't read. She must keep his confidence, for whatever reason.

"Calm down. Just saw him there that one day and then again today. You know I won't tell on you," Lucy reassured her.

Before Jane could say any more, the music below them cut off. Loud, angry voices echoed up the stairwell.

"Damn it, that's Zeke yelling," Lucy said heatedly.

Both women scrambled out of the apartment and downstairs to try to diffuse whatever situation was about to blow up.

CHAPTER 21

About ten minutes after Jane had gone upstairs for her interview, Martin swaggered into the inn with all the confidence in the world. Calvin, a few steps behind his brother, shook his head. Martin loved to make an entrance.

"Howdy, partners!" Martin called out to the room.

He received nods from a few patrons, but most people ignored him. That didn't faze Martin one bit.

Calvin hoped not to attract as much attention. He surveyed the bar and was disappointed not to see Jane. There was her idiot husband, playing cards at the table right in front of him.

Abigail dropped off a fresh mug of beer to Zeke, now seated at a table playing cards, then came over to them.

"Hey boys! You eating tonight or just drinking?" She motioned them to follow her to the counter. The Drake brothers sat on two empty stools.

"We're eatin' some of your sister's delicious beef stew tonight, darlin'. My brother here is treatin' me." Martin clapped his hand on Calvin's back. "But that don't mean we'll pass on the beer, of course."

"Sure thing." Abigail moved around the counter to get them plates of the beef stew.

George Maxwell strode over, depositing a drink in front of each man. Martin thanked the big man and Calvin almost choked. When they'd first moved to town, Martin had joined Zeke and a group of men who'd tried to persuade George to leave Morley. Calvin suspected it had more so been about causing trouble than any true animosity towards the black man. As the years have passed, and Martin has become less of a fan of Zeke's, he and George seemed to have reached a silent agreement of civility.

As Abigail set the plates down, Martin asked, "Just where is that pretty sister of yours? Anyone ever tell her she'd look so much prettier in a dress?"

Abigail laughed, "She's actually wearing a dress tonight! But I don't think she's wearing it for you. Besides, you know she'll deck you if you tell her that."

"Might be worth it." Martin licked his lips, then frowned. "She really not around?"

"She's upstairs with Jane. They're doing an interview with that reporter from New York."

Calvin's head came up at the mention of Jane's name. He saw Martin's eyes narrow. To deter Martin from opening his big mouth, Calvin directed the conversation away from Jane.

"What's a reporter doin' in Morley? Up until this week, nothin' exciting happens here. No way in hell he made it out from New York when all this freaky stuff started happenin'."

"It's true, he was here before the weird stuff started. Probably thought the Wild West would be good to write about." Her eyes fell on Calvin. "Hey, I wonder if he might be interested in talking with you? You have a direct connection with that Indian tribe nearby, right?"

Calvin looked down at his plate. He didn't advertise his trading with the Apache because some people had problems with having to share the land. With how much land there was, Calvin didn't see why they couldn't all get along. People with attitudes of entitlement made things difficult. He just shrugged, a typical answer for him, and Abigail smiled, leaving them at the calling of another customer.

Martin scooped up the last of his stew, making satisfied noises as he wiped the back of his hand across his mouth. From behind them, the door swung open. Martin spun around to observe two new people entering. "Well, who do we have here?" Martin said in a very low voice.

Calvin thought his brother meant the older man in the dirty white cowboy hat, but as he twisted his head back, he realized Martin was focused on the woman behind the man. She was younger than the man but there was a strong resemblance. Her hair was very dark and wavy, falling well below her shoulders. Her frame was small but wiry, dressed in more of a Mexican style than usual around these parts. They watched as the two newcomers went to the last empty table across the room.

Calvin answered his brother's question. "That's the farrier, come to work on the horses' hooves for a few weeks. The woman with him is his daughter. I think her name's Lydia or something. They're stayin' on the McKenzie farm."

Martin leaned closer to Calvin. "How do you know so much about what's goin' on in this town?"

Calvin shrugged again. "I have them comin' over for Sky next week. Don't want her throwin' a shoe."

Martin's eyes roved back to the dark-hair woman, seeming to lose interest in what Calvin was saying. "May not have ta leave ta find a woman after all," he muttered with a smirk on his lips.

Calvin just snorted.

The loud screeching sound of a chair being dragged across the wood-planked floor drew their interest. The piano playing halted.

"What did you just say to me?" bellowed Zeke as he lifted his large frame out of the chair to tower over Isaac.

Everyone in the bar fell silent, watching the men face-off.

Isaac leaned away from Zeke, his eyes wide and face pale. Isaac's wife was behind him, clutching her husband's shirt. Then the older man drew himself up and looked Zeke in the eye. "I said you'd better watch how much money you're losing, because you have other expenses to consider."

Zeke's face turned red, he stepped flush with Isaac, and jabbed a dirty finger into Isaac's chest. "Don't you tell me how I should handle my money, you meddling old man!"

Several people got on their feet now, including the Drake brothers.

George stepped around the counter. However, before anyone else could move, Jane flew down the stairs.

"Zeke, please don't do this here," she hissed at him as she grabbed his forearm.

He turned towards her, his rage now redirected. "How dare you talk to me like that, you bitch!" He wrenched his arm out of her hands and backhanded her hard across the face.

Everyone watched in shock as Jane's body hit the floor with a brutal sound.

Calvin tried to intercept Zeke but there was an unexpected barrier in front of him. He realized it was his brother's large hand firmly planted on his chest, keeping him in place.

"This ain't none of our business," Martin whispered urgently to him. At the moment, Calvin didn't care.

Zeke towered over Jane, and she flinched as his fingers wrapped around her arm. He dragged her to her feet, and her other arm rose to try to push him away. Her eyes scanned the room over Zeke's shoulder, locking onto Calvin.

Zeke spun around. His vise-like grip on her arm forced Jane to move with him as a mean smile spread across his face. "You gonna do something 'bout this? Huh, you stupid Indian lover?" He shook Jane by the arm until her head snapped back on her neck.

It was all Calvin could take. Rage exploded in his head. He shoved his brother out of the way and lunged at Zeke. Calvin's fist connected solidly with Zeke's face. He ignored the pain in his hand, getting more satisfaction out of the feel of Zeke's nose crunching. A spray of blood spurted out as Calvin landed another punch before hands pulled him away.

Zeke's body fell against his chair. The man seemed much better at dishing out punches than taking them. Blood ran from his nose and into his mouth. His eyes were glazed and his finger gingerly examined his mangled nose, eliciting a wince. When he saw Calvin restrained by Martin and George, he smiled with red-stained teeth. He pulled himself to his feet and pointed at Calvin. "If I ever see you on my farm again, your brother's out of a job. Only reason he ain't gone now is because he has some sense to mind his own business."

The sound of a shotgun cocking stilled all of them. Lucy stepped around the counter holding a long gun in her hands. "Get out."

After spitting red blood on the floor, Zeke turned and walked out of the inn.

Jane stood there, fingers rubbing at her arm where he'd gripped her. Her cheek was already bruising. She stared at the open door he'd walked through.

"Jane!" came the bellowing voice from outside.

Her entire body flinched. A little sob escaped from her throat, but she didn't move. Her head swung around to face Calvin where he was still restrained, a look of longing covering her expression.

"You'd better get your ass out here right now or you'll regret it later!"

She turned to look at her friend. Lucy shook her head at Jane, silently advising her to stay. Jane pressed her lips tight before her face crumbled into silent crying.

She put her head down and walked out of the inn to whatever fate held for her.

CHAPTER 22

The inn was silent as everyone listened to Zeke and Jane's footsteps fade into the distance. Calvin shoved away from Martin and George. They didn't resist him now. All eyes followed as he stormed out the back door. Then people started moving again. There was a mass exodus from the inn. Even though it wasn't very late, there'd been enough excitement for them.

Calvin paced back and forth outside the building. He clenched his jaw until the muscles hurt. His stomach burned and rolled. He wanted to destroy Zeke, just rip the asshole apart. Unfortunately, that wasn't an option at the moment. He wondered if it ever would be.

With a growl of frustration, he punched the wall. The thick wood creaked but didn't split. Pain radiated up his arm, and he welcomed it as a distraction from his anguish. He blew out a deep breath of stale air, turned and slid down the wall he'd just assaulted. He laid his bloody hand in his lap. His other hand covered his eyes, as he unsuccessfully tried to block out the images in his head.

He kept seeing Zeke backhanding her across her face, hearing the sound of her body crashing to the floor. The way she'd looked at him, like he could save her, just tore his heart apart. He didn't feel like he could save anyone.

After a while, when his hand began to throb, Calvin decided he needed a drink. The place had practically cleared out with no bodies left at the bar. Where the hell was Martin? He finally spotted him at a table across the room. Next to him sat Lydia, the farrier's daughter.

Calvin didn't know whether to laugh or be pissed off at his brother. No matter what was happening, Martin always thought about Martin. Didn't matter that not even half an hour ago, there'd been a major brawl involving his brother and his boss. Martin's mind was on women.

Martin raised his glass to Calvin and motioned him over. "Hey, little brother! This here's Lydia. She was just telling me all about the exciting world of being a farrier."

Calvin nodded at the woman.

She smiled nicely at him, although it seemed like she wasn't sure what to make of him after seeing him fight. "Nice meeting you," she offered. "This town is pretty exciting." She pointed at the chair next to her. "My father is having a smoke outside. Want to join us?"

Calvin glanced at Martin, and the look in his brother's eyes said he didn't dare sit down. "Nah. Gonna get a drink." Calvin went back to the stool at the counter.

George looked up from the glasses he'd been cleaning as Calvin sat down. Without being asked, George filled a mug with beer and set it in front of him. "On the house."

Calvin thanked him by downing the first beer. As he started on the second beer, Martin clapped his large hand on Calvin's back.

"Gonna walk this pretty lady and her pa home. Make sure none of those wendigos get them. You gonna be okay gettin' home?"

Calvin was actually kind of touched that Martin seemed to give a crap about him getting home. That was new for him.

Lucy called out to Martin, "I'll stick him in one of the empty beds upstairs if he can't!"

"Thank you kindly for lookin' out for my baby brother here!" Martin called back and left. He briefly laid his hand on the small of Lydia's back as he held the door for her. Calvin chuckled when Martin snatched his hand away as her father came into view.

Abigail bounded down the stairs, a big apple in her hand.

"You're going out to the stable now?" Lucy questioned.

"I'm taking Wildfire a snack. I haven't been out there all day and he's a jumpy horse when I don't pay attention to him." Abigail tossed the apple up and caught it in her other hand.

"Do you have your knife with you?"

Abigail rolled her eyes but pulled out a small knife. "I doubt those monsters killing the animals would come this far into town."

"Just keep your eyes open," Lucy warned.

Abigail stuck her tongue out at Lucy and walked out the back door.

A quiet descended over the room for a few minutes before George spoke up. "I'm awful jealous that you got to smash that bastard in the face. I've been itching to do that ever since my first day in town when he called me a goddamned nigger."

Calvin was definitely feeling more comfortable, a good way to loosen his tongue. "Yeah, felt good. I don't think he liked it as much as when he's doin' the hittin'."

"Poor Jane, having to deal with that jackass. I don't know why she left with him. She should just stay here. He's probably beating the blazes out of her right now." George clunked the glass he cleaned down on the counter with a loud thud.

Calvin's stomached clenched. He wanted to go up to the farm right then and beat Zeke into oblivion.

Before he could say anything, Lucy responded without looking up from washing dishes. "She went because she has a child to think about, and she's not ready to leave Morley yet."

Calvin frowned. "What do you mean 'leave Morley'?"

Lucy turned around to face them, still holding a dirty dish, her brow furrowed and lips a thin line. "Isn't it obvious? If she ever leaves that mean bastard, they'll need to run far and fast to stay ahead of his wrath." She stopped and took a deep breath. "She is going to run. Run far away. Zeke threatened that if she ever left him, he'd kill her. I think he'd do it, too. So when she leaves him, she's leaving Morley."

Calvin sat stunned. Jane couldn't leave Morley. She was a fixture in this town. He didn't want her to leave. The thought of never seeing her again made him cringe. He still didn't really understand these feelings, but he wanted to be rid of Zeke all the more.

CHAPTER 23

Jane treaded about ten paces behind her husband as they walked home from the inn. He remained silent, but she could tell by his hunched shoulders that he was fuming. She wrapped her arms around her middle. Silent tears coursed down her face, dreading what was to come.

Zeke threw open the front door and stomped inside.

Jane hesitated at the threshold. She steeled herself for the inevitable beating, Zeke's temper had to be at full rage after the humiliation he'd suffered at Calvin's hands. Despite the pain coming, she couldn't help but take a grim satisfaction that Calvin had pummeled her husband in her defense. It made all of this worth it. She drew in a deep breath before stepping inside her house.

It took a moment for her eyes to adjust to the darkness in the hall. A heartbeat passed. She blinked. Nothing. Perhaps he decided to go to bed after all?

With a feral roar of anger, he rushed at her out of the living room. His body slammed her into the wall. "Never disrespect me!"

Alcohol fumes from his fetid breath assaulted her nose. She cringed away, bile rising in her throat. As Zeke's hands gripped her shoulders and he slammed her into the wall again, she wondered if this might be it. A spike of fear slashed through her. Would he wrap his fingers around her neck and squeeze the life from her once and for all?

When his hands released her, she dropped to floor. Her bruised back ached but she was relieved to be out of his grip. Then he kicked her hard in the gut, stealing her breath from her. Droplets of spittle splattered on her as he gnashed his teeth.

As she'd laid there gasping, looking up at her husband towering over her, pure hate for him flooded through her. Her hands curled into fists. If he were going to kill her, he wouldn't get out of it unscathed. She'd kick and hit and scratch and bite. She'd fight for her life, for the life of her daughter. An image of Calvin flitted through her mind.

Then he stopped and stepped away from her. She watched as he gingerly touched his nose, winced, and walked upstairs. Their bedroom door slammed shut.

She lay on the floor, letting the adrenalin coursing through her body abate. She'd been ready to die fighting him when he'd backed off. She smirked as she hauled herself up, realizing that he'd suffered worse injuries tonight than she had. She almost laughed as she thought once again of Calvin smashing his fist into Zeke's face. Alone, she curled up on the little bed in Emily's room and slept in peace.

CHAPTER 24

Abigail walked out the back of the inn, clutching the apple. The darkness pressed into her. She grabbed one of the lanterns to push it away.

One of the horses squealed. Abigail stopped, frowning. A scraping sound whispered out of the stable door. Jogging the last few steps, she burst in and turned the lantern up for maximum light. Shadows lingered in the corners, but she could see around most of the stable.

Putting the lantern down in its usual spot for the best illumination, she peered around cautiously. Nothing looked out of place, all the horses stood in their stalls. Lucy's horse, Sally, and Harold's horse, Barlowe, gazed back at her from one side. Her horse, Wildfire, stood in the last stall on the other side. Even though a gelding, the tall chestnut-colored Quarter horse remained spunky and fidgeted when he wasn't exercised. She'd neglected him the last week since all the strange happenings started. She offered the apple to him, almost as an apology.

He nickered at her and stamped his feet nervously, refusing the fruit. The other horses responded in kind, shaking their heads and making noises of discontent. Something was wrong, even if she couldn't see it. She carefully removed her knife from her pocket, holding it out in front of her as if to ward off danger. Thoughts of the mutilated chickens at the McKenzie farm and the dead woman at the Lansing farm swirled through her head.

From behind, a pair of burly arms wrapped around her like a steel trap. One of the arms compressed around her midsection while the other hand covered her mouth. Absolute terror engulfed her, and she urgently tried breaking free from the hold. Slashing with her knife, she aimed at her attacker's thick body.

In an attempt to avoid the knife, he spun her around with his arm still clutching her middle, and a third hand came out of nowhere, gripping her wrist firmly. A handsome man with boyish features moved out of the shadows. He confiscated her knife easily.

"Don't want you hurting yourself, sweetheart," he said in a smooth voice laced with menace. His eyes scanned her, roaming down her body.

Sour acid swirled through her stomach and threatened to come up. Her breath quickened and her knees shook when he smiled at her, a mean smile.

Taking her knife, he ran it lightly down her neck as he stepped closer. She tried to flee but the other man behind her held strong. "Don't be shy now, little filly," he cooed. "We can be real nice when we want to."

"Yeah, real nice," whispered the other man.

His hot breath on her face brought the bile up her throat. The man in front of her pressed into her, and she was sandwiched between the two of them.

Reacting with pure instinct, she smashed her foot down with all her strength on to the foot of the man holding her. He cried out, and the arms around her released as he stumbled backward. Abigail let out a scream, hoping desperately that someone would hear her. She twisted toward the door in an effort to escape.

Abruptly, her scream cut off as her own knife pierced into her abdomen. There was no pain, at least not yet. Her whole body stopped moving, and she stood there, contemplating how the knife felt inside her.

"Shit! What do we do now, Warren?" The fat man with the beard was suddenly visible in her sight. He sounded frantic.

Warren wrenched the knife out, holding the bloody weapon up like a sword.

Abigail's hand flew to her wound, distressed to feel blood oozing between her fingers. She hunched over and backed up against the stable wall. The first slivers of pain laced through her side.

"Someone must have heard her. We've gotta get the hell out of here, Jimmy!" Warren hissed.

Before either man could budge, the door to the stable slammed open, and George rushed in, shotgun up and ready for action. Lucy and Calvin followed behind him.

"Don't move!" George shoved the shotgun into Warren's face.

Crying her sister's name, Lucy ran to Abigail. The strength left Abigail's legs and she rapidly collapsed in her sister's arms. Lucy carefully lowered her to the ground.

Jimmy squealed and ran for the other door across the stable. Calvin motioned for George to stay put and sprinted after the fleeing man. He easily caught up and tackled him to the ground. Jimmy screeched as his body hit the floor.

"Ya stay down there or George's gonna put a bullet through yer back," Calvin threatened him.

Jimmy panted heavily, but he put his arms up.

"Oh god, she's bleeding a lot! Abigail! Abigail, can you hear me?" Lucy sounded frantic, her words running fast together.

"I can hear you," Abigail said quietly. "Stop shouting. It's really not that bad," she tried to assure her sister, even though she really wasn't sure if that was true. Numbness crept through her limps.

A hysterical giggle interrupted Lucy's sobbing. "Even now you're going to be contrary?" Lucy looked up at George. "We need to get Doc Silverstein right now."

"I can run and get him if you keep the gun on them," George offered.

Calvin spoke up. "No. I can run faster than you. I'll get the Doc and the Sheriff so you three ain't alone with these bastards too long."

Abigail shifted, the numbness spreading. "Don't dawdle now."

Nobody laughed.

CHAPTER 25

Doctor Israel Silverstein hurriedly stocked a bag. He needed more supplies for an injury this severe.

Calvin fidgeted, unable to stand still. The Doc's slow pace was unbearable and he needed to move. "I'm goin' over to the Sheriff's. They need to know. If ya get there before the lawmen, wait."

Israel nodded and shoved another bottle in the bag.

Calvin ran as fast as he could to the sheriff's office. He flew through the door, startling the sleeping Deputy Victor Wade awake. Calvin shook his head in disbelief.

Victor sat at the desk, his chair tilted back and his feet up. He almost lost his balance as Calvin barreled in but righted himself just in time. "What the hell, Drake?"

"Abigail's been stabbed in the stable behind the inn. George's got two men cornered."

"No kidding!" Victor exclaimed.

The deputy sounded more excited than concerned, and Calvin narrowed his eyes. The deputy never seemed quite right to him, like he didn't actually want to be bothered with the townsfolk. "I'm gonna get the sheriff too," Calvin informed him.

"You do that." Victor strapped on his gun belt. He was acting like a kid going on a trip, not a lawman faced with a potentially life-threatening situation.

Calvin headed to the sheriff's house a few yards down the road. He dashed up the stairs and pounded on the door.

It didn't even take a minute for Sheriff Bill to appear at the door. He was in his nightclothes but appeared fully awake. Martha stood behind him with her eyebrows raised.

"Calvin?"

Calvin repeated what he'd said to Victor.

Bill swallowed hard, his movements becoming stiff as he wiped at his face. "Poor Abigail."

That was the concern that Calvin felt he should see from an officer of the law. "Deputy Wade and the Doc are already on their way. I'll meet ya down there."

Bill nodded. "I'll be right there."

CHAPTER 26

Bill closed the door even as Calvin took off. Martha stared at the closed door and then screamed out, "What is going on in this town? This place is supposed to be safe!" It sounded to Bill like she was accusing him of not doing his job.

He sighed loudly and ran to change his clothes. His head hurt again, but he was out of the house in less than two minutes. He let the door shut behind him, muffling the sounds of Martha's arguing as he ran to the inn. He understood she was scared and didn't want him leaving but why couldn't she understand? He was the sheriff of Morley, and it was his job to keep them all safe. At the moment, he felt like a failure.

Pushing those self-deprecating thoughts aside, he focused on the job he had to do. Slipping through the door, he saw that the inn was empty. He strode through the room to the back door.

He whirled around at that loud sound of footsteps flying down the stairs behind him. A man he didn't recognize stopped short of crashing into him.

Bill pulled his gun out. "Hold it right there!"

A yell escaped the man as his hands flew up and he stumbled backward. "Wait! I'm a reporter!"

Bill took a good look at him. His disheveled clothes were high quality and store-bought. A pair of fancy eyeglasses rested on his face. Even though mussed, his hair was clean. He remembered Lucy telling him about the boarder from New York City writing articles on the territories.

"Harold?" Bill questioned.

"Yes, sir."

Bill lowered his gun.

Harold pushed his glasses up his nose. "What's going on? I thought I heard a scream but nobody's here anymore. I just checked upstairs, and it's empty, too."

"There's been an incident. I need you to stay here." Bill pointed to the floor and turned to the back door.

Harold scoffed. "Obviously you've never met a reporter before, Sheriff." He turned to follow Bill.

Bill sighed, accepting the inevitable. "Just stay behind me."

They walked quietly to the nearby stable.

Before they got into the building, Bill could hear Victor ranting. It was very unprofessional, and Bill ground his teeth. He wondered if Victor had even followed any of their training when dealing with criminals. Even though it was a rare occurrence, they'd both still been trained rigorously by the previous sheriff.

"You think you can come into our town, steal our horses and hurt our women? You stupid jackasses got it all wrong!"

Bill entered the stable and surveyed the situation. Victor immediately shut his mouth, not looking at his boss. Bill looked over at Lucy cradling Abigail in her arms as she pressed a handkerchief to the wound on Abigail's abdomen. He noted that Lucy had tears on her face but no longer cried, her mouth set in a grim line as she tried to stop her sister's bleeding. Abigail looked pale and sweaty.

"How's she doing?" Bill directed at Lucy.

Abigail answered instead, her voice raspy. "Sentiment appreciated, Sheriff, but you gotta deal with getting the scum out of our stable right now."

Bill tilted his head. Abigail's spunk remained intact. A good sign.

Harold immediately knelt down next to Lucy, putting his hand on her shoulder. "Oh gosh, Abigail! What can I do to help?"

Lucy tilted her head up to give him a little smile. It seemed to Bill like she was relieved to have him there. "The doctor's on his way. But she's still bleeding. Can I borrow that? I promise I'll wash it." She pointed to the cravat around his neck.

Harold hurriedly pulled the cloth off and handed it to her.

Lucy removed the bloody handkerchief and pressed the fresh cravat against Abigail's wound. Abigail whimpered.

Bill looked at the two men who had attacked Abigail and instantly recognized them as the men from the wanted poster, Jimmy Blythe and Warren Olson. Wanted dead or alive for murder, rape and possible kidnapping, considered extremely dangerous.

Without alerting them to his knowledge, he spoke quietly but firmly to Victor. "Have you disarmed them yet? Restrained them?" He knew Victor hadn't. The man was too busy exercising his muscles of authority to deal with proper procedure.

Victor grimaced. "I was just about to do that." He tucked his gun in the holster and brought out the handcuffs. He paused briefly, observing the two criminals.

Warren stared down the length of George's shotgun, lips pursed and eyes narrowed. Bill wondered if the man was stupid enough to try taking the shotgun from the muscular black man. Jimmy had gotten up on his knees but his beady, little eyes leaked tears while he muttered for mercy. He held his hands high, definitely not the mastermind of this operation.

Victor walked to Jimmy, side-stepping Warren by a good margin. He pulled the gun out of Jimmy's belt and shoved it into his own waistband. Then he hauled the large man to his feet, eliciting a whimper of fear from Jimmy. The handcuffs snapped shut on Jimmy's wrists. Victor stood there, this hand gripped around Jimmy's arm, making no move toward Warren. Bill realized that Victor had no intention of securing Warren, that he expected Bill to handle the more dangerous one. Coward.

Bill looked to George and said, "He makes one move, shoot him."

George growled deep in his throat. "Please, make a move. It would brighten my whole day."

Warren seemed to think better of it as Bill disarmed and cuffed him.

"George, do you think you could assist us by lighting the way back to the post?" Bill asked.

George looked at Lucy and Abigail. "I don't want them here alone, unarmed. Just in case there are any more of them."

"I can help you out, Sheriff." Harold grabbed the lantern and headed out in front of them.

Bill jerked Warren into motion out the door, keeping his gun trained on the criminal's back. Victor followed, pushing Jimmy with such force the bearded man went down on his knees in the dirt. He stumbled back up on two feet before Victor could inflict any more trauma.

Before leaving the stable, Bill turned back to those remaining. "Doc Silverstein should be back any time now." He just hoped it was in time.

CHAPTER 27

Calvin sprinted down the road, seeing the Doc lugging his medical bag toward the stable. Without a word, Calvin grabbed the bag away from him, allowing the Doc to speed up. They flew into the stable, and Calvin was relieved to see the outlaws gone.

Lucy sobbed in relief as they walked in.

Israel took back his medical bag and rushed over to Abigail. He kneeled down beside her, gently moving the bloody cloth off her wound.

Lucy gave it up readily so he could examine her sister. "I think the bleeding might be stopping."

"Oh, good. I love this dress and the blood is going to be quite a chore to wash out of it," Abigail grumbled.

The Doc chuckled.

"Abigail! Stop that. This is serious!" Lucy chided her.

Calvin nodded to George. "They take those assholes away?"

"Yep, probably got them all locked up in cages by now," George replied. "If they'd taken any longer, I would've shot the one that stabbed Abigail."

Israel stood up. "We need to get her into bed."

"I'm pretty sure I can walk." Abigail tried to push herself up.

"No, my dear, that's not advisable," Israel said calmly but firmly.

Abigail bit her lip and accepted Lucy's helped to lay back down.

Israel motioned to George and Calvin. "Would you two be able to carry her up the stairs?"

They nodded in unison, shuffling towards the prone woman. George lifted Abigail under the arms as Calvin lifted her legs at the knees.

"Ow!" Abigail's hands flew to her wound.

George struggled, almost dropping her but then straightened himself.

Once they got her settled in her bed, the men stepped back. The Doc leaned over Abigail with a pair of scissors and cut the cloth around her stab wound.

"My dress," Abigail whined.

"I'll buy you a new one, just like this one," Lucy assured her.

Once the wound on Abigail's abdomen was fully exposed, Israel glanced at Lucy. "I need to get some supplies from your kitchen. Can you come with me?" He looked pointedly at Lucy.

Lucy reluctantly disentangled her fingers from Abigail's, who had her eyes squeezed shut.

"I'll stay with her." George took Abigail's hand.

Lucy patted George's shoulder and followed Israel out. Calvin joined them.

Israel's weathered eyes surveyed Lucy as he reported his diagnosis. "The good news is that it doesn't appear any major vessels were cut. She's not bleeding internally. However, I am concerned by the location of the wound, that the knife may have cut into her intestines." Lucy's eyes widened, but before she could panic, he put his hand on her arm. "Hold on. We don't know if that's actually happened."

"But if it did, she's going to die. Isn't she?" Lucy's voice broke.

The Doc's mustache dropped down in a frown. "Yes," he answered truthfully. "I could try to take her into surgery but there's an even higher chance of her not surviving if I cut her open to find the wound. It would already be too late by then. She's not going to feel too bad at first, but she'll become septic within a few days, and that will take her. All we can do is keep her comfortable and wait. In the meantime, I am going to suture the wound closed."

Lucy nodded, tears running down her face as she walked back into the bedroom.

Calvin's eyes wandered around the apartment, a place he'd never been before. It was homey, more so than the run-down place he shared with his brother. Pictures actually hung on the walls, and cute little figures stood on the mantle. He shifted from foot to foot, unsure how to fit into a room like this. "I'm goin' over to the Sheriff's. Make sure they ain't having any problems with them outlaws."

The Doc nodded as he prepared his suture material.

Calvin slipped out the door, not wanting to attract any further attention.

Across the road, Bill, Victor, and Harold stood in front of the sheriff's office. Light illuminated the window, silhouetting the men. Harold leaned against the wall several paces away from the lawmen, writing in his little pad of paper. Neither of the other men seemed to notice him. They argued in whispers. Calvin slowed down, not wanting to interrupt.

"I was getting to it!" Victor hissed.

"Those two men should have been disarmed and handcuffed before I even walked through that door. These are dangerous men, wanted for murder and rape! The notice said they're suspected for kidnapping too. Do you see a hostage? Probably means they already killed that kid." Bill turned as Calvin strode from the darkness. "What's the news on Abigail?"

"Doc said she ain't bleeding no more. But the knife mighta sliced somethin' in her gut. If it did, she's a goner. Won't know for a few days."

Nobody said anything for a minute. Harold even dropped his pad down to his side, like he forgot it for a moment.

"We need to hang them," Victor stated.

Despite his dislike for the deputy, Calvin agreed with him.

CHAPTER 28

Jane awoke to the sound of heavy pounding on the door. The sun barely peeked through the window, early morning. She leapt up, instantly on guard. Her legs cramped from sleeping in Emily's small bed. She was sure Zeke had come to finish the beating he'd started the night before. Her fists clenched at her side as she stared at the bedroom door.

The pounding sounded again and realized it came from downstairs, the front door. She quickly slipped into the dress she'd worn yesterday and shoved Emily's little chair out from under the doorlatch. She peered into the hall.

Zeke slowly stepped down the stairs. He glared at her as she stepped out of the bedroom. The damage to his face made her cringe. His nose was askew and swollen to twice the normal size. A large bruise ran from his left cheek to his hairline. He snarled at her, and she shrank back behind him.

"Who is it?" he called belligerently at the door as he finished going down the stairs.

"Sheriff," she heard Bill say from the other side.

Zeke glanced back at her, his teeth clenched and his eyes wide. Had someone reported them to the law about what happened last night? Had Lucy finally gotten fed up with Zeke's temper? Pulling open the door, Zeke faced the sheriff.

The man recoiled at Zeke's appearance. Apparently, he hadn't heard about the fight between Zeke and Calvin at the inn. Zeke's voice was deep and angry. "What?"

Bill stuttered a little. "Um…good morning…ah… Zeke. I was actually here to see Jane."

Without a word, Zeke swung the door open and walked away. Jane strode down the stairs.

"Good morning, Sheriff. What can I do for you?" Jane pulled the door shut as they stepped out on the porch. She noticed him studying her face and realized she must have a bruise or two as well.

"So sorry to be bothering you this early. I need to discuss some things with you." He spoke slow, like he was hesitant to talk.

Jane braced herself for whatever bad news might come. "Okay."

"Abigail was stabbed last night."

Jane's hand flew up to her mouth as she gasped in shock. "What? We saw her last night at the inn, and she was fine! Did this involve one of those wendigos? Is she all right?"

Bill took her hand gently. "Two wanted criminals were hiding out in the stable. She's not doing too badly right now, but the Doc's a little worried she might get worse. Something about infection if her insides were cut. Only time will tell. Since it's Saturday and there's no school, would you go down to the inn to be with Abigail? Lucy refuses to leave her bedside, and I'm getting worried about her. Maybe if you were there, she'd be willing to lie down for an hour or so. Emily is having a grand time at our house with Simon, so she can stay with us for the rest of the day."

"Absolutely. I'll go right now," Jane assured him.

Bill nodded his thanks then hurried off. Jane rushed upstairs to change, not even caring what Zeke was doing. Her thoughts never left the possible fate of her best friend's sister.

CHAPTER 29

Calvin awoke with Jane's voice in his head. He'd been dreaming that after he'd punched her husband last night, the bastard had fallen into a bottomless pit. She'd thanked him profusely, calling him her hero. Then they'd left the inn together, hand-in-hand. It was a pleasant, albeit unrealistic, dream and it faded out of his mind as soon as he awoke.

The sun shone fully through the window as he pried his head off the pillow. Judging by its position in the sky, it was almost noon, much later than he was used to getting up. Confused momentarily by his surroundings, he knew he wasn't in his house. The smell of fresh baked bread wafted through the air, and he breathed in deeply. Then the memories of last night's events surfaced.

He'd spent a good portion of the night at the sheriff's office. It had seemed like Bill wanted him there. Even Victor hadn't said anything about his presence, just ignored him. The outlaws had been locked tight in their cells, handcuffs removed, but there was no way they were going to be left alone at any time. Jimmy had muttered about not deserving this, and Calvin wasn't sure if he was talking to them or himself. Warren had remained deadly quiet, staring intently at them.

Around three in the morning, he'd checked on those at the inn. He'd found Abigail sleeping, but Lucy and Harold softly talked outside her room. Lucy had offered the empty room next door and he decided if he was going to get any sleep, he'd feel better if he was close by.

He swung his legs over the side of the bed and pulled on his pants. Jane's voice echoed in his head again, and he shook his head to clear the sleep. Then he realized her voice was actually coming from just outside his door. She talked with the sheriff's wife, her soft voice stilling him.

"Abigail seems as comfortable as possible. Still painful if she tries to move, and she has no appetite. According to Doc Silverstein, we shouldn't force her to eat. Harold went to sleep when I got here early this morning, but I only got Lucy to sleep about an hour ago. I doubt she'll sleep long but every minute counts. Thanks so much for coming over, Martha, and arranging for the kids to go to the McKenzie farm with Tommy. Emily loves Clara like a big sister. I have to take care of a few things at the schoolhouse."

"It's no trouble. Emily is as good as gold. She is so good with baby Harry. I heard about what happened last night...um, with you and Zeke. Emily can stay with us until everything is okay at home," Martha offered.

Jane's voice was just a whisper of emotion. "Thanks."

He heard feet on the stairs and looked out the window as Jane came out of the building below him. She walked stiffly, and it tore him up just thinking about what her bastard husband must have done to her after they left. Figuring he'd already gotten the update on everyone at the inn, he slipped silently down the stairs and outside.

CHAPTER 30

Jane escaped to the schoolhouse to lick her wounds. She wrote Monday's lesson on the board. The smell of chalk was as soothing as summer sunshine. Zeke never came in here. She thought of the bundle hidden beneath the floorboard under her bed, still far too lean. She needed more supplies and she'd be ready to flee somewhere safe. In the meantime, she needed to keep up appearances of her normal activities.

She almost jumped out of her skin when Calvin walked into the schoolhouse. After what had happened the night before, she'd expected him never to interact with her again. It was a loss she hadn't even begun to process. Yet here he was in her doorway, his eyes darting around and his muscles tense, just like he had every other time he'd come to see her.

"Got time for a story?" He motioned to their book.

She wanted to kiss him. Last night he'd come to blows with her husband, and here he was asking her to read him a story. He didn't even mention her bruised face. It made it seem like life was normal, despite all the surreal things happening around them.

"Yes, of course." She motioned for him to sit down and flipped open the book to a random page. "This one's called 'The Pact of the Fire.' It is about how the first people and dogs came together."

When she finished reading, Jane turned the book so Calvin could see the drawing of a dog by the fire, a tiny puppy clutched in her mouth. Then Jane put the book down on the desk, and her eyes glided over him.

"Oh Calvin, your hand!" She reached for his right hand. The knuckles were scabbed and bruised. He stood up quickly, and she mimicked him, her focus completely absorbed in his injured hand. "You did this last night, because of him." Her voice cracked as her eyes found his. "Thank you." Without thinking, she leaned toward him and kissed him lightly on the cheek.

He leapt away from her, yanking his hand out of hers.

Horror gripped her as she realized what she'd done. Judging by how he cringed away from her, it had been an unwelcome gesture.

"Calvin, I'm sorry," she breathed out as tears came to her eyes.

He bolted out the door, slamming it as he left.

Jane tried unsuccessfully to hold in her choking sobs, but finally they tore out of her, releasing all the anguished she'd been holding back.

She shook her head hard. She'd gone and done it, done exactly what she wasn't going to let herself do. She opened herself to the feelings she harbored for Calvin Drake. Despite his defending her the night before, his extreme negative reaction to her kiss confirmed those feelings were not reciprocated.

As her sobs slowed, her mind drifted back to the first time she'd realized just how attracted she was to Calvin. It had been over two years ago, around the time when Zeke had started his odd behavior of going out into the fields without accomplishing anything. That was also when he'd become more erratic and crueler with his moods. Jane had accepted long ago that she was stuck in a loveless marriage, but when it had started to get dangerous for her and Emily, that's when thoughts of escape began nibbling at her brain.

The water pump's handle at the schoolhouse had frozen in place again. Martin, who hadn't been working on the farm for very long, had offered to send his brother out to fix it when she'd mentioned it to him. She'd only known Calvin from the barest interaction at that point, but not wanting to tell her husband, she'd accepted the offer. She would rather pay Calvin's fee than bear her husband's annoyance at having to do the task.

He'd arrived just after the children had left for the day. She'd been sitting at her desk after straightening up. Her mind had wandered and she'd been just staring out the window. His movements at the broken water pump had caught her attention. She hadn't been able to tear her eyes away from the sun-bleached blond god as he stood confidently over the pump, examining the parts. She'd become mesmerized by his strong hands wrapping around the handle, trying to get it working again. The handle had budged but then stuck again. He'd whipped out another tool to screw the base of it and tried again. The handle had resisted for a moment but then grudgingly moved and got easier as it slid down.

Jane hadn't been able to tear her eyes off the muscles bunching in his arms as he worked the handle up and down, up and down. A fine sheen of sweat had covered his body, and it glistened in the sunlight. Her heart had been pounding in her chest, and her breathing quickened when he'd leaned over to look at the pump where it entered the ground.

She'd jumped when he'd straightened back up, tested the handle and fresh water flowed out. Then he'd turned toward the schoolhouse, and Jane had a flash of fear that he might see her, might know she'd been watching him. Luckily, he hadn't seemed to notice her. He'd looked nervous, running his fingers through his blond hair and squinting in the sun.

Jane had tried to control her breathing. She had been sure he would come in for his payment and see her all flushed. Then he'd turned and walked away. He'd just fixed her water pump and never asked her for anything. She'd been ashamed of herself, a married woman, for thinking of him in such a way. She hadn't even been able to face him and had given his pay to Martin to pass along. She's pushed those feelings of attraction deep down. He made it easy, never talking to her or hardly even looking at her. Getting the vibe that he didn't like her, especially in that way, helped her to better associate with him. That offer to read him the Indian legends book had changed everything. Had she just ruined their blossoming friendship?

95

CHAPTER 31

Calvin Drake kicked a rock in the road and watched it skitter off into the grass before ripping open his front door. He grabbed his hunting rifle and escaped into the forest. He couldn't delude himself into thinking he was actually going hunting, because he was just crashing through the woods, his feet kicking up dead leaves and snapping brittle branches. He could check his traps at least.

Thoughts of Jane flooded unwelcome into his mind. He shook his head, trying to dispel them, but they kept coming. Her face had looked so shocked when he'd wrenched his hand away from her. Her sobs as he'd left her standing there still rang in his ears. Why'd she kiss him? Why'd it bother him so much?

What was it about her? He'd been drawn to her quiet but kind manner, even when he'd first met her. A lot of people hadn't been nice to Martin and him when they'd first come to Morley, but Jane had always treated them both like they mattered. He suspected she was actually the one to get Zeke to hire Martin after he'd been dismissed from the McKenzie farm.

For years, he'd avoided her, only seeing her when absolutely necessary. Why did he get so nervous around her? He couldn't even talk to her until just recently. Truthfully, he got nervous around women a lot. Whereas Martin could turn on his silver tongue and have a woman in his bed readily, Calvin would mumble and make a fool of himself. He was inexperienced and downright frightened of that kind of intimacy.

Calvin's father had been a worthless drunk, taking out any frustrations with his fists on his family. Zeke reminded him of his father. His mother had taken the worst of it until she died in childbirth along with their baby sister. Then Calvin had taken the brunt of the beatings because Martin was old enough to dish it back to their father. There'd been a strange feeling of giddy relief when the sheriff had come to their boarding house to tell them their daddy had been knifed to death in a saloon brawl. After that, he and Martin had moved from town to town as his older brother chased his own demons.

One disturbing memory drifted through his head. Martin had taken Calvin to a whorehouse in Texas and bought him a night of fun. Calvin, barely fifteen, couldn't even look a girl in the eye. Martin had wanted to make sure his baby brother didn't become a sissy. They'd locked him in a room with this woman who barely wore anything. She may have looked good from a distance, but up close, the flaws showed through her heavy make-up. Her eyes had been red and tired, and when she'd sat in his lap, she'd smelled like ash and stale alcohol. He'd had to fight off vomiting, and she hadn't gotten the hint when he'd pushed her off. Then she'd touched him there. He'd reacted violently, shoving her off him and kicking down the door. Martin had tackled him as he'd tried to run out, kicking his ass something awful for wasting his money. It had been a humiliating night, and Calvin had been glad Martin had since laid off him about women. Well, except for the occasional snippy comment just to embarrass him.

Calvin had been somewhat wary about coming to Morley after Martin had won their little property in a poker game. The place wasn't exactly glamorous. However, just a few years later, he felt like he'd become a productive member of the community. Even Martin was working and starting to act like an adult. It was something Calvin had never thought he'd live to see. He'd always figured Martin would be in jail or dead like their daddy by now.

Jane invaded his thoughts again, her pretty smile welcoming him whenever he saw her. He hated her husband so much for laying his hands on her. Seeing that bruise across her cheek had made him want to reach out and…

What? What had he wanted to do? He didn't know, and that made him mad. He kicked a tree, and the jolt of his foot colliding with the wood traveled up his leg. It jogged his senses a little, and he came out of his fog of thoughts.

CHAPTER 32

Victor sat at the sheriff's desk, simmering in frustration. He'd never written so many damned reports as he had in the past week and a half. Seemed kind of pointless to him, when Bill was going to write a report also.

Jimmy kicked at the bars in his cell across the room. Victor glanced up. The fat man had gotten more agitated as time passed, practically crying now. His mumblings had become loud enough to hear. Some of them seemed aimed at Victor and others just rantings to himself.

"I can't hang. I just can't die like that. This isn't my fault. None of this was my idea. I don't want to die. We never should have come to this shitty little town. We weren't even gonna steal those horses! We were just hiding out there 'til everyone went to sleep so we could get some supplies. Why'd that girl have to come out there so late?" He went on and on, blaming everything in the world for his circumstances except himself.

Victor smiled a little, enjoying the show. He liked watching the fat man squirming. Didn't matter what he said, Victor would make sure they hanged. He'd only seen one hanging before, and the thought of it made his heart quicken and the small smile widen to a grin. He was almost sure Bill would be willing, considering how dangerous these men were and what they'd done to Abigail.

His eyes shifted to Warren, and his grin fell. That man had been completely silent since they'd caught him. His malevolent eyes bored into Victor's soul until Victor looked away.

Jimmy cried full out now, gripping onto the bars with both hands. "Please, man, please. Warren's the one who made all this happen. He's the one that stabbed the girl. Not me. He planned all of this. Killing the rancher, raping his daughter, all of it. I only went along with him because I felt I had to. Please don't hang me. We've still got the kid. Got him tied up out there!"

Victor whipped his head around to stare at Jimmy. Warren sat up and shifted towards Jimmy's cell.

"What did you say? You've got a hostage?" Victor got up from the desk.

"Yes! Yes!" Jimmy cried, a huge smile blossoming on his face. "It's that rancher's farmhand. Warren says he's our insurance policy but I'm cashing that in right now. Got him tied up at our camp outside of town."

"He hurt?" Victor questioned.

"Nah, although he hasn't had anything to eat or drink since we got here. Let me outta here, and I'll take you right to him." Jimmy rattled the cell door.

Victor paused, rubbing his chin in thought. "Hmmm, we might be able to take hanging off the book for you, if we find the boy with your help."

"Is that so?" Warren spoke up for the first time. "Let us out and we'll show you where he is."

Jimmy fell silent, looking sideways at Warren now that the man had joined the conversation.

"No way in holy hell are you getting out of here." Victor settled back into his seat. "But ya'll tell me where I can find this boy, and we might forget about hanging either of you if he comes out of this safe and sound." He hoped his lie passed for truth.

Jimmy opened his mouth to speak, but Warren talked over him, shutting out the weaker man. "Two miles south of town, just off the road toward Santa Fe. The camp is behind a large thicket, and our horses are tied up there as well."

Victor knew he'd be in deep trouble with Bill if he left these criminals alone. Yet to save a hostage would make him the celebrated hero in town, not Bill. Not this time.

Pulling out his gun, he aimed it at the men. "Get back against the far wall."

They both complied. Without taking the gun off of them, Victor tested the locks on both doors. They held firmly.

Stepping away, he put the gun back in his holster. "All right, you two be good while I look for this boy. It'll go a long way in helping your case." Then he strode out the door, heading south.

CHAPTER 33

Jimmy laid on the cell's uncomfortable bed. He fidgeted and finally couldn't contain his curiosity. "Why'd ya tell him the kid was south when we left him north?"

Warren had taken off the stained sheets from the bed and was tying them up into a thick rope.

"Warren? Warren, what are you doing? I'm sorry about what I said. You know I just get scared. I'm on your side, always. Okay?" Jimmy wrung his hands, grimacing at the sweat between his palms.

Warren looked up at Jimmy, the rope of sheets in his hands. He smiled brightly, and his handsome face seemed so friendly. "Don't worry, Jimmy. I sent the guy on a wild-goose chase to get him out of the way. I know you're on my side, buddy."

Jimmy breathed out, his shoulders relaxing. Everything would be okay after all.

"Hey Jimmy, give me your sheet. I want to try to rope the sheriff against the bars when he comes back, get his gun from him." Warren pointed at Jimmy's bed.

Jimmy nodded, picturing the plan. He liked any plan from Warren, especially since he wasn't so good at coming up with ideas himself. He gathered up the sheet, hoping Warren's plan would work and they could get the dickens out of this damned town. He passed it to Warren through the bars connecting their cell. Then he turned back to his bunk, cringing at the disgusting stains now evident on the thin mattress.

"Hey, Jimmy, what's that on your back?"

Jimmy turned his head sharply, rotating around as he tried to see his own back. "What is it?"

"Looks like a spider."

Jimmy squealed. "Get it off!" He jumped up and down, twisting around.

"Come over here and I will."

Jimmy, still twitching, put his back against the bars dividing their cells.

Suddenly, the tightly wound sheet slipped through the bars and looped against his neck. He had no time to move as it constricted tightly around him. He clawed frantically at the material, his head pounding and his jaw opening and closing as his airway cut off. He tried to scream, but no sound could force its way past the tightening rope on his neck. Minutes passed as he fought, breaking off a grimy fingernail in the coils of the bed sheet rope, but unable to feel the pain. His body spasmed against the bars in a last effort to break his deadly bondage. Reality blurred, and his vision swam as Jimmy's brain started to die from the lack of oxygen.

Even after he stopped struggling, and his heavy body fell to the floor, Warren didn't let up on the pressure of the sheet rope. Jimmy's last vision before death was of Warren's boyish features twisted into a murderous grimace.

"That's for backstabbing me, you traitor."

CHAPTER 34

Calvin brought his rifle up when he heard a quiet, snorting noise to his right. Might have been a deer. The lingering thoughts of Jane finally dissipated. If he caught it, then this stupid, emotional foray into the woods wouldn't have been completely worthless.

Another noise, louder, more like a whinny of an upset horse, made him stop for a moment. He moved forward again as he crossed into a clearing near the road leading to Morley. His finger rested on the trigger, knowing there wouldn't be any deer in front of him but possibly something more dangerous.

A horse stood tied to a stake in the ground with a good amount of leeway to the rope. However, almost all of the grass around the stake had been clipped off, indicating the horse had been there a while. The frustrated beast pulled at the rope attached to his head, nervously skittering away from him.

Two other horses, similarly staked, seemed unconcerned. A camp lay on the other side, the fire dead in the middle. All the gear had been packed up for an imminent departure but had been left behind.

A muffled sound from behind the skittish horse caught his attention. Carefully leaving room so the frightened animal couldn't kick him, Calvin eased around the camp. His eyes landed on a young man, bound and gagged. A rope attached to his hands tied behind his back was firmly anchored to another stake. Flaking blood was dried to the side of his face, and he blinked at Calvin for a moment before struggling against his restraints.

After making sure they were indeed alone, Calvin strode over and pulled the gag out of his mouth.

"Help! You've gotta help me!" he cried.

"Shhh, calm down kid." Calvin noted that he couldn't have been much over the age of seventeen. "What in tarnation happened to you?"

"Got kidnapped. They killed my ma and pa and raped my sister. I think they're trying to ransom me off to my older brother. Told me they'd be back in a few hours, but that was more than a day ago." His voice held a note of hysteria.

"What's yer name?" Calvin asked as he shifted behind the boy. Pulling out his knife, he swiftly cut the ropes.

"Alexander."

"So ya got kidnapped by a pretty boy and a fat jackass?"

"Yeah, that's them! Warren and Jimmy. What happened to them? They get killed?"

"Not yet," Calvin growled.

CHAPTER 35

Utterly exhausted, Bill made his way back to the office. He'd been up a good portion of the night dealing with the prisoners and then spent the day alerting the townsfolk about the situation. Now late afternoon, he was just finishing at the inn with Doc Silverstein, checking on Abigail's progress. The young woman was still very weak. The Doc was worried about her, as was the rest of the town.

For the next six hours, Bill hoped things would be quiet, but there was no way he was going to leave those men locked up without supervision. He would relieve Deputy Wade and let the man sleep until about midnight. Then Bill would finally get some sleep until morning.

As he walked through the door, he noticed Victor wasn't at the desk. He frowned. There weren't exactly a lot of places to hide in the little office. Then he looked over at the jail cells, and his breath caught at the horrific scene before him.

Warren pressed up against the farthest wall of his cell, his body jammed into the corner. His eyes bulged open as he panted, his chest heaving as he tried unsuccessfully to make his body smaller. Stark terror had replaced his usual expression of self-assurance. He spotted the sheriff and his hoarse voice whispered, "Help me."

In the other cell stood Jimmy. Or at least what used to be Jimmy. His arms pushed through the bars connecting the cells as far as they could possibly go. He'd rubbed the skin off as he struggled, and large areas lay open, oozing dark, clotting blood. His fingers clutched, trying to claw forward in the air. Warren, obviously his target, cowered only inches from Jimmy's bloody grasp. Without care for the iron bars holding him back, Jimmy smashed his body against them with bone-cracking strength.

"Hellfire!" Bill cursed.

Jimmy stilled, which was more disturbing than when he slammed against the bars. His body shifted sideways towards Bill's voice, like he hadn't noticed Bill until he spoke. Jimmy's arms slid out from between the bars separating the cells, and the left one hung at a strange angle. The blank eyes moved over Bill, the unreadable gaze seeming to drink him in.

Seeing Jimmy's face was more horrific than he'd could have believed. The large man looked like the dead risen. Gray skin bordered on blue in some places. Red rimmed his wide open, solid white eyes. From his mouth poured garbled groans and snaps as he gnashed his jaws together. His neck had turned purple and swelled up to an even larger diameter than it had been in life.

Jimmy rushed the bars again, this time at Bill. At this new angle, he now crashed his head into one of the bars. His nose was mashed instantly into his face, spewing black blood down the front of his already disgusting shirt. It did nothing to slow him down.

"Jesus Christ, what happened to him?" Bill shouted.

"I don't know! I swear!"

The monster opened up his mouth, emitting a horrid gurgling noise. A huge spew of black blood flowed out through the bars. Bill jumped backwards with a cry, narrowly avoiding it striking him. Warren retched at the atrocious smell. Jimmy seemed to take a moment to recovery and returned to thrashing against the bars.

Bill's stomach tightened, and his hands shook. He clenched them to keep Warren from seeing the weakness.

Warren crouched down in the corner as Jimmy swiped his arms through the bars. "Kill the bastard!" Warren shrieked.

Bill drew his weapon, aimed carefully, and fired a bullet straight into Jimmy's chest. Black blood sprayed from the exit wound. Jimmy's legs hit the bunk, and his body sagged down on the bed, pushed backward by the impact. Bill stepped closer to the cell to investigate.

Jimmy's head flew back, and he roared, his mouth gaping. With a speed uncharacteristic for a man his size, Jimmy launched himself off the bed at Bill. The sheriff backpedaled as the monster ran full force into the bars again. Bill brought the gun up again and shot three more bullets into him. It didn't seem nearly as effective as the first one.

Another bullet buried itself in Jimmy's head. The dead, fat man tottered unsteadily before crashing to the ground, truly dead now.

Bill and Warren both whirled around to see where that last bullet had come from. Calvin Drake stood in the doorway, his rifle aimed at Jimmy's cell. Seeing that the monster wouldn't get back up, he lowered it and tilted his head at the shocked lawman.

"Balls, Calvin! How'd you know that would work?" Bill whispered, still stunned.

"Heard it in a story."

Bill turned to the only living convict. "You tell me what happened here."

"He just grabbed his chest and fell over. I thought he was dead, and then it was like he came back to life like this!" Warren shouted back, not daring to move out of the corner.

"Where's Deputy Wade?"

"Your deputy bailed out of here." Warren was trembling, but suddenly seemed eager to be helpful.

"After Jimmy died?"

"Nah, before that."

"This bastard changed into a wendigo," Calvin chimed in. "Just like that woman when Martin killed her, already dead but still moving."

"What the hell is a wendigo?" Warren questioned.

Bill responded. "An Indian myth about a demon that possesses dead people, making them rise again to feed on living flesh. I thought it was a bunch of hogwash when Martin brought it up."

"Don't seem like hogwash at the moment," Warren snorted. "Does anyone just become one of these wendigos?"

Calvin frowned, unsure about the answer. "I think you've got to get bit by one."

"Jimmy didn't get bit or scratched or anything." Then Warren's mouth gaped open as he inhaled sharply. "Oh shit! The deer! It was all chewed up. We ate it! Oh God, it tainted me, too! There's a demon in me!" Warren's frantic hands ran all over his body.

"Excuse me, Sheriff." Calvin moved aside, revealing Alexander. "Found this guy tied up out by the south road. Says he was kidnapped by those two." Calvin's eyes darted to Warren.

Bill, starting to compose himself, nodded. He strode over to the desk and grabbed the wanted poster. After scanning it quickly, Bill looked at the young man. "Alexander."

Alexander had been staring at Jimmy's dead body, but his head whipped up at the mention of his name. "Yes, sir."

"You've got to be kidding me," a fuming voice said from outside the doorway. Victor Wade spat on the ground, glaring first at Alexander then at Calvin. "You found the kid? Damn you, Drake." It looked like he'd been in a fight with a large plant. Grass stains covered his pants, and dirt painted his disheveled shirt. Pieces of foliage clung to his hair, and a tiny cut ran along his cheek.

Warmth flooded Bill's face as fury pounded up through his skull. "Where have you been?" He gritted his teeth to keep his temper in check.

"Been searching for this guy, the kidnapped rancher's son," Victor stated as if he'd done nothing wrong. "They told me they had him stashed north of town, so I figured I'd better find him soon, or else he'd die of dehydration or exposure."

"You left them here alone?" Bill sucked in a breath and let it out slowly, forcing himself to remain calm.

"They were both locked up tight in their cells and I knew you'd be back soon. I thought the kid was more important." Then Victor's brows knitted together. "Why? Did something happen?"

"Come look." Bill stepped out of the way.

Victor made a strangled cry when he saw Jimmy's dead, grotesque body. "How did that happen?"

Bill stepped face to face with the other man. "I don't know! No one was here watching to know how this happened! You weren't doing your job!"

Victor held his hands up, looked at the ground and shook his head. "I'm sorry. I thought it would be better to find the kid."

"Well, you can think about that decision while you're cleaning up this mess!"

Victor put his head down and nodded. Bill swiftly walked out to cool down, but stayed within earshot.

"What happened?" Victor asked Calvin.

"The fat one became a wendigo."

"I thought that was a bunch of made-up Indian bullshit."

"Does it look like made-up Indian bullshit to you?" Calvin stomped outside, hauling Alexander with him. Bill had closed his eyes, drawing in cleansing breaths of fresh air. He gained control of his anger but noticed Calvin scrutinizing him.

"Calvin, can you get Doc Silverstein? He's probably still across the street with Abigail. We need to get this body back to his place and figure out exactly what happened to him. Warren is not exactly a trustworthy witness." Bill heard the exhaustion in his own voice.

Calvin nodded then said to Alexander, "Come on, kid. This inn has got the best beef stew in the whole territory of Colorado."

CHAPTER 36

Sheriff Bill Anderson walked slowly up the road to Doc Silverstein's office. He wasn't in a rush to be near the dead body of his prisoner, who had essentially died under his watch. Even though Victor was the officer in charge at that moment, his incompetence was a direct reflection on Bill. Jimmy was going to hang for his crimes anyway, but what had happened in that jail cell had been unacceptable. Only Warren knew the truth. He insisted Jimmy had a heart attack and turned into one of those monsters. One of those wendigos. If it was true that he'd been tainted by the deer meat they'd eaten, then Warren harbored a demon, too. Maybe leaving the dead bear in the woods for the scavengers had been a bad idea.

Stepping up to the door of the small building that served as Doc Israel's office, Bill held back a gag. The smell of rot rolled out the open window, and he steeled himself as he pushed the door open and stepped inside.

Jimmy's body lay on a table, some of him poking over the edges. The bodies of the woman with the bear and the unknown traveler had already been removed. There had been quite a debate about whether to bury them in the cemetery outside of town or to burn them. Due to the mysterious circumstances of their demise, burning had won out. People were still twitchy in Morley about possible communicable diseases ever since they'd lost so many to cholera a decade ago.

"Good day, Sherrriff," Israel greeted him in his faint Russian accent.

"Hopefully today stays a better day than yesterday, Doc." Bill's eyes felt so heavy and he rubbed his face in an effort to bring his mind away from thoughts of sleep. "What've you found?"

Israel walked him closer to the corpse and pointed at the swollen, purple neck. "This is not norrrmal, even in death."

Bill pointed at the bullet wounds in the middle of his forehead and in his ample gut. "These aren't exactly normal in death either, not unless they're the cause."

Israel's mustache twitched at the Sheriff's sarcasm. "They werrren't. All of those vounds came after death."

Bill opened his mouth to speak.

Israel held up a hand to quiet him. "I know. You said he vas still moving, trrrying to attack you thrrrough the bars. Based on my examination, he vas technically already dead by that point. I don't know vhy his body was still moving. Same with the voman vith the bear. Maybe they rrreally are dybbuk."

Bill looked at him sideways, silently demanding an interpretation of the unknown Yiddish word.

"Possessed by demons." Israel shook his head, frowning deeply. Bill had never known the doctor to be superstitious, but this was a very strange string of occurrences.

"So it was a heart attack that killed him," Bill concluded for him.

"No, he vas strangled to death. Hence the swollen and brrruised neck."

Bill processed this information for a moment, coming to the logical conclusion. "Warren killed him."

Israel nodded.

"He's a dangerous man. We're going to have to hang him."

Israel nodded again.

"I'm going to look for more evidence at their camp, although it's going to have to wait until tomorrow. Don't want to disturb anything tripping around out there in the dark. But I want this man gone fast."

"That is very wise, Sheriff."

CHAPTER 37

Jane wiped her eyes and smoothed out her dress. She'd cried enough after Calvin had stormed out on her. She locked the schoolhouse and headed back to the inn.

She pushed through the door and pasted a smile on her lips as she nodded to George at the counter. Over the years with Zeke, she'd learned how to adequately bury her feelings. Unfortunately, Calvin's very negative response to her kiss had been unexpected and the intensity of her emotions had overwhelmed her.

Harold opened the apartment door wide, motioning her in. "I'm glad you're here. Maybe you can get her out of that room. She's driving Abigail crazy."

"How daunting of a task." Jane could already hear the sisters arguing.

"Stop touching me! I don't have a fever!" Abigail yelled.

"You feel hot. That's a fever." Lucy's tone sounded of barely restrained frustration.

"Jane!" Abigail cried, seeing her in the doorway. "Help me! She won't leave me alone!"

Jane noticed Abigail's skin wasn't as pale or sweaty as before. She still had dark circles under her eyes though. The girl's spunky attitude gave Jane hope.

Lucy smacked the night table. "Abigail Daisy Rodgers! Stop acting like such a child! You want to sleep? Good, I'll get some dinner. Don't you dare get out of that bed." Lucy stormed out of the room, pulling Jane along with her.

Jane managed to get the door closed behind her.

Out in the living room, Harold looked up from the book he was reading. He and Lucy made eye contact, little smiles on their lips.

Oh yes, there's definitely something there.

Lucy turned to her and sighed. "That girl is driving me crazy, but at least she's alive to do it. For that I'm thankful." Lucy then gave her a good look over and frowned. "What's wrong?"

Uh-oh. Jane turned up the brightness of her smile. "Nothing. I'm just worried about Abigail."

Lucy narrowed her eyes and turned around to the man reading. "Harold? Can you grab us a couple bowls of that corn chowder that George's serving downstairs?" she asked sweetly.

"Absolutely." He jumped up, seemingly relieved to have a job to do.

As soon as he left, Lucy pulled Jane down on the sofa. "Don't tell me there's nothing wrong. You've been crying, I can tell. What happened? Zeke hit you again? I swear if he did, I'll-"

"No, it wasn't Zeke. It's nothing for you to worry about. Just let it go." Jane knew the effort was futile.

Lucy was like a dog with a bone once she set her mind on something. "Jane."

"Fine!" Jane huffed and looked up at the ceiling. "I did something stupid."

Lucy waited.

"Something really, really stupid."

"Come on, Jane. Your idea of doing something stupid is typical behavior for some people. How bad could it be?"

"I kissed Calvin Drake."

Lucy wasn't easily shocked but at that, she was speechless.

Jane rambled, trying to explain herself. "It was only a kiss on the cheek. I wanted to thank him for what he did for me last night. It didn't go over well."

"What do you mean?"

"It was like I slapped him, he was so disgusted. He jumped away and bolted out of there. It was awful. He'll probably avoid me forever now." Jane put her head in her hands.

114

"I can't believe you kissed him." Lucy shook her head. "That is so unlike you."

"Well, it won't happen again."

"Would you want it to happen again?" Lucy questioned, and continued when Jane didn't answer. "The way he acted last night, those weren't the actions of a man who's disgusted by the woman he's defending."

She was saved by Harold arriving with two bowls in his hands. Both women thanked him and ate the delicious chowder in silence.

Standing up, Jane gave them an appreciative smile. "Thank you for the chowder. I need to get home to Emily. I'm sure Rebecca and Clara have brought her back by now." To Lucy, she added, "If you need anything, just send for me."

Lucy stood up and hugged her friend. "It wasn't stupid. Give my love to Emily."

Jane thought about Lucy's words as she walked home in the dwindling light. It was easy to dismiss them.

CHAPTER 38

The bright sun had dimmed as it descended to the west. Martin Drake awoke from his late afternoon nap in the hay loft. He stretched and lay back in the soft hay for a few more minutes, collecting his thoughts.

He hated to admit it, but he really loved this job. He'd never been at a job as long as this one, usually getting dismissed for sleeping on the job or insulting the boss with his filthy mouth. Okay, sometimes the boss's daughter too. Not that he didn't want to provoke Zeke Lansing. This boss was a complete asshole. Yet, it seemed like the guy didn't care a lick about his own farm. On many days, he'd go out into the fields, and Martin had no idea what he was doing out there.

His thoughts drifted to the woman he'd met at the inn the night before, Lydia. She was a pretty thing, although a little older than what he normally went for. Granted, he was getting older as well, and it'd been a couple years since he'd had to employ his charms. She'd responded positively and he'd been sure he was going to get her in bed once her father went to sleep. That was until they'd arrived at the McKenzie's guest house and he met her kid. Martin Drake did not mess with women with children. He'd made a hasty retreat, which she didn't seem to notice. Perhaps Lydia had though him a gentleman, delivering her home safe and sound? He laughed at the thought.

In the past, that would've been the end. He wouldn't have bothering thinking about her again, would've just moved onto the next woman to come his way. Yet, here he was, thinking about her again.

He frowned as his thoughts shifted to his brother, who hadn't come home the night before. Had he really drunk so much he couldn't drag himself up the road?

"Hey, Martin, you up there?" a voice interrupted his thoughts.

He scrambled down from the loft but relaxed when he realized it was a feminine voice. Before him stood Rebecca and Clara McKenzie, Tommy Anderson, Emily Lansing and Lydia's son, whose name he never bothered committing to memory.

"Taking a little nap? We could practically hear the snoring from the road," Rebecca goaded him.

A smirk came to his lips as he jumped off the ladder. "Well, what're you babies doin' on this side of town?"

Rebecca rolled her eyes. "Shove it, Martin."

"I know where I'd like to shove it." He chuckled as Rebecca's eyebrows shot up, and Clara grabbed her arm.

Lydia's son snickered.

Rebecca smacked the boy on the arm. "Stop laughing, Jacob!"

The kid quieted, but he couldn't keep the smile off his lips. Maybe this kid wasn't so bad.

"Don't listen to him. He says stuff like that all the time, but he really is soft underneath," Emily piped in.

"Whatcha doin' callin' me soft? Bollocks to that," Martin spat out.

Clara and Rebecca's eyebrows flew up, but Jacob laughed. Emily kept smiling at him.

Rebecca took a calming breath. "Look, Martin, we're bringing Emily back. Jane's still helping with Abigail, and we have no idea where Zeke is. He's not in the house. Can you watch Emily until one of them gets back?"

"I'm not a damned babysitter. I got stuff to do." He waved his hand around the farm. Then he blinked. "What happened with Abigail?"

"Didn't you hear?" Tommy asked. "She got stabbed in the stable last night."

Martin gasped. "By who?"

"Two outlaws hiding out. Your brother helped stop them, then got my dad," Tommy explained.

"My brother?" Martin clutched his chest in shock.

They all nodded their heads. Including the fight with Zeke, his brother sure did have an interesting evening. No wonder the guy didn't make it home.

"She gonna be okay?" he asked, surprised he was truly concerned for the girl's well-being. She'd always been sweet to him, even if she blew off all of his advancements. Then again, she was really was too young for him, her sister being more his type. Not that she'd responded any more favorably.

Clara's eyes teared up. "The Doc's not sure. He says only time will tell."

Tommy put his arm around her.

"We've got to get back before dinner time. You'll watch her?" Rebecca glared, as if daring him to say something else to set her off.

"I'm just gonna watch you a little longer as yer leavin'." He smiled slyly at her.

Rebecca stepped forward, smacking her fist into his shoulder. Martin laughed loudly, even if she did pack a bit of a punch. He stumbled back, continuing to laugh.

"Boy, that stockboy is sure gonna have his hands full with you!" he cackled.

"Don't you dare talk about Daniel like that! He's a gentleman, something you've got no clue about!" Her fingers curled into fists.

Jacob laughed so hard he couldn't catch his breath. Gulping air, he got a hold of himself and said to Martin, "Daniel is already completely under her thumb."

"Jacob!" Clara grabbed his arm and dragged him off.

Martin watched the boy go with a new-found respect. Maybe he could consider getting with a woman who had a kid like that.

Martin side-eyed Emily as she waved good-bye. "What's that in yer hand?"

"A book. It's called Jane Eyre. Isaac gave it to me. I've never read a book before."

Martin shrugged. "Books never much interested me. Let's go, ya little imp." He walked back in the barn. "Gotta milk yer old-as-dirt cow."

Emily ran ahead. "Don't be mean to Bessie. Her milk makes the best cheese in town." She petted the cow's neck. Martin got down to the business of milking, and it was silent for a moment before Emily spoke up again. "Were you at the inn last night?"

"Yep, but I was gone before that thing happened with Abigail." Martin didn't look from his task.

"Were you there when your brother punched my father?"

Martin glanced at her. "Where'd ya hear that?"

She shrugged. "Sheriff Bill was talking about it to Isaac when he stopped at the store. They didn't know I was listening."

Martin grinned. "You are a crafty little thing, ain't ya?"

"So did Calvin break my dad's nose? How many times did he hit him?"

Martin took note at the interest in her voice. She sure wanted to hear the details of her father's beating. "Couple times in the head."

Emily grinned back at him. "Was he bleeding?"

"Oh, yeah. His nose gushed all over the place. Why so many questions? Not very lady-like of you wanting to hear 'bout your daddy getting beat."

"I hate him!" She crossed her arms and ducked her head.

Martin nodded. He could understand that. His feelings towards his father hadn't exactly been warm and fuzzy.

"What did you just say?" Zeke Lansing stood silhouetted in the door like a giant shadow devil blocking out the light. His face was purple and swollen, but his eyes focused intently on his daughter. In an instant, Emily's smile melted away and she bit her lower lip. Zeke advanced on Emily, who cringed away from him, but he grabbed the front of her dress.

"You will respect me as your father, you little whore!" he screamed in her face.

Martin leapt to his feet, the bucket of milk spilling across the floor in his urgency, but he just couldn't react fast enough.

Zeke pulled Emily off her feet and flung her away from him with all his might. Her small body sailed through the air across the barn and collided with the wall. She fell to the floor with a thunk.

A beat later, Martin was on top of Zeke, his fist landing in the same spot on Zeke's face as his brother had the night before. It didn't take much to knock the large man off his feet. Zeke crumpled onto his hands and knees. Martin then kicked him squarely in the ribs before taking a quick look back at Emily. She was starting to sit up.

From the ground, Zeke bellowed, "I told you to mind your own business, you deadbeat! You're gone! Get the hell off my farm, and don't come back!" He spat blood on the floor as he brought his body up on his hands and knees.

"Oh, yeah, well I quit!" Martin kicked his boot hard into Zeke midsection again, flipping the man onto his back.

Emily got to her feet, a little wobbly at first, but then she took off out of the barn. Martin spit on Zeke and ran after her.

CHAPTER 39

As she neared her house, a light burned in the kitchen. She had mixed feelings about arriving. On the one hand, she missed Emily. It had been over a day since she'd seen her little girl. However, the thought of running into her husband made her stomach churn.

It wouldn't be long now until she would take Emily and run from Morley. The road would be hard. She'd hidden some money, but they had no place to go, no shelter or friends elsewhere. It would mean giving up her family's farm, the schoolhouse her parents had built, and all her friends. She just didn't see any other options to get away from him.

"Blackjack!" was the first thing she heard as she walked into the kitchen. Emily sat at the kitchen table, but Zeke wasn't the man sitting with her. Martin Drake appeared to be playing cards with her.

"Martin Drake! Are you teaching my daughter to gamble?" While it was sort of sweet that he was taking the time, it wasn't appropriate for a lady to learn.

"Hell, yeah. And she's winnin', too!" He stood up from the table.

"Hi Mama! I'm learning Blackjack," Emily squealed.

"That's the way I learned counting," Martin commented.

"Well, thank you so much for your interest in Emily's math skills, Martin." Jane laughed. Then her smile faded. "Where's Zeke?"

"Your idiot husband and I had a little disagreement over his parentin' skills. Even though he let me go, I wasn't gonna leave the little one alone."

121

Addressing Emily, she said, "Sweetie, why don't you get washed up for dinner?"

Emily looked between the two adults, nodded, and left the room.

Jane leaned toward Martin, her voice low. "What did he do?"

Lowering his usual exuberant voice, he said, "That bastard heard Emily tell me she hated him. Then he threw her into the wall. I might've lost my temper a bit and added a few more bruises to what my baby brother did last night. Got dismissed for it."

Jane gasped, and the room swam. She clutched the back of the chair to keep from falling to the floor.

Martin wasn't done. "Ya gotta do somethin' about him. I ain't gonna be around now, and you ain't safe."

Jane nodded, closing her eyes at hearing his advice. "Thank you, Martin. I know what I need to do."

Martin patted her roughly on the shoulder, which Jane took to be a comforting gesture. He left out the back door, and Jane climbed up the stairs to Emily's room.

"Emily?" she asked gently.

The girl looked up at her mother, biting her lip. Jane could barely hold back tears. "Martin told me what happened. Can I see?"

"It's not bad, Mama. I don't want you to cry."

"Please...," Jane whispered, trying desperately to keep the tears in.

Emily relented, and unbuttoned the back of her dress. Jane couldn't help the little cry that escaped her lips when she saw the large purple bruise across Emily's upper back.

She composed herself by drawing in a deep cleansing breath as she kneeled down in front of her daughter. "Does it hurt anywhere else?"

Emily slipped her dress back up. "No. But Mama?" Emily reached out and laid her hand over Jane's bruised cheek. "We need to leave him."

This time Jane couldn't stop the tears from leaking out of her eyes. "Yes, baby. Right now." She gathered her little girl into her arms, and they both cried.

After a time, Jane drew away. She wiped the wetness off her cheeks.

"Gather up your things for the road. Remember, the more you take, the more you have to carry."

Emily nodded.

Jane dashed to her bedroom. She threw open a small carpet bag on the bed. She pulled out a pair of trousers she'd managed to alter, complete with pockets, from an old skirt and a warm shirt. She quickly changed into them, stuffing her dress into the bag. She added her other two dresses, her old shoes and a blanket. But she still needed the most important item for their journey.

She pushed the bed over towards the wall using all her might. Digging at a loose floorboard with her fingernails, she pried it up. Underneath lay a handgun, a gift from Lucy several years earlier when her friend had learned the extent of Jane's abuse. Jane had never had the guts to use it. She loaded the gun shoved it in her pocket. A cloth bag filled with more ammunition and a small stack of bills went into the carpet bag. It was all the money she had.

"Look, Mama! I can use this basket for my things. It all fits!" Emily handed her the basket Jane usually used to collect vegetables from the garden.

Jane scanned the contents. A book, Jane Eyre, lay on top. Jane wondered where it had come from but decided that conversation could wait until they were on the road. Her clothes filled most of the basket. Underneath she found Emily's stuffed rabbit. She couldn't help but run a finger along its worn little head. While not exactly necessary, it was the first toy she'd made when Emily was born. The little girl had carried it with her constantly, right up until she started school. Jane wouldn't force her to leave it, especially since she'd probably never see it again otherwise.

"I can carry it myself."

"Good. Now grab your blanket off your bed. I'll put it in my bag."

Emily ran to get it as Jane replaced the floorboard and shoved the bed back into place. Downstairs in the kitchen, Jane got down on her hands and knees in front of the cabinet. She pulled out a pan and some cooking utensils.

"Emily, gather up as much food as you can in the basket for the eggs."

"Yes, Mama." Emily ran off.

In the very back of the cabinet, Jane drew out two beautifully made silver candlesticks. Behind that she removed four place settings of silverware. Years ago, after her parents had died and Zeke had started gambling, Jane hid away these precious possessions. It broke her heart to sell them, making her feel like she was abandoning her legacy. But Emily was her real legacy, and she needed to be protected.

Once out in the night, Jane kept a watchful eye out for both Zeke and wendigos as she guided Emily towards town.

Emily paused. "I thought we were going to Denver. This is the wrong way."

"It's too dark. We can barely see out here. We'll stay at the inn and leave tomorrow." Jane tried to get them moving again, but Emily stayed rooted to the ground.

"What if he comes looking for us?" Emily whispered.

"He won't."

Emily pressed her lips together, wincing at the hooting of an owl nearby.

Jane sighed. "Your father acts brave and tough, but he's a coward. He's afraid of George, and even Lucy. He won't confront them." While her words were true, she didn't know how far Zeke would go to catch them if he realized they were running.

Emily nodded.

They moved quickly through town to the inn. The front door opened easily, unlocked.

George walked out the door behind the front desk. He rubbed his sleepy eyes and blinked at them.

"George! Please, we need help. We have to get away from Zeke." Jane could hear the panic in her own voice.

George held up his hand. "No need to explain. Just hearing that man's name explains everything." He took the carpet bag from Jane's hand. "Lucy and Abigail have finally fallen asleep so I'm not inclined to wake them. But you'll be safe here, I promise."

Emily stepped forward and hugged George around his waist.

The big black man smiled as he looked down at her, his hand patting her back.

Emotion almost overwhelmed Jane. In a broken voice, she said, "Thank you."

CHAPTER 40

Zeke passed out near the edge of his field, not able to fight the pain inflicted on him by Martin. Time passed quietly around him as the sun set and a three-quarter moon rose in the night sky. When he regained consciousness, he took a long drink of whiskey he'd had hidden under the barn. It helped to dull the pain some but not enough. His face still throbbed, and each breath was difficult. He crawled through the turnip field, a specific destination in mind.

Almost at the end of the field, Zeke came to a place where the soil had been previously disturbed. His hands dug in the dirt, intensifying the throbbing in his side, but he didn't stop. He uncovered a small box and pulled out a little bottle of thick, reddish-brown liquid. The label on the front read Laudanum: Tincture of Opium. He took a sip and grimaced at the bitter flavor. The bad taste was worth it. His body relaxed, and he took another swig. The pain ebbed.

He'd become addicted to laudanum when a salesman came through Morley selling his snake oil products, claiming to cure any ill. Once Zeke had tried it, he was hooked. Since then, he'd sunk a lot of the money from the farm into laudanum to feed that addiction.

He knew Martin and Jane were suspicious of his jaunts out into the fields without him accomplishing anything, but he couldn't care less about what either of them thought. The deadbeat was gone now after laying hands on him, and he had plans for his wife and daughter. He just had to do it in such a way that would keep the law and the other nosy townsfolk out of his business.

Perceptions swirled as the drug soothed his brain, and he fell back onto the soft earth as consciousness fled again.

A snapping sound nearby, just beyond the field, woke him. He looked through the turnip plants. A woman shuffled by, unaware of him. In his drug-addled vision, she was beautiful, an Indian woman with long, black hair flowing down her back. With a shapely body and skin shining in the moonlight, she seemed a gift that came out of nowhere.

He wanted her. Damn it, he would have her. He would get rid of Jane and her idiot child. Not that he'd let them leave him. Oh no, nobody leaves Zeke Lansing. He'd daydreamed so many ways to do it. This stray was Jane's perfect replacement. His own Indian princess.

He whistled, and she stopped to slowly turn in his direction. She limped, probably the reason she moved so slowly, but his focus remained on her lovely hips. She shuffled in his direction, a crooked smile on her face. She wanted to be with him, too.

Just for good measure, he sipped a little more of his precious laudanum and stood up. The pain in his face and ribs had gone. He moved on his own unsteady legs towards her, the drugs affecting his entire system. When she reached him, he embraced her, and her mouth tilted up for a kiss.

His emotions soared. An Indian princess had come right out of the countryside and into his arms. His hands slipped down her back as he kissed her. Then the pain returned, now focused right on his lips. It was more than even the laudanum could suppress. His Indian princess moved her head back, and the excruciating pain intensified. His eyes cleared.

Her dead, white eyes stared at him, almost unseeing. Moonlight had given the illusion of a shine on her gray skin. No longer did it have the tanned, reddish hue of healthy Indian skin. Her teeth seemed too big for her mouth, and red gore covered her face as she chewed something.

Terror stabbing into his gut as he gasped and cringed, realizing she was chewing on the remnants of his lips. He tried to push her away, to run back through the field, but her claw-like hands clutched at him, pinning him against her. She growled as she opened her bloody jaws wide again.

He screamed with all his might as she ripped into his throat. The sound changed into a burbling noise as his trachea opened in a gush of blood. He collapsed to his knees. His body was racked with pain as he felt his lungs gasping for air. None could be had as it all whooshed out the hole in his neck. She stood over him and bit him again, this time pulling off his ear. He could no longer scream, but waves of pain kept coming.

Hours passed in minutes as his brain died. During that entire time, he felt every bite and scratch from the dead Indian woman.

CHAPTER 41

Calvin returned home from his morning hunt and laid three rabbits and a squirrel on the wood block behind his house. He strolled to the barrel of rain water. The cool water splashed over his face and neck, removing the layer of sweat he'd built up out in the forest.

He startled a little when the back door flew open and Martin stepped out into the sun, smiling.

"Drat, Martin! What are you still doin' home? You should be at the farm by now," Calvin yelled.

"Oh, yeah, I lost my job," Martin told him, the smile still on his face.

Calvin spit on the ground. "God damn it! Why didn't you tell me that when I saw you last night?"

"Last night I was quite enjoyin' myself with some homemade moonshine, and I didn't want you ruinin' my mood." Martin climbed up on the fence post of Sky's enclosure. The horse slowly walked over and nudged Martin with her nose. He scratched behind her ears roughly, which she relished.

Calvin snorted, annoyed by his brother. "What did you do?"

Martin twisted his lips. "Well…" He drew out the word. "Seemed me and Zeke had a little disagreement on his parenting techniques."

Calvin squinted at him, cocking his head to the side. What did Martin know about parenting techniques? Then again, he had some strong doubts about Zeke's knowledge on the subject as well.

Martin's smiled disappeared. "Son of a bitch started smackin' his kid

129

around in front of me. I couldn't let that go. Gave my resignation with a fist to his face and a boot to his gut."

Calvin nodded. It was how he felt when he'd seen Zeke backhand Jane earlier in the week. Perhaps she would leave Morley now, and all his emotional turmoil would end. His heart clenched, like someone was trying to rip it out. What if he never saw her again?

Shaking those thoughts away, he glared at Martin. "Since ya seem to have nothin' to do at the moment, ya can dress these for dinner." He pointed to the prey he'd hunted.

"Okeydokey, boss man." Martin saluted him.

Calvin's annoyance flared again. He grunted and got Sky out to meet up with the Apache tribesmen.

After picking up the barter items from Isaac, he rode Sky into the countryside. The sun beat down hotter today, and sweat wet his skin as he traveled. Luckily, he didn't have to travel far without cover to get to the usual meeting place.

The Indians were already there, Nantan in front with only one younger brave behind him instead of two. Nantan slid off his horse when he saw Calvin approaching. Calvin did the same when he reached them.

The Indians fidgeted, looking around in different directions. It reminded him of last year when they had first started meeting, but he had slowly gained their trust since then. He wondered if only sending two of them was a sign of that trust, but it didn't explain why they were anxiously scanning the territory as if expecting to be attacked.

Calvin waited for Nantan to greet Sky as usual.

Nantan ignored the horse today, simply saying "Trade."

Calvin blinked, surprised. Nantan loved Sky, loved petting her before trading. Now he rushed with getting out his wares, as though they just wanted to get their business over with and get the hell out of there. Calvin pulled the bag of goods off Sky.

Only Nantan focused on the trade. The younger man kept glancing around, sometimes even lifting his body off his horse to get a better view. Nantan and Calvin quickly examined each other's items and began packing them up.

A wisp of wind brought a foul scent toward them. All three horses whinnied in discontent, shifting unhappily on their feet.

"Wendigo!" shouted the young brave on top of his horse. He pointed toward a figure shambling towards them. It appeared to be moving as fast as it could, frenzied to reach them. A dirty, tan-colored cowboy hat sat on its head, a brown vest on its body, and tall leather boots covered its feet. What had once been a blue bandana lay around his neck was now stained with clotted blood. As it hobbled closer, they heard quiet hissing sounds emerging from it.

Nantan said something to the other man in their native tongue as he climbed back on his horse. The young man took off, heading in the direction of their village. The undead cowboy glared at him with blank, white eyes, as if debating whether to follow the running horse or not. Seeing the other two remaining, it continued the same course.

Calvin slung his rifle off his back and cocked it. Nantan's horse tried to jump away, but he held the beast steady and watched Calvin closely. Stepping away from Sky and into the direct line of sight of the oncoming monster, Calvin aimed carefully and pressed the trigger.

The bullet flew across the distance in a blink. It buried itself into the dead flesh just between the creature's eyes. The wendigo fell gracelessly to the ground and lay still.

Calvin and Nantan made eye contact before Calvin walked slowly toward the prone body. Nantan slid off his horse and followed. They examined it, trying not to let the rotten smell bother them.

Calvin frowned as he looked down at the wendigo's face. The full beard and underbite reminded him of his brother. Anyone of them could become a wendigo. He shivered at the thought. Looking for this wendigo's cause of death, he found long, bloody scratches that had ripped right through the vest and into the skin underneath on his back.

Nantan clamped a hand on Calvin's shoulder. Calvin flinched a little at the unexpected physical contact.

"You kill wendigo. Need guidance from spirits now. Come." Nantan guided him back to their horses and waved for him to follow. Calvin had always hoped for an invitation back to their settlement, although his excitement was tempered by this most recent wendigo attack.

As the horses moved away from Morley, Calvin glanced back at the dead monster that resembled Martin. Flies already buzzed around it.

CHAPTER 42

The Apache village had no direct roads leading to it from Morley, so they traveled over the countryside. Smoke drifted lazily up into the air, floating over crude structures made of grasses applied to elliptical frames. Nantan rode them to an enclosure for the horses.

Nantan smiled as Calvin handed over Sky's reins. "Spirit Walk, Calvin Drake." He put a hand on Calvin's back and guided him forward.

Calvin didn't flinch. People stared at him as they walked by. His mouth went dry realizing everyone in the village had their eyes on him. Little children ran up to peer closely at him but ran away shyly when he looked back. Some of the men, a few carrying spears, addressed Nantan. With a word from him, the men nodded and walked away, except for one who ran ahead of them.

They came to a larger structure covered with a buffalo pelt instead of brush. Before they went inside, Calvin stopped him. "What's a Spirit Walk?"

The man took a moment with his response, trying to find the right words in the foreign tongue. "Answers."

Calvin didn't really know what the questions were that needed answering but accepted it and entered the structure.

Steamy heat filled the room. A small fire burned in the center, the smoke floating out an air hole at the top. A stack of rocks sat just outside the border of the fire, the innermost ones glowing red. Sweat trickled down his body. An old man with long, straggly gray hair entered behind them and sat off to the side. He started rhythmically beating a drum, and the sound filled Calvin's ears.

Nantan pointed for him to sit across from the drum-beating man. Grabbing a scoop from a pail, he poured water over the hot stones. The water sizzled loudly, sending more puffs of steam into the already saturated air. Then he poured greenish liquid into two cups. Handing one to Calvin, he kept the other for himself and sat down equidistant from him and the elderly man. He drank deeply from his cup and told Calvin, "Drink."

Calvin took a tentative sip. The cool liquid made him take a bigger drink, which choked him with the bitter flavor. Nantan chuckled a little. Calvin gritted his teeth and narrowed his eyes, unsure the goal of this torture.

Nantan finished his cup. "Drink," he said more forcefully.

Calvin downed the remaining contents in one large gulp, then coughed heavily.

Nantan crossed his legs and closed his eyes, relaxed. Calvin followed suit. He closed his eyes and listened to the pounding of the drum, coaxing his normally tense body into relaxing. Did the spirits really talk to people when they did this? Did he even believe in spirits?

A wave of dizziness washed over him. He opened his eyes and found he was alone. Strangely, the beat of the drum still sounded clearly in his ears even without the old man. Calvin tried to move his hand, but he was so sluggish. He wasn't alarmed though, which he found strange considering his normal reactions. Still relaxed, he watched his hand as he flexed his fingers, lost in the movement.

Laughter floated through the air, increasing in volume. A hazy figure stood in the mists of the steam, becoming more defined as he watched. Martin solidified, still pleasantly laughing, like they were joking around with each other. Calvin smiled, still dizzy and sluggish.

"Martin, whatcha doin' here?" Calvin noticed his words slurred together.

Martin laughed, and Calvin chuckled a little with him. Then the laughter got quieter, and Martin faded out of view, as if enveloped by the steam. Calvin closed his eyes again, falling into the drumbeat.

The falling began to feel like floating, and he opened his eyes, unsure when he'd closed them. A large, still body of water surrounded him, large enough he couldn't see the shore in any direction. The warm water buoyed him up, letting him stay afloat while hardly exerting any energy. He splashed around some, noticing he was naked. His hands reached to cover himself, but the sense of relaxation overcame his modesty, and he lay back in the water again.

"Calvin." Her voice sounded softly behind him.

Jane.

He tried to jerk away from her, not wanting her to see him so exposed. Her hands clasped onto his shoulders, keeping him in place. Her mouth was right by his ear as she whispered reassuringly. "Shh, just relax."

Her words soaked into him with the water, and the tension left him. Her hands moved against his skin, massaging him, her fingers kneading into his muscles. He'd never had hand work into his muscles like that before. Her hands worked across his shoulders, moving inwards. Then her thumbs rubbed against his neck, swirling in little circles against his backbone.

He moaned reflexively, and heat grew in his lower belly as he became aroused. With horror, he tried to wrench himself away from her, afraid of her reaction to his growing condition.

She refused to let go, her arms coming over his shoulders as she clung to him. Her naked body pressed against his back, and he grabbed her hands around his chest and tried to pry them off him. His heart pounded, his breath rapid, whether from fear or excitement, he wasn't sure.

"Calvin, it's okay. Please let me in," she whispered in his ear. Her voice soothed him, and he stopped resisting her. Her warm breath in his ear sent shivers over his skin. Her lips touched his neck, kissing the sensitive skin gently. Sensations he'd never experienced washed through him. Never had he been this intimate with a woman, and he almost forgot where he really was. He closed his eyes, moaning again.

"Calvin?"

"Mmm…?" He didn't want to move. He just wanted her to keep touching him.

"You know I'm going to leave," she said, her tone firmer.

His eyes flew open. "What?"

"I'm going to leave Morley. I can't stay there, not with Zeke threatening us. It's going to happen soon."

"No." This time when he tried to twist around, she let him. Even in the wavering water, her beauty overwhelmed him. He reached out and cupped her cheek, and the whirlwind of emotions inside him stilled into peace. A realization dawned on him. She was meant to be with him. "You can't leave. I can protect you."

"Then you've got to find me before I leave."

He reached for her, needing her to be in his arms, but she, like the lake, faded away into darkness, and he slipped into unconsciousness.

It could have been minutes or hours that passed when he finally woke up. The oppressive heat was gone, and the drum no longer beat in his head. A cool, wet cloth lay over his eyes, and his head swirled as he tried to sit up.

A giggle came from next to him.

"Jane?" he croaked out, his throat feeling raw.

The giggle came again, but it wasn't Jane.

He pulled off the cloth and sat up fully. A young Indian girl smiled shyly at him. "Um, thanks." He handed her the cloth and scrambled to his feet. Where was Sky? He had to get back to Morley before Jane left.

CHAPTER 43

Jane snapped awake. Her heart pounded, and her breath came in rapid gasps. Confused for a moment, she sat up and looked around the bedroom at the inn. The sun streamed in through the window, indicating morning had come a while ago. Her daughter slept in the bed next to her.

After they got dressed, Lucy caught them at the top of the stairs. A huge smile graced her face. "George told me you were here. Come see!" She sounded like a gleeful child as they made their way to Abigail's bedroom. The young woman slept peacefully, her skin a rosy color. Even the dark circles under Abigail's eyes had lightened.

"Last night, her fever broke. Then she fell asleep. A real, deep sleep. Doc Silverstein said to let her sleep as long as she could. This is such a good sign!" Lucy cried excitedly.

Jane hugged her friend hard. "I'm so glad, Lucy. She's a strong girl and can beat anything in this world."

Lucy gripped her fiercely before pulling away, wiping tears off her cheeks.

Jane glanced around the room, missing someone. "Where's Harold?"

"Writing one of his articles. He's been so sweet, spending all his time helping me up here or George downstairs. Now that everything has settled down, he's catching up on his own work." Lucy glanced at Emily, who looked back up at her. "How about some breakfast?"

Once she got Emily settled at the tiny kitchen table with a plate of eggs, Lucy guided Jane to the living room sofa. "You're leaving, aren't you?"

"Today."

"Is this because of what happened with Calvin Drake? Because I think he may have real feelings for you and just doesn't know how to own up to them."

"Oh, yes! Calvin likes you, Mama! He punched Father in the head for you." Emily piped in, speaking around a mouthful of eggs.

"Emily Lansing! You mind your business," Jane shot back. Her voice dropped to whisper as she looked back to Lucy. "No, this has nothing to do with Calvin. Zeke hurt Emily last night."

Lucy gasped. "That bastard! How dare he lay hands on her!"

"That's why I have to leave now. I have to protect her."

Lucy shook her head, lips pursued. "But you don't even have a horse."

"We're going to walk to Vigil. I'm going to sell my mother's candlesticks and buy a horse there. It's not that far. Remember when we walked it together, back when we were young and rebellious."

"Your brother was escorting us and you didn't have a child back then."

"I don't have a choice, Lucy."

"What am I going to do without you?" Lucy whispered.

"You're going to have Abigail nagging you instead." She put her hands on Lucy's shoulders. "I need you to do something for me."

"Anything."

"I didn't see Zeke last night before we left. If I'm not at home, he's going to come looking for me eventually. Can you tell him Emily and I are helping with Abigail, and you'll send us home when we're done? It should put him off for at least a day. That'll give me a good start."

"I bet I can keep him distracted with beer and food for days." She laughed through her tears. "Wait here, I have something for you." Lucy slipped into her bedroom for a minute then came back and pressed a wad of bills into Jane's hand.

"No, I can't take this." Jane pushed it back at Lucy.

"Yes, you can. It's not that much, and it won't leave me destitute, I promise. Maybe it'll help you not to forget me in your new life."

Jane wrapped her arms around her friend. "I would never forget you in a million years."

Emily slipped off the chair and stood before them. "Can I go over Simon's house? I want to say good-bye to him."

Jane frowned. "I don't think that's a good idea. I don't want anyone knowing we're leaving."

Emily crossed her arms over her chest. "But I have to say good-bye to Simon! He's my best friend. Lucy's your best friend, and you got say good-bye to her. It's only fair." Then Emily paused, her eyebrows drawing together. "Where's your cameo necklace? The one from Grandma."

Jane paled as her hands flew to chest. "Oh, no! I must have left it on the dresser when I changed. I can't leave without it! I can't!"

Lucy grabbed her hands. "You won't. Emily will go over to the Anderson's so she can discreetly say good-bye to Simon. I'll run to the store and get you any more supplies you need. Just make me a list. You go get the cameo." Lucy squeezed her hand. "Just be careful of Zeke."

Jane pursed her lips. "Okay. But, Emily, you must swear Simon to secrecy until after we're gone. He's not even allowed to tell his parents. If your father finds out too soon, he'll come after us."

Emily nodded her head slowly. Jane wasn't quite sure her daughter completely understood what it would mean if Zeke caught them running away, but she had a feeling Emily realized it was a dangerous prospect.

"Simon can keep a secret."

CHAPTER 44

Victor idly traced random designs with his finger on the top of the desk. He was supposed to be cleaning but he didn't feel like it. It was useless busywork to punish him. Bill had barely spoken to him since yesterday when he'd walked in on the mess that had once been Jimmy.

Warren sat on the bed in his cage, his shoes dirtying the already grimy mattress. His sat against the wall and drummed his fingers repetitively on his knee. His eyes stared at the bars. His cocky attitude had melted into boredom now that Jimmy was gone.

Victor still struggled to accept this living dead idea. There had to be a more logical explanation than some hogwash about demons possessing dead people. Maybe it was rabies. Even the nicest dog can become vicious with that disease, foaming at the mouth and brutally trying to bite anyone that came near it. They weren't really dead though.

The door opened and the beautiful Martha Anderson walked in. A smile played at the corner of Victor's mouth as she sat up.

She smiled sweetly when she saw him, although it did seem a little tentative.

Simon followed her, shoving baby Harry's carriage through the door. Harry shrieked giggles at the bumpy ride. Simon then abandoned the carriage, barreling around his mother and skirting out of her reach before she could grab him. He ran right up to the desk, but his eyes weren't on Victor. They were focused squarely on Warren behind the bars. "Is that the prisoner?"

Victor ruffled his hair, loving Simon's enthusiasm. "Yep, it is. He's a real bad guy." Victor took a quick look at Warren, noting the man's attention rested solely on Martha. He didn't like that.

"You gonna hang him?" Simon questioned.

"Yep."

Martha grabbed Simon's arm and dragged him behind her, the smile gone from her face. "Don't tell him things like that. He's just a boy."

Simon twirled around behind Martha, and that was when Victor noticed Emily Lansing in the doorway. The shy girl hardly ever said a word to him, and he found her presence disconcerting as she watched him. Simon whispered in her ear, but she shook her head. Her eyes glanced at the bars across the room, and then down at the floor.

"Do you know where my husband is?" Martha brought his focus back to her.

"He took the hostage kid out to the campsite. Collecting evidence and such," Victor explained, a little annoyed to have to talk about Bill.

"Okay, thanks." She guided the baby carriage outside. "Come on, you two. We've got to get some things at the store."

The door closed and the room fell silent again. Victor's didn't like the coldness he sensed from Martha, but now loneliness swamped him with only a murderer across the room. He slumped back into the desk chair.

"She's pretty," came a cool voice from behind the bars.

Victor flicked his gaze over the convict.

An ugly grin spread across the man's lips. "She's just pretty enough to eat. I'd like to take a bite out of her."

"Shut up!"

"I think I'll save her for last. Yes, once I'm done killing everyone in this god-forsaken town, I'm going to take my time with that one," Warren mused.

Victor stood up at the desk, his rage now finding a new target. "You better shut your mouth about her," he growled through clenched teeth.

Warren continued on, goaded further by Victor's warning. "Gonna have to tie her down, because she looks like she might be a wild filly.

Then I'll have to shove something in her pretty little mouth because I don't like `em talking. Then I'm gonna just rip that dress right off."

Victor slammed his gun against the bars. Heat washed though his face, and he pointed the gun at Warren, the pounding of his heart screaming in his ears. "Not one more word."

"Then I'm gonna ride her `til she's broken."

The gunshot was deafening as it bounced off the walls, but Warren's scream of pain matched it. He clutched at his thigh, which had a bleeding hole through it now. The cocky grin had fled his face.

"You think you can come into my town and threaten my people like that!" Victor stomped to the far side of the room and unwound a long piece of rope from a hook on the wall. "I'll tell you, this town is in need of a hanging. I don't give a damn how much evidence Sheriff Anderson thinks he needs before you swing, because it's happening right now. I'm the man who's going to get done what needs to be done." Victor carefully tied the rope into a noose. He unlocked the cell and swung the door open wide. "Get up!"

"I can't! You shot me in the leg!" Warren gripped his ruined thigh.

"You'd better get up, or I'm going to shoot you in the head instead." Victor thrust the gun forward, aimed at the center of Warren's forehead.

Warren's eyes narrowed and his lips turned down despite the pain of the bullet wound. Using the edge of the bed as leverage, he struggled to his feet. Putting most of his weight on the undamaged leg, he limped out of the cell. Behind him, Victor had the gun in one hand and the rope noose in the other.

Victor harshly jabbed the gun into Warren's back. "Outside."

With only one good leg, Warren hobbled along with Victor close behind. Once out the door, he directed Warren left toward the gallows at the edge of town. The place hadn't been used in several years, and was somewhat weathered, but would function as needed. Thank goodness he'd rallied some of the townsfolk around him to keep it up when Bill had wanted to tear it down to reuse the wood a few years ago.

"Victor! What are you doing?" Martha screamed from the walkway in front of the general store. The two children stared wide-eyed at him. "Does Bill know about this?"

"Get back in the store, Martha!" he commanded.

By then, Isaac and Daniel had come to the doorway to see what the yelling was about. Duncan McKenzie stood behind them. Martha shoved the children back inside and ordered them not to come out. Both of them nodded, afraid of this unknown situation.

"Victor, are you hanging that man? Where's the sheriff? He was supposed to make a formal announcement about this matter to the entire town," Isaac said loudly.

"Bill doesn't have the balls to do this kind of work. I'm the one who's taking care of business!" Victor yelled back at him.

Across the street at the inn, Lucy and George emerged, the latter gripping the trusty shotgun in his hands. Another three farmhands exited behind them.

"What's going on?" Lucy stepped out on the dirt road.

"I'm getting rid of this scumbag," Victor informed her.

"Yes! He needs to pay for what he did to my sister and everyone else he's hurt."

George nodded and they both followed Victor.

Isaac scratched his head and licked his lips. "Lucy, I agree this man is dangerous and needs to be dealt with accordingly, but I think the sheriff needs to make that decision. We shouldn't let this turn into a lynch mob."

"I think it's too late for that, Isaac," Lucy told him.

Martha fell into step with the rest of the townspeople walking towards the gallows. "Victor, please wait for Bill before you do this! You know he's already angry. He just needs to do things right, and it will get done. Don't throw away your friendship with him over this. Please!"

Martin and Lydia walked down the road from the direction of the McKenzie farm. They sped up and joined the crowd when they saw the commotion.

"Ho boy! We ready to hang this asshole?" Martin hooted loudly at no one in particular, drawn into the charged emotion hanging in the air.

Lydia remained silent as she walked along.

When they reached the old gallows, Victor pushed Warren toward the stairs.

With his shot leg, he couldn't climb up so sat heavily upon the middle step and chuckled. "Oops, found a little loophole in your plan."

Victor's fist lashed out, catching him right along the jaw. Warren bit his tongue as his teeth snapped shut. He chuckled some more as he spit out red blood. Sweat beaded on his pale face and a red mark welled up where Victor had connected, but he still managed an attitude.

George and Martin both stepped forward, and each grabbed one of Warren's arms.

"This is for Abigail, you murdering piece of trash." George dragged him up the rickety contraption, he and Martin helping hold him tightly as Victor secured the rope around his neck and tied it to the wooden bracket above.

"This isn't right. I demand a trial," Warren pleaded, struggling to stand on his injured leg.

"Victor, I promise he's going to hang. Please just wait for Bill!" Martha also tried again, her words getting faster and higher pitched.

Victor didn't even look at her. He placed his hand on the trap door lever, and hesitated. His eyes swept over the crowd gathered at the gallows. This was where he belonged, in charge of things, with all of them looking up at him. In the back of his mind, he knew he could possibly lose it all because of his actions, but at that moment, he didn't care.

Warren laughed loudly, a chillingly evil sound. Blood steadily dripped from his wounded leg. "Hope I see you all in hell. This town is cursed."

With that, Victor pulled down the lever. The trap door under Warren's feet opened. In Victor's mind, he floated in the air for a moment before gravity took over and he fell. Before he hit the ground, the rope snapped taught, the sickening crack of his neck breaking echoing across the crowd. He hung quietly about two feet off of the ground, his body swaying lightly back and forth.

CHAPTER 45

Bill finished packing up the outlaws' camp and climbed on one of the horses. Alexander had been eager to help, and Bill was grateful for the extra hand. He'd go through everything thoroughly once he got back to town, but he couldn't leave the horses tied up out there. They poor beasts had finished clearing all the grass they could reach and strained to get to the fresh blades just out of range.

Alexander climbed onto the other horse with a lead rope for the third horse. "I gotta say that it's much easier to ride a horse when you ain't tied up." He gripped the reins in each hand.

The two men guided the horses to the road back toward town. They rode at an easy gait, the third horse trailing behind them.

"What're you planning to do with Warren?" Alexander asked tentatively.

Bill turned his head to examine the young man. The kid stared at the ground, lips pressed together. Bill didn't know all that had happened after the two criminals had kidnapped him, but he knew Alexander had witnessed the murder of his parents and the rape of his sister. The young man would have a vested interest in his kidnapper's fate. Interesting he didn't mention Jimmy. "He's going to be hanged."

Alexander blew out a heavy breath. "When?"

"Soon. I'm going to go through all his stuff and things from the camp and make sure there isn't anything else that needs to be addressed before that. I'm still hoping that he'll tell us more about his activities the last few years."

Bill veered his horse off the road and Alexander followed. They unloaded everything in front of the sheriff's office.

"Can you settle the horses into the open stalls in the stable behind the inn? I need to check in with Deputy Wade. Then you can tell Lucy and George about the horses. I'm sure they'll give you some lunch."

Alexander nodded, taking the reins of the other horse, and trotted away.

As Bill bent to lift one of the bags, he spotted something peculiar sticking out of it. He pulled out a double barrel shotgun. "Damn," Bill muttered, impressed by the firepower. Looking back in the bag, he found a slew of ammunition for it. Warren and Jimmy had been well-stocked for battle. He decided to take it along with him until he had time to get it in the safe.

Walking into the office, Bill studied the shotgun, its double barrels gleaming in the dim light. "Victor, you've got to see this."

No answer. Bill scanned the room, registering the empty desk and the utter silence. His stomach sank.

Whirling around, he faced the jail cell. Shock welled up inside when he saw the open door. Blood covered the floor, and a trail of it led across the room and out the front door, still relatively red, fresh. Neither Victor's nor Warren's bodies lay in sight. Not that there couldn't have been a wendigo-form of one of them walking around causing havoc at the moment.

"Shit!" The ugly word bounced off the walls in the quiet room.

The front door flew open, and Alexander ran in, panting. "Everyone's gone!"

Bill looked up at him, a kernel of dread forming in his chest.

Alexander noticed the blood-splattered but empty jail cell. "Where is he?" The color drained from his face, and his hand shook as he steadied himself on the desk.

"That's what I'm going to find out," Bill told him with resolution but then frowned. "What do you mean 'everyone's gone?'"

"The restaurant's empty. Not even George was there. There were still full glasses and one table looked like it had had a good card game going. But there wasn't nobody in there."

147

"Come on, I've got to find Victor." Bill patted Alexander's shoulder.

Bill burst into the general store next door. "Isaac! Daniel! Anyone in here?" His words echoed with no responses. "Anyone!" he tried again but it was useless. The place was empty as well.

Bill closed the door and looked out on the main road. At that instant, Morley felt like a ghost town, with no obvious signs of life anywhere. Panic rose. Where the hell was everyone? Bill resisted the urge to run home and make sure his family was safe. He'd be lost without them. He rubbed his face, trying to focus. Then he spotted the trail of blood in the dirt.

"Here." He nudged Alexander and pointed. It led them through the rest of town and veered sharply to the right. Bill realized where the trail led. Right to the gallows. Fear mutated into anger. "Damn it, Victor," he muttered.

Sounds of a crowd increased as they neared the seldomly visited area outside of town. One voice sounded out louder than the others.

"That's what you deserve for trying to kill my baby sister, you monster!" Bill recognized Lucy's voice. A murmur of consent issued from the crowd.

Bill and Alexander came into view of the gallows, and it took a moment for them to take in the entire scene. A small crowd faced the gallows. Warren's neck had obviously been broken during the hanging as his head now hung at an unnatural angle. The bloody trail they'd followed appeared to be coming from him, as blood soaked his pants, still dripping into a little pool underneath him.

Atop the gallows, right on the edge, stood Victor. He looked out at the crowd, as if surveying his kingdom, not one wound evident on him. His eyes found Bill's as Bill paused at the back of the crowd. For a split second, Victor smug smile faltered. The moment passed and Victor's head tilted ever so slightly, his expression hardening. Bill saw the challenge in his eyes, as if to say he'd done what Bill didn't have the guts to do.

"Victor," Bill said loudly, his firm tone just barely concealing his burning rage. Everyone in the crowd turned and stared at him. Most of them looked shocked that the sheriff would come now, right after the deed had been done. Others just looked interested in what was about to transpire between their sheriff and his deputy.

Martin stood on the top of the other side of the rickety wooden structure. He initially had a look of satisfaction on his face as he looked at Warren's swinging body, but his head turned with interest as he watched the two lawmen staring at each other.

"Oh, thank goodness you're here! Isaac and I tried to stop him, but he wouldn't listen to us!" Martha pleaded.

Bill nodded to her and moved to the gallows stairs. Victor stomped down them, and the whole structure swayed. Martin grabbed on to the hangman's beam to steady himself.

Victor stood before him, meeting his eyes with a glare. Bill didn't say a word, waiting for an explanation and working hard to keep his temper under control so not to physically attack his deputy. The hanging was coming, just as soon as Bill had completed a full investigation. Victor had been trying to undermine his authority in subtle ways a lot lately, but this was a clear betrayal. Bill gritted his teeth.

Victor started to ramble. "That lunatic told me that he was going to rape and murder your wife. He threatened to murder everyone in this town! I couldn't allow that to happen. I did what was necessary to protect all of us!"

Bill took a deep breath. "Give me your badge."

"What? No," Victor took a step back, his arrogant swagger gone.

"Give me your badge," Bill repeated.

"No! That brute was going to hang no matter what. I just did it a little early!"

Bill just shook his head, not accepting anything Victor had to say.

"You're going to regret this!" Victor unpinned the deputy badge from his vest, violently threw it on the ground, and spat on it.

Bill watched him, his heart aching for the man he once considered his friend.

A great gasping sound came from the crowd in front of the gallows. Bill groaned that such a spectacle between him and Victor had to be done in front of half the town. He glanced over and discovered not a single set of eyes on them. They all looked at the hanging dead man.

Warren continuing to swing slowly with his feet dangling off the ground. His head still tilted at an odd angle, but his eyes were open and now completely white. One of his arms extended, the fingers reaching out toward the people in front of him. Everyone cringed back but none ran.

A growling, hissing sound issued from Warren's mouth. All other noise had stopped. Sensing how near his prey was, Warren struggled, agitated. His other hand extended, clawing at the air as he strained to reach them. The hissing sound became more of a dreadful moaning, and his teeth snapped open and shut menacingly. His legs kicked, swinging him closer to the crowd.

All of them leapt back at the sharp crack of gun fire. Warren's head exploded, and he hung limply from the rope again. The crowd's attention shifted upward to Martin on the top of the gallows.

A huge grin played on his face, his pistol still smoking. "That makes two on my scorecard!" he laughed.

CHAPTER 46

Emily browsed through the wares in the general store. She hoped to find another book to take with her on the road. She'd been surprised at how much she loved reading Jane Eyre, especially when the orphaned girl fell in love. The wonderful story gave her hope that maybe it wouldn't be so bad on the road.

"I can't see anything," whined Simon, his face pressed up against the front window.

The crowd outside had moved out of view up the road, leaving the two children alone in the store with baby Harry. He cooed loudly in his carriage, not at all frightened by all the excitement.

Emily ignored Simon, glancing behind the counter.

"They're hanging that guy, and we're missing it!" Simon complained loudly to the empty store.

Emily didn't answer. After the incident with the dead woman eating the bear, she had enough with death for a while.

"I'm going to see if I can make out anything from the back door," Simon said, turning away from the front windows.

"Wait! Your mama said not to leave the store!" Emily reminded him as she followed. She glanced back at the carriage, but Harry seemed to be entertaining himself by trying to shove his foot in his mouth.

"I'm not going to leave the store. I'm just going to take a peek out the back door." Simon weaved around the counter and through the storage room. Emily trailed behind.

Simon gripped the doorknob and yanked it open. He put one foot only out of the store and strained to see past the buildings. "Ugh, still can't see." He glanced at Emily, his lips pursed. Then he walked out the back door.

"Simon, you get back here right now!"

He ignored her, stomping in the direction of the gallows.

Emily glared at his back, huffed and whirled back into the store. Wheeling Harry's carriage out the back door, she chased after Simon. The baby laughed with abandon at the bumpy ride. When she got close enough, she grabbed his arm, but he wrenched it away.

"My father's the sheriff. I'm going to be sheriff one day. I need to see that outlaw hang!" Simon skirted past Deputy Wade's house.

Emily, unhappy with disobeying Martha's order, frowned but followed silently with the carriage. Just past the Wade house, they saw the gathering at the old gallows in the distance.

Simon crept up to a patch of bushes at the top of a small hill overlooking the gallows. He peered over them.

Curiosity won Emily over. She scooped Harry out of the carriage, hugging him against her chest. He snuggled into her, resting his head on her shoulder as she walked up next to Simon behind the bushes.

Emily could hear the cheering as Martin and George hauled the man up the wobbly stairs. Deputy Victor tied the rope around the outlaw's neck, then placed his hand on the trapdoor lever. Emily closed her eyes as he pulled it down.

"Whoa," Simon breathed out.

Emily peeked out of one eye, but closed it quickly when she saw the dead man hanging. "Please let's go back to the store," she pleaded to Simon.

"Uh, oh."

Emily opened her eyes full. "What?"

Simon pointed to the back of the crowd. "My papa just showed up. I was wondering why he wasn't there. He looks awful mad."

They watched as all heads in the crowd followed Bill, who stalked over to the gallows. Victor stamped down the stairs, his face red, confronting Bill. The distance stole the words away from the children's ears, but their body language conveyed the mounting tension as they argued. Victor threw something on the ground, the light bouncing of the metallic object.

"His badge!" Simon gasped.

Emily barely heard him, her eyes glued to the swinging dead man. She whimpered with dread and clutched baby Harry to her as she saw the outlaw's arm stretch out toward the crowd. It was too far away to see his eyes, but she knew they had gone white.

Wendigo.

Simon's eyes shifted off his father, and he screamed. His fear echoed in the volume of the noise emerging from him. A few heads from the back of the crowd swiveled in their direction, but Simon didn't seem to acknowledge them. He backpedaled away from the bushes, tripping on a rock and falling on his backside. It cut off his scream, but he cried as he scrambled to his feet and ran away.

"Simon!" Emily yelled. A gun shot echoed in her ears.

Harry began to cry.

Emily tried to sooth him as she ran after Simon. She grabbed the carriage, and gently but quickly laid Harry inside. He whined but the crying died down as she pushed him toward his house.

Simon crashed through the door, leaving it open.

Emily wheeled the carriage inside and closed the door. She breathed a sigh of relief to see Harry had fallen asleep. She smoothed down his mussed hair. Then she climbed the stairs to the bedroom Simon and Tommy shared.

He huddled under the blanket on his bed, his body trembling.

Emily sat down on the bed next to him and rubbed his covered shoulder.

He pulled down the blanket. His face had gone pale and tears streaked down his cheeks. "That robber changed into one of those monsters."

"Calvin called it a wendigo." She wiped his tears away with her finger.

Simon nodded. "It was like that wendigo in the woods was coming after us all over again." His voice dropped to a whisper. "They're everywhere."

Emily's stomach clenched, fear welling up inside her. She shook her head. "No, it was just two." She wasn't sure she believed her own reassurances.

He didn't acknowledge her words. His hand reached out and gripped hers. "Can you stay over again tonight?"

Emily opened her mouth to say yes when she suddenly remembered everything with her parents over the past day. She gasped, surprised she'd forgotten something so monumental as leaving Morley.

Simon must have misinterpreted her expression. "It's okay. You don't have to stay if you don't want to. I know I'm acting like a scared baby." He pulled his hand away.

"Simon, I've been meaning to tell you something all day, but I forgot." She took a deep breath. "I'm leaving Morley."

"Leaving?" He sat up, the covers falling off him. "Where are you going? Denver? How long will you be gone?"

"A long time. Maybe forever."

"Forever? No! Why are you leaving forever?" Simon frowned.

"My father. You know he hurts us, right?"

"Yes, he's a bad man," Simon agreed.

"He hurt me worse than ever last night." To illustrate her point, she turned around and pulled down the neck of her dress. It revealed the top of the large purple bruise that encompassed most of her upper back.

Simon gapped, mouth open wide. "He should go to jail."

"It wouldn't work." Emily turned back around. "They couldn't keep him in there forever, and then he'd come back and hurt us worse than ever. Mama and I have to leave."

Simon's whole face fell, and the tears that had dried welled up again. Emily's chest tightened, her own tears spilling over. The two children wrapped their arms around each other. Both of them bordered on adulthood and had spent their entire lives believing they would be together forever. Now circumstance pulled them apart, and there was nothing they could do.

"You're my best friend, and I love you, Emily. I'll never stop missing you," In that moment, he sounded more grown-up than Emily had ever heard him.

Emily pulled back and wiped the tears from her eyes. "I love you, too. You're the only true friend I've ever had. I promise I'll send you letters from wherever I go. You just can't tell anyone. We can't have him finding out."

He nodded, then pulled her back into the hug.

CHAPTER 47

Jane slowly pushed the front door inward. She winced as it made a loud creaking noise in the silence. Had it always been that loud? Before entering, she listened for any noises that might indicate Zeke was in the house.

"Zeke?" she whispered, her fear not letting her speak any louder in that moment. No response. She tried again, louder. "Zeke?" Still nothing.

Concerned he was waiting to ambush her, she slowly made her way up the stairs. She checked the two bedrooms, both empty. Her spirits started to lift, daring to believe that he hadn't come home yet. She could potentially get away scot-free!

On the dresser lay the cameo necklace. She snatched it up, holding it tightly in her hand. How could she have forgotten it? It was the most precious possession she had except for Emily. She looped the chain over her hand. The cameo rested comfortably on her chest.

A low scraping noise downstairs caught her attention, and she stilled her breathing. Her heart clenched in her chest, knowing Zeke must be coming home. As quiet as possible, she took a few steps to the fireplace and picked up the heavy metal poker. It was true that she could have used her gun if he threatened her, but she wanted to save the ammunition. Besides, it would be worse for her if he took the gun out of her hands than the poker.

Another noise sounded in her ears, closer, a creak on the stairs. Silently, she hid against the wall next to the doorway, holding the poker ready.

CHAPTER 48

Calvin leaned against the large oak tree in the front yard of the Lansing farm. He'd seen Jane slip inside a few minutes earlier, but he'd been reluctant to call out to her. She'd looked skittish, her eyes darting around then she'd cautiously entered the house. He hadn't wanted to startle her.

Other than Jane sneaking into her own house, there were no obvious signs of life. In fact, it seemed like the whole farm was abandoned, and he briefly wondered if anyone had fed the animals since Martin was dismissed. He hoped Zeke would at least be responsible enough to handle that task on his own farm. On second thought, he might check on them later if he didn't run into the bastard.

He took a deep breath. Time to stop hiding behind the tree and find Jane. He was thankful he didn't have to chase her out into the wilderness. Rounding the house, the back door opened easily. He eased his head inside, examining the kitchen. Empty. Peeking into the living room, he found that empty as well. Footsteps crossed the floor above him. He glanced up at the ceiling, trying to determine if they were the light steps of Jane or Zeke's heavy ones. Difficult to determine from where he was listening. As silently as he could, he walked up the stairs.

One of the stairs creaked under the pressure of his weight, and he almost cursed as the sounds from the bedroom went silent. He inched along the hallway, keeping against the wall, trying to catch a glimpse of whoever was in there. He poked his head into the room, his hand on the holt of his knife.

Sudden movement out of the corner of his eye caused him to pull his body back into the hallway. A heavy object held in delicate hands flew down the length of the doorway, just narrowly missing him. He grabbed the object as it was descending, ripping it away from his attacker.

"Calvin!" Jane gasped. "I'm so sorry! I thought you were Zeke! Did I hit you?" Her hand covered her mouth, her eyes wide.

"Nah, ya missed me." He tried to smile reassuringly as he handed her back the fireplace poker.

She took it, her eyes never leaving him.

"You better be careful with that thing. Ya could do some real damage with it."

That got a little smile out of her. Then she tilted her head. "What are you doing here?"

He stepped closer to her, looking her in the eye. "Yer leavin'."

Jane looked down on the floor, her voice a whisper. "I have to. He's getting worse. I think one day soon he'll kill us if I stay."

"That ain't gonna happen." He picked up her hand, a move so out of character for him, but he squashed down all feeling of being uncomfortable. "You both'll come with me. Where's Emily?"

Jane looked at him like he was crazy. "Wait, why?"

"'Cause I can protect ya." He turned to walk out of the room, her hand still in his.

She stayed in place, tugged on him to halt his forward progress. Her big, beautiful, brown eyes looked up at him, searching his face. "Why?"

He met her eyes, then his gaze flicked down to her lips. She must have caught it as he saw the beginnings of a blush sweep across her cheeks, but her eyes stayed on him.

Uncertainty fluttered in his stomach at this critical moment, or maybe it was that stupid drink from the ceremony causing the flip-flops. The vision he'd had made him so sure that they were meant to be together. Yet, he knew the wrong words could ruin it all. To hell with words.

He kissed her, sweet and gentle. He tried conveying his love for her in the kiss, but tentatively as he was unsure how she felt about him.

After a brief moment, he broke the kiss and stepped away from her. Silence filled the room as his green eyes met hers. After the way he'd treated her, she had every right to slap him or throw him out. Hell, she'd just pecked him on the cheek as a thank you for helping her. Maybe she didn't even feel the intense emotions he did.

The iron fireplace poker slipped out of her hand and landed with a heavy thud on the floor. Neither of them even glanced at it, their eyes holding one another. She blinked, then she moved.

Her arms came around his neck, her hands in his hair, pulling his head down as her body pressed tightly against him. His mouth met hers, and this time, the kiss was not gentle, but fiery and full of passion. He dropped her carpet bag, wrapping his arms around her waist. The feel of her lips against his was intoxicating as she moved her mouth. His heart pounded, and fireworks exploded in his chest. Her tongue ran across his lower lip, eliciting a shiver. Her mouth opened a little, and he slipped his tongue in. It scraped seductively against her teeth before her tongue was tangling with his. She tasted so sweet.

He pulled his tongue back into his own mouth and captured her lower lip between his own lips, sucking gently. A throaty moan pushed from her throat, and the sound resonated through his body. Leaving her lips, he trailed kisses down her jaw and across the sensitive skin on her neck. The vision of her kissing his neck in the lake whispered through his mind. A little whimper escaped her lips, and he smiled against her skin to think he caused that.

His hands traveled over her hips, and her body tensed. She pulled away from him, her eyes darting around. Was she having doubts what had just happened? His stomach clenched, bile rising in the back of his throat. What had he done?

"Zeke could come home any second! He'll kill us both if he finds you here. We've got to get out of here!" She grabbed his hand again.

He swallowed back bile. His knees weakened from relief that he hadn't been mistaken about her feelings. If Zeke did come before they left, he'd just kick his ass again. They rushed down the stairs.

At the front door, he halted her with a hand on her arm. "If Zeke ain't been back since yesterday, ya think he fed your animals?"

Jane frowned. "I doubt it. He doesn't seem to do anything on this farm. I fear for it with both Martin and me gone."

"Wasn't this your parents' farm? Why can't ya kick him out?" Calvin was perfectly willing to assist in said kicking.

Jane smiled, her hand rubbing up and down on his arm. "Calvin, you know it doesn't work that way."

"Ain't fair," he grumbled. "This farm is gonna go to shit without ya."

"I know." She rubbed his arm some more. It was very distracting and yet very appealing. "Why don't I go throw the chickens some feed while you milk and feed Bessie the cow?"

He nodded, and she gave him a quick kiss on the cheek before heading to the chicken coop. He was glad he didn't feel the urge to flinch away from her this time. His hand went to his cheek, touching the spot in a happy daze.

CHAPTER 49

Jane practically skipped around the farm, floating, almost in disbelief at what had just happened with Calvin. Never in her wildest dreams would she have thought he would come for her like this.

When she'd heard the noises in the house, the only person she thought it could have been was Zeke. The second the iron poker was ripped from her hands, she knew she was dead. He would kill her for trying something like that. It was a complete shock when she saw that it was Calvin. Then the kiss. Her lips still tingled.

She got to the chicken coop and threw in large handfuls of feed. In the back of her mind, it registered that the birds seemed agitated. Most likely because they hadn't been fed all day. A lot of them flapped around the food, but some of them were reluctant to leave the hen house. Odd.

It didn't matter. She smiled again. Calvin really wanted her to come away with him. Her and Emily. Something must have changed because the last time she saw him, he'd acted like her tiny peck had been the kiss of death. She shook her head, confused but certainly happy. She'd been harboring feelings for him for a while with no hope of reciprocation. With him, she could stay in Morley. It wouldn't be easy because Zeke would be a constant threat, but they would survive.

As she finished feeding the chickens, she turned toward the barn and caught movement out of the corner of her eye. She spun around, the bucket of chicken feed falling from her numb fingers. Her heart fought to rip itself from her chest, the beat pounded in her ears, blocking all sound but the scream that shredded the air. Her scream.

The sound pierced through the air, but she could barely hear it over the roaring sound of the blood pumping in her ears. Her legs stumbled backwards, and she ran as she recovered from the shocking site.

The reanimated corpse of her abusive husband pursued her. Other than his lack of coordination, there was nothing wrong with his arms and legs as he stumbled after her. His head and neck were a ruined mess. One of his ears had been pulled off, leaving him looking lopsided. A huge, jagged hole disrupted the middle of his neck, the dried gore from his shredded jugulars still thick and gooey down the front of him. The absolutely worst part was his face. His lips had been ripped away, leaving a wide skeletal grin.

Seeing his ghastly smile as he reached out to grab her, Jane flashed back to all the times he'd beaten her senseless and stood over her, smiling down at her like he'd done something good. A choking sob escaped her as she dodged away from his grasping hand. She picked up speed and put some distance between them as she ran toward the barn. Her salvation lay there.

Behind her, Zeke groaned loudly as he lurched through a shallow hole in the ground. It almost sounded like he was calling out her name, the word drawn out. "Jaaaannneee…" He swayed drunkenly on his feet as they tripped mindless on the short lip of the hole, but he unfortunately stayed upright.

Jane turned to the barn, hating to take her eyes off him but needing to find a weapon. There it was, their hatchet, resting against the barn wall. Martin never remembered to hang it back up inside after using it. She pulled it up, gripping the smooth wooden handle with both hands. Spinning around, she swung it just as he neared her. The hatchet wobbled in her unsteady hands and sunk into the groove connecting his neck to his shoulders. Black blood sprayed out and slowed his forward movement, but it didn't stop him.

His arm sprang out in front of him, and his fingers clutched the front of her dress. The stitches ripped as she fought against his grip. With a cry of effort, she wrenched the hatchet out from his decaying corpse and backpedaled a few feet.

Out of the corner of her eye, she saw Calvin come tearing around the barn. Ghostly pale in the darkness, he clutched the rifle in his hand. Even though he ran at full speed, he wouldn't make it in time to stop dead Zeke from ripping into her. Both of them knew it.

With a burst of strength, she brought the hatchet up and swung it straight down. The blade sliced cleanly through the center of his head, coming to stop in the middle of his chest. He wavered for a moment and then crumbled to the ground.

Jane dropped the handle, letting it fall with his body. He was truly dead now. She panted, her whole body shaking. She looked down at her dead husband and wanted to spit on him for all the pain he'd caused.

Calvin stopped several feet away from her. He aimed his rifle directly at her. She froze, her eyes wide as her hands extended in front of her in a gesture to stop. Did he think she'd been bitten? Was he just going to end her like that? His eyes did not meet hers, a bead of sweat coursing down his cheek.

Calvin, wait! she thought, but there was no time to say it.

He didn't, his finger depressing the trigger to send the bullet flying at her. She squeezed her eyes shut, her body jerking in anticipation for it to pierce through her.

It never came.

It whistled as it flew past, the feel of the wind of it on her face.

The thud of something heavy behind her landing on the ground had her opening her eyes and swiveling around. There lay Zeke's dead Indian princess, a bullet right through her eye. Jane just gaped at the rotting woman.

Pinpricks of bright colors flashed in front of her vision, and her legs wobbled. She was about to pass out and there was not a damn thing she could do about it. A little whimper left her as she fell, barely registering Calvin's arm around her waist, cradling her head and neck as he slowly lowered her to the ground.

Once the blackness faded, sobs racked her body. He gently pressed her face against his chest, letting her tears drench his shirt. She had to stop, had to pull herself together. He would think she cried for Zeke, but she didn't. She cried from the fear of what had happened to Zeke, of what might happen to any of them now that the myth of the wendigo seemed to have come to life, infecting their tiny corner of the world.

Calvin's hand fidgeted in her hair awkwardly, as if trying to reassure her. His efforts helped, and the sobbing tapered off. She pulled away from him, but his hands gripped her head on either side. He looked into her eyes.

"Are you okay?" He stroked her cheek, worry etched into the creases where he'd drawn his brows together.

She nodded, her head moving his hands. "Yes," she whispered. "Thank you."

"Sorry I scared ya. There just wasn't any time to tell ya that thing was behind ya," he explained, seemingly worried she still thought he was going to shoot her.

"I know. You saved my life."

He smiled lopsidedly and stood up, holding out his hand. She took it gratefully and lifted herself off the ground. He didn't let go, watching her carefully as if to make sure she didn't drop again. After a moment, apparently satisfied, he crept to Zeke Lansing's carcass.

"Nice hit," he complimented her as he examined the hatchet cut.

She blushed but took several steps away from all of it. It was bad enough that she would see it every time she closed her eyes. She didn't want to keep looking at it now.

"Calvin, we need to get the sheriff," she told him, her voice still a little shaky. He nodded, walking to her and taking her hand again. Together, they walked into town.

CHAPTER 50

Once it was clear Warren was truly dead this time, the crowd around the gallows dispersed. Bill stared numbly down at the deputy's badge, thrown so carelessly in the dirt. Behind him, his wife argued with Lucy about the hanging. He tuned them out, not wanting to deal with those heated emotions at the moment.

Martin bounded down the gallows stairs next to Bill. The heavy footfalls made the rickety structure creak loudly, and anyone left standing nearby stepped away. Martin stopped, spotting the badge on the ground, and scooped it up before Bill could stop him.

"Hey, looky what I found here. A real sheriff's deputy badge! Guess that makes me yer new partner, huh?" Martin grinned broadly and slapped Bill hard on the back.

Bill looked at him, shocked at that prospect.

Martin let out a loud cackle. "You thought I was serious, didn't ya! Don't you worry your pretty little head, Sheriff. Ain't nobody gonna make a lawman outta me. But it was worth it just ta see that look on yer face." Martin handed Bill the metal emblem of the law.

The men looked up when the heated words between the women behind them halted, both of them gasping.

"Jane, what happened to you?" Lucy questioned.

Jane's dress hung in tatters, splattered with black flecks of gore. Calvin held her hand firmly in his and led her toward the sheriff with a determined look on his face. That is, until his eyes spotted Martin gawking at their clasped hands. Calvin blushed and dropped her hand quickly, eyes shifting away. Jane didn't notice because Lucy was practically on top of her with worry.

"Did Zeke do this to you?" Lucy fingered the torn material. "What is this black stuff?"

"It's blood," Jane stated, almost without emotion. She'd cried out all her tears. "Zeke came after me, but he was dead. He was one of those wendigos, like that woman in the woods. I killed him, but there were two of them."

Lucy pulled Jane into her arms. Jane was stiff at first, but then melted into her friend's comforting hug.

Bill pulled Calvin to the side, and Martin moved with them, still staring at his brother. Bill didn't want to make Jane upset, but he needed the whole story. "What happened?"

Calvin told him all about Zeke. He went into detail about how Jane had killed him and about the wendigo Indian he'd shot through the head. He didn't say why he happened to be at a farm that he'd been banned from, and Bill didn't ask.

Calvin noticed the body hanging from the gallows. "Somethin' excitin' happen here?"

"Just an old-fashioned hanging!" Martin chuckled. "Of course, most guys tend to die when they break their necks, but this guy decided he weren't done with this world till I introduced a bullet into his brain. Almost got to be the deputy, too." Martin winked at him.

Calvin's eyebrows shot up and he looked at Bill. Bill shook his head, a little smile on his face as he started to relax slightly.

Lucy pulled away from Jane. "All that matters is you're okay. I need to go check on Abigail, because I'm sure she's crawling out of her skin with curiosity over what's going on out here. If I leave her much longer, she's going to get out of that bed and tear her stitches open." Lucy pointed at Jane. "You and me gotta talk soon. You've got to come get your bag anyway." She waved good-bye as she headed to the inn.

"Hey, Martha. Where are the kids?" Jane looked around.

"They're in the general store," Martha answered.

Bill's head snapped up. "No, they aren't."

"What? They have to be," Martha stated, her voice rising.

"I'm telling you, they aren't there. When Alexander and I were trying to figure out where everyone was, I checked. It was empty."

Daniel, heading back to the store, paused by them. "Sheriff? I swear I caught sight of your boy up there by those bushes during the hanging. Emily was there too, holding your baby."

Martha's voice rose again as she became more frantic. "I told them not to move from that place!"

Bill's focus stayed on Daniel. "Did you see where they went?"

Daniel scratched his head. "Think they bolted off toward your house. But I'm not really sure."

The group hustled up the hill, past the Wade house and right through the front door of the Anderson's house.

Martha flew through the door first. She ran to the baby carriage in the middle of the living room. She breathed a sigh of relief as she looked down at her baby sleeping. Then her hands clenched and she stomped back to the hall. "Simon Matthew Anderson, where are you?"

A tiny voice from upstairs answered. "Here."

Martha bounded up the stairs, Bill behind her and the rest of them following. Simon and Emily sat on his bed, holding hands. They cringed back from Martha's angry glare.

"I told you to stay in that general store! Did you watch that hanging when I told you not too?" Martha screeched.

Simon and Emily bolted to their feet, gasping. Not a word came from them.

Martha took a step towards them. "Answer me, young man," she ground out between clenched teeth.

Emily spoke up in the face of her best friend's angry mother. "Simon's going to be sheriff someday. He needed to see a hanging or else how would he know how to do it when he grows up? But then that bad man changed into a wendigo. We got so frightened, we ran away."

Martha's face fell and she scooped Simon up in her arms. "My poor baby! To have to see such a frightful sight!"

167

Jane stepped past Calvin and stood beside Emily, her hands on her daughter's shoulders.

"Don't ya worry, babes. I shot that wendigo piece of shit dead!" Martin assured them from back of the group.

Calvin rolled his eyes, grabbed Martin by the arm and hauled him downstairs.

"Good!" Emily shouted out the doorway.

Bill clamped his teeth shut to stop from laughing when he heard Martin laugh heartily and gleefully say, "Damn, those kids crack me up sometimes." Then the front door slammed shut.

Bill caught Jane ducking her head, trying to suppress a smile as well.

CHAPTER 51

Jane ducked her head, barely containing the laughter at Martin's comments. The hilarity had a touch of the hysterical, so much she feared that if she started laughing, it would overwhelm her and never stop. They'd commit her to the mad house. She swallowed it back down, needing to get back to the awfulness of the day.

"Can I talk to Emily alone?"

Bill nodded, led them downstairs to the fancy little parlor and closed the door behind him. They sat down on the plush sofa.

"What happened, Mama?" Emily touched the torn and stained fabric of Jane's dress.

Jane took a deep breath. "I was getting my necklace, and Calvin asked if anyone had fed the animals today. With Martin gone and-"

"What was Calvin doing there?" Emily's brow knit.

Jane paused. How could she explain to her child? "Well…he was there for…" She cleared her throat. "He was there to protect me while I was getting the necklace." It seemed close enough to the truth.

Emily smiled. "Aww, that was sweet of him."

Jane wished they could've only talked about Calvin, but she didn't want to stall any further. She touched the girl's forehead, running her fingers through her daughter's hair. "Emily, your father died today."

Emily's eyes widened slightly, her lips pressing together. Then she whispered, "Did Calvin kill him?"

Jane blinked, stunned. "Why would you think that?"

Emily shrugged. "Calvin doesn't seem to like it when Father hurts you. If he was there protecting you, and Father tried to hurt you, he might get mad enough to kill him."

Emily seemed so calm, saying the words matter-of-factly. Even though Jane had no love or remorse left for her husband, she still found it very sad that her daughter didn't either. The girl never really got to have a father. She had learned to deal with the monster he eventually became.

"No," she answered. "Calvin didn't kill him. He was bitten by one of those wendigos. And I stopped him from hurting anyone else."

Emily whole face brightened with her smile. "He's gone. We don't have to leave!" She jumped up and hugged her mother fiercely. Then she composed herself and sat back down on the sofa. "Maybe now Calvin can keep coming over, and we can let Martin work our farm again?"

Jane couldn't help but smile. "Of course. Are you ready to go home now that we don't have to leave town?"

Emily frowned. "Actually, Simon was real upset when I told him we were leaving. I think I should sleep here tonight to reassure him I'm staying."

Jane thought about it and couldn't think of a reason why not. She didn't want to deny her. "As long as it is okay with Simon's parents."

"Thank you, Mama!" She jumped up and ran to the door. Before she opened it, she spun around. "Maybe Calvin can stay with you tonight so you won't be alone. You know, since I won't be home." Then she was gone.

Jane sat on the sofa, not sure how to take that last remark.

CHAPTER 52

The sun headed for the horizon, and shadows stretched out in front of them. Jane wrapped her arms around her body as she walked down the road towards her farm.

Calvin walked beside her in a comfortable silence, each of them absorbed in their own thoughts. Occasionally their shoulders brushed against each other, but they didn't hold hands. Calvin had made a quick stop at the inn to get her carpet bag, which he carried for her.

While Jane explained the situation to Emily, Calvin and Bill had arranged to have the bodies at the farm taken away. After Bill gave permission for Emily to stay at the Anderson house for the night, there was an unspoken agreement that Calvin would escort Jane home. Nobody was to be outside alone anymore, especially someone who'd already been through a trauma like Jane had today.

As the farmhouse came into sight, Jane stopped by the road. Calvin didn't realize it for several strides until he glanced back at her. Her body faced away from him and she looked down at the ground. Calvin walked back, stopping in front of her.

"I can't," she said. Her eyes didn't come up from the ground.

Calvin frowned. "Can't what?"

Now her eyes met his. "I can't stay here. Not tonight."

Calvin glanced at the farmhouse, not huge or in great repair but comfortable. However, for a person who'd been through what she had, he could see how it could be eerie all alone in the dark. "I'll stay with ya," he offered, having already planned on doing just that. "On the

171

couch," he quickly added, not wanting her to think he was planning on taking advantage of her vulnerability.

Her eyes went back to the ground, and she shook her head. "No, I can't stay here. It'll be better tomorrow, but not tonight." Her voice fell to a whisper. "Can I stay with you?"

Calvin stared at her. What should he say to such a request? His little house was not like hers. Sure, he'd been fixing it up slowly over the past few years, so the roof didn't leak now and the holes in the floor had been repaired. He'd even built a nice table and chairs. Yet, it still didn't have a pump to run water, and the floor was bare wooden slats. "Jane…"

"Please?" Her eyes rose again. "I promise I'll sleep on the sofa and not bother you about anything. I'll even cook you breakfast in the morning. Please, just for tonight." Her voice sped up, as if she sensed he was relenting. He couldn't bring himself to tell her that he didn't own a sofa.

He huffed, knowing he would agree to it. The image of the dead Indian woman looming behind her, hands outstretched to tear into her vulnerable body, flickered through his brain. A chill ran across his shoulders. He'd almost lost her. Nausea washed through him, and he swallowed back bile. He couldn't, wouldn't leave her alone. He nodded.

A huge smile brightened her face, and for a moment, she seemed as if she might jump up and down with joy. "Thank you, Calvin. Neither you nor Martin will even know I'm there."

Oh, no, Martin. He hadn't thought about that. His big brother would never let him live this down. Also, he didn't want Martin messing with Jane either. She didn't need that. Considering it carefully, he knew he could work it that Martin would actually never know she was there. At least he hoped. Maybe he'd get lucky, and Martin wouldn't come home tonight. It wasn't an impossible prospect.

He clutched the carpet bag and guided her back to the road. She almost skipped beside him as they neared his house. His stomach flipped and twisted. With almost anyone else, he wouldn't give a damn what they thought of his living conditions, but he was somewhat uncomfortable with the idea that she would judge them.

As they approached, he appraised his home from the new viewpoint. The roofline sagged over to one side, while the patched front door hung crooked to the other side, giving the structure a lopsided appearance. The wash from two days ago still hung on the uneven fencing on the side. He cringed. However, when he glanced at her, her smile never dimmed. He loved her for that.

Darkness shrouded the inside as the sun descended past the horizon. Calvin lit a large lantern on the table. It flamed to life, illuminating the room with a soft golden glow. Jane paused in the living room, surveying the space.

"No sofa." She eyed one of the larger chairs, which was fairly well padded if not a little worn.

"Here." He took her bag into his bedroom. She stopped in the doorway and surveyed his room. Its sparse furnishings included a thin mattress on a simple bed frame, a woven yellow blanket and lumpy pillow heaped on top. A beat-up dresser holding a small lantern sat in the corner. Calvin lit it and placed her bag on the bed. "You can sleep in here tonight."

She stepped in, and as she was acclimating to her surroundings, he slipped out. When he returned, he carried a saddle roll. Jane watched silently until he started unrolling the saddle roll on the floor. "What are you doing?"

"I don't want Martin knowin' yer here. Don't want him givin' ya any trouble. I know it really ain't right, us in the same room and all, but I'll sleep over here by the door."

"Calvin, I'm not kicking you out of your own bed. I'll sleep on the floor." She strode over to the makeshift bed.

"No, yer not sleeping on the floor," he said just as stubbornly. He blocked her from getting any closer to the door. "Yer sleeping in the bed, and I'll make sure nothin' gets through that door."

"Don't be ridiculous, Calvin. I pressured you into letting me stay here. I get that you don't want Martin to know I'm here, even though I doubt he'll give me nearly as much trouble as he'll give you. But I'm not having you sleep on the floor." She attempted to dodge around him, yelping as he caught her around the waist and threw her on the bed.

He knew he shouldn't have done that. She'd been handled badly by a man for years. He wanted to sink into the floor when he saw her curl in on herself and lean her head against the wall. She'd turned her face away from him, but he was afraid she was about the cry.

"I'm sorry. I never meant…" He reached out to gently touch her shoulder.

She was up and around him before he'd even blinked, a self-satisfied grin on her face as she plunked herself down on the blanket on the floor.

His mouth hung open in astonishment. "You faker!"

"Now I know where your weaknesses lie, Drake." She snickered.

"You ain't sleepin' on the floor," he ground out, more determined than ever to get his way as he lifted her off the floor and slung her over his shoulder.

"Calvin!" She shrieked then dissolved into giggles.

He carried her the two steps across the room and pulled her off him to throw her back on the bed. However, she locked her arms around his neck. With her forward momentum, he struggled against gravity from being dragged down with her. Unfortunately, his foot caught the edge of the blanket on the floor, and he slipped. His body crashed down on top of hers on the bed.

He tried to sit up, to move off her, but she twined her hand in his shirt and pulled his lips against hers. He froze, and she froze, breaking contact.

Her teeth bit into her bottom lip. "I'm sorry."

"For what?"

"I shouldn't be so forward."

"It's okay." He put a foot down on the floor, moving to get off the bed.

"Wait!" Her hand pressed against his chest. "Can I kiss you again?"

He licked his lips and nodded. Her mouth moved over his, and she gently sucked his bottom lip between hers. Her tongue flicked out, touching his lips, asking for entrance. His lips parted, and her tongue scraped against his teeth. He opened his mouth more, deepening the kiss, sliding his tongue against hers, dancing. The room spun, and he closed his eyes, tilting his head to aid her movements.

She moaned, the noise echoing through his mouth, the vibration delicious. Electricity jolted through his body, and he felt himself getting hard.

Panic, fear, insecurity joy. He couldn't identify the emotion, though maybe it was all of them. But he didn't want her to think he'd lured her into his bed just to please himself. It hadn't been on his mind, not after what they'd been through that day. Not that he hadn't had a few dreams about exactly this, ones that left him drenched in sweat and needing to take care of himself before getting back to sleep.

He shifted his hips away from her, trying to hide his predicament. She whined against his mouth. The hand twined in his shirt clutched tighter to stop him. His breathing quickened, and the blood rushed in his ears. He needed to stop this or he wouldn't be able to stop.

Her other hand moved up his thigh, and he fought to keep reason. Panic. It was definitely panic now. Yet, he didn't want to stop.

Then her hand slid over his pants, and her fingers caressed the length of him through the material. He broke the kiss, his hand gripping her wrist. Her hand retreated.

"What're ya doin'?" He hated how hoarse his voice sounded, full of lust but also fear in it. It perfectly reflected the turmoil inside him.

"I'm sorry," she repeated.

His grip softened hearing her apologize again. How many times had she had to apologize to her bastard husband for everything she did?

"I can stop if you want. I know this is so improper and I'm acting like a sinful woman." Her eyes fell to his chest, refusing to make contact with his. "I just...I just want to thank you. For saving my life and letting me stay here tonight."

"Ya don't have to do that."

"I know. I thought, maybe, you might want me to." Her cheeks burned red and she blew out a held breath, almost seeming to deflate. Her eyes remained glued to his chest.

175

He realized she must have thought he didn't want her. That thought was far from the truth. He released her wrist. "Ya know I want to. I just ain't good at this stuff."

Her eyes tracked up his neck, lingered on his lips and finally met his eyes. "Maybe we could learn together."

He licked his lips and nodded again. Capturing her mouth with his, he fanned the flames that had been burning so hot just a moment earlier. Slowly, she eased him over so he lay fully on the bed, only his legs hung off the side with her pressed between him and the wall. He clamped down on the panic stirring in his belly, panic that demanded he bolt out the door. No, he wanted this more than he'd ever wanted anything. Instead, he toed off his boots without breaking the kiss, and his legs curved up on the bed with the rest of him.

She tentatively slipped her hand into his pants, her fingers encircling him. He forced himself to stay relaxed, to concentrate on her lips and caressing the back of her neck. Her fingers slipped against him a fraction of an inch, but the sensation flashed through his body, sending more blood rushing down. Her hand moved up him, now with more purpose. Her long fingers stroked him, once at first, but then again.

Every muscle in his body tensed, and he broke the kiss, moaning. Her hot breath puffed against his cheek. Up and down, her fingernails barely grazing his sensitive skin and sending little streams of fire through his nerves. The heat built into a river. His hips moved at the same pace as her hand, and he wasn't sure if he was supposed to be doing that.

All of his thoughts and doubts dissolved as the river of heat within him exploded. His hands twisted in the blankets as a strangled moan escaped his lips. Stars flashed in front of his eyes as he went over the edge.

He fell back against the pillow, unable to budge. His heart thudded so fast in his chest Jane probably heard it. If this was how it could feel, he understood Martin's drive for bedding women.

Staring up at the ceiling, he recovered as Jane moved around him, squeezing under his arm and laying her head on his chest. His arm wrapped around her instinctively.

"Was that right?" she whispered.

He wanted to tell her how he's never reached such heights of pleasure. How she was absolutely amazing. That only with her, could he let himself feel a level of intimacy he's never allowed himself to feel with anyone else. All that came out was, "Hell yes."

He felt the smile on her lips through his shirt, and his arm tightened around her protectively.

They lay there, holding each other. For the first time in longer than he could remember, he drifted into an easy sleep.

CHAPTER 53

Dusk descended on the little house behind the sheriff's post. Cora Wade hid in the corner behind the bed, listening to her husband's ravings in the next room. For once, his temper wasn't directed at her. That didn't mean it couldn't turn at the slightest provocation, so she dared not risk it by showing herself.

Cora didn't venture out of the house often these days. She'd go to the general store for supplies when needed, but both the Waller and McKenzie farms delivered food to the house. Interacting with other people was a problem. She knew she was different, that she saw things nobody else saw and that it was getting worse. Sometimes it frightened her and other times made her angry. They all looked at her like she was crazy. Why didn't they see the bugs?

It had been over a week since she'd been bled by Doc Silverstein, and she hadn't left the house since then. She hated the cutting and could tell that Doc felt bad doing it. Yet her husband pressed the poor man, having decided before that it was the only treatment for her visions. It wasn't working, just made her too weak to react to anything she saw. Only now her strength returned bit by bit.

A crash echoed through the house from the other room, and she squeezed more tightly into the corner.

"That lunatic was threatening his wife! His wife! He was a danger to the whole town that I took care off. Me! Bill was sitting on his ass, babbling about investigations and evidence while I did his dirty work!"

Cora flinched when Victor kicked the wall separating them. What had gone so wrong between him and Bill regarding the hanging of the outlaw? Victor had been itching for a good hanging in Morley, so she didn't understand why he'd be so angry about it.

Planning things out had never been a strength for Cora, so when she came to the snap decision to visit her parents, it was going to be that night. When the noise outside the door had stopped for a while, she silently stood up and put on her shoes. Her nerves were so rattled, she didn't even think about changing out of her night clothes. She didn't pack a bag, nor did she arm herself, despite the fact that Sheriff Bill himself had come to her door warning of the dangerous wendigo monsters.

She crept out of the bedroom and saw Victor slumped on the sofa, a bottle of whiskey clutched in his hand, half of it gone. He snored loudly. She immediately noticed the absence of his beloved deputy badge. She frowned, knowing how much he adored that symbol of his authority. Yet, it wasn't enough to stop her from leaving.

A beetle scurried past her feet, and she almost jumped backwards. She had to resist stomping on it, part of her knowing there was a very good chance it wasn't even real. The insect ran across the room and was gone. Unfortunately, the shifting of her weight caused the wood to let out a loud creak. She froze, her eyes snapping to her sleeping husband. Her heart skipped a beat as he snorted and rolled on his side. After her settled, Cora eased the door open and closed without disturbing him further.

The fresh air enlivened her senses, and she breathed in deeply. The stars twinkled above her, and she smiled at them as her eyes adjusted to the darkness. Giddy at the prospect of freedom from her husband for a few days, not at all thinking about her controlling parents, she dreamily walked down the empty main road. The inn was open but quiet, which was understandable since Abigail Rodgers still lie injured upstairs. She strolled past the Waller farm and out of town. She giggled as she began the three-mile trek.

She hadn't gone far when she heard a strange noise, a groan, accompanied by shuffling. She stopped, squinting her eyes to see down the road. The shuffling grew louder, and the outline of two figures came into view.

She thought of the murdering outlaws. What if they stabbed her like Abigail? Or raped her like that farmer's daughter? Before she could draw their attention, she darted off the side of the road and into a tall patch of swaying grass. She crouched down and watched as the figures approached, trying to control her breathing to be as quiet as possible.

A scream rushed up her throat, and she crammed her fist in her mouth to stop herself from making any sound. Her heart pounded in her chest, and air rushed in and out of her nose as she tried not to panic.

Bugs completely covered the three man-shaped figures. Every inch of them was crawling with insects. Flies, wasps, beetles, worms, moths, fleas, maggots. The bugs fell off them as they walked, leaving a trail of squirming horror. One of them looked like it had a huge set of antlers growing out of its head, but it was actually a branch tangled in its hair. The creatures seemed unsteady on their feet, one dragging his foot along the ground creating the shuffling sound while the other lurched along beside him. Despite their slow, apparently aimless saunter, the straight road was going to lead them right into town.

Were the bugs real? Were the men? Was this all an elaborate hallucination? Bill's warning about wendigos popped in her head. These could be wendigos, although he'd made no mention of insects. If they could hurt someone, she knew she had to warn them.

They shambled past her, and she waited for them to get further down the road. Before they completely disappeared from sight, Cora crept out from her hiding place and followed them. As they passed the Waller farm, she held her breath again. She wondered if the pigs acted up, would the noise attract the wendigos' attention? It was a stroke of luck that everything stayed quiet.

The road forked, one direction leading to the McKenzie farm while the other led to the main street of Morley. More importantly, the road curved, and if the bug creatures continued to just move forward, they'd walk right off the road and into the uninhabited wilderness. Cora hid behind a tree and almost cheered when they stepped off the road and headed away from town.

Then the wendigos stopped, their bug-covered heads swinging toward the McKenzie farm. Whistling. Someone was coming down the road whistling a happy tune. The creatures shifted their direction. Cora waited to see who it was, hoping it was the sheriff or someone else who could defend themselves. Then again, maybe the creatures weren't even real, just figments of her imagination, and the person would walk right through them.

The moaning intensified as the wendigos picked up the pace. The whistling stopped. Cora covered her mouth, choking back a sob of fear. A young man strode into view. She didn't recognize him at first, not having socialized with people for years. When she realized who it was, she was surprised how much he'd grown-up.

It was Tommy Anderson.

"Tommy, run!" Cora screamed from her hiding place.

Tommy looked around, unsure where the warning came from. His eyes widened as the creatures neared him. They were real! He took a few steps backward, fumbling for his knife on his belt. His mouth dropped into a gaping O, and his wide eyes held a look of sheer terror. One of the wendigos was almost upon him.

Cora stepped out from behind the tree and ran straight at the monsters. "Tommy, run!" she repeated. She attacked the wendigos, pushing them away from the young man. The insects swarmed off them and on her. She desperately clawed at her arms, trying to rake the bugs off.

Tommy dodged around them, the knife trembling in his hand.

"Get help!" Cora yelled at him.

He nodded and took off, running for home.

She watched Tommy instead of paying attention to where she was going as she scrambled away from the approaching wendigos. Her feet caught under her, and she fell hard on the ground. Pain split her head, blurring her vision. The scream caught in her throat as the creatures descended upon her.

CHAPTER 54

Tommy burst through the door of his house, almost collapsing in the threshold. "Help! Help!" He gasped for breath. His face was bright red and tearstained.

Martha sat on the chair in the living room, stitching her latest needlepoint project. Bill dozed on the sofa with his eyes closed as he massaged his forehead. Simon and Emily lay on the floor, playing blocks with baby Harry. Tommy's abrupt entrance ruined the idyllic scene.

Martha ran over to her eldest son, touching his face and trying to smooth away his tears. Bill jumped to his feet, instantly behind her.

"What happened? Why aren't you staying over at the McKenzie's?" Bill questioned.

"Wendigos! They got Cora at the crossroads! We've got to help her!"

Bill buckled on his holster and checked his gun. "Tommy, show me exactly where this happened. Martha, get Victor, and meet us at the crossroads. Take your pistol and aim for the head. Simon, you and Emily stay here with Harry. Lock the door. Got it?"

Simon saluted, back stiff and knees locked. "Yes, sir."

Martha held up her small pistol. Bill nodded, and then they all ran outside in their respective directions. She crammed her terror deep down as she made her way to Victor and Cora's house, stumbling in the darkness. Everything looked sinister. She breathed a sigh of relief when she got on the front porch and pounded on the front door. "Victor, it's Martha! Open the door!"

"Go away, Martha!"

"Please Victor, open the door. It's Cora. Something's happened!" Martha clarified. She heard Victor yell for his wife, knowing there would be no answer. She cringed back when the door swung open, her nose assaulted with the fumes of booze.

"Where the hell is she?" Victor wobbled on his feet, clutching at the doorframe to steady himself.

"Tommy said she needs help! Come on!" Martha urged.

Victor didn't bother shutting the door. He followed behind her, still not quite right on his feet. Martha stayed with him, guiding him down the road through town. The inn was already closed, and there were only a few lights in the windows in the center of town. Martha wanted to move faster, but Victor was too drunk to run.

Two gunshots rang out through the night. It seemed to instantly sober Victor up. He shook his head and ran full speed down the road, leaving Martha in the dust. She picked up her skirts and ran, fear giving her speed.

She'd almost caught up with Victor when he rounded the corner to the fork in the round and staggered to a halt. Two dead mean slouched on the ground, their heads blown open, the smell of rot and death surrounding them like a cloud. Tommy's face had lost all color, and he stood behind his father. Bill held his gun up, lips pursed and steel in his eyes as he aimed it at the third figure crouching on the ground.

Cora was dead. And yet, not. Blood soaked her white nightclothes, and huge chunks of skin had been torn off along her torso and down her arms. Most of her fingers were gone, possibly from trying to defend herself from being eaten alive. However, her beautiful face had been spared. Victor focused on that angelic face as she struggled up on her knees, reaching greedily for Bill, growling and snarling.

Victor watched Bill steady his arm. "Cora!" Victor screamed.

Her head turned to him, looking at him with blank, white eyes. When the bullet cracked through her skull, Victor fell to the ground also, sobbing.

Martha dropped down next to him, wrapping her arms around him.

For a moment, he let her do it as he sobbed for the loss of the woman he once loved. Bill crouched down at Cora's side, closing her blank eyes. Then he stood, put his arm around his terrified son and walked over to them.

Victor wrenched himself away from Martha, glaring up at Bill. "You killed her! YOU KILLED HER!"

Bill stepped back. "N-no. She was beyond help."

The muscles under Victor's shirt bunched up, as if he was about to attack, and Bill shifted Tommy behind him. Martha reached to comfort him again, hoping to calm him. They'd lost enough this night. But Victor pushed her hand away, jumped up from the ground and ran into the woods.

CHAPTER 55

Darkness covered the countryside. The half-full moon deepened the shadows, giving an advantage to anything lurking outside. Yet the crickets chirped their happy songs.

Calvin lay stretched out on his bed with Jane's head on his chest and his arm wrapped around her. He'd drifted in and out of his easy sleep, not dreaming, just comfortable in her arms. A small smile touched his lips.

The peace shattered when the front door slammed shut, both of them jumping awake.

Martin's loud voice boomed through the house as he sang out a bawdy ballad. "Roll me over in the clover, roll me over, lay me down, and do it again. Now this is number one and I'm buttering up her bun. Roll me over, lay me down, and do it again." A fist pounded on Calvin's door. "Ya sleeping in there? Have a drink with me!"

Calvin scrambled off the bed. He held his finger against his lips. She nodded and settled back in the bed. He left, pulling the door shut behind him.

Martin's eyes lit up a little too brightly at seeing him, and Calvin knew he'd been drinking.

"Hello, baby brother!" Martin greeted him warmly. "I didn't wake ya, did I?"

"Nah, I was up," Calvin lied, hoping if he reassured Martin, he could just get his brother off to bed without much effort.

"Oh boy, that woman Lydia. I ain't even knocked boots with her yet and I think I'm in love," Martin gushed.

"Thought you didn't like women with kids?" Calvin questioned.

"Eh," he shrugged. "Her kid's growin' on me. He laughs at all my jokes. I could get used to that." Martin stopped smiling for a moment, focusing fully on Calvin. Then the smile returned, big like the Cheshire cat's. "What about you with Jane? Holdin' her hand today? Didn't think I'd caught ya doin' that, did ya?"

Calvin snorted.

"She finally gonna be the one, boy?"

"Balls, Martin! Shut up," Calvin spat out. He knew Jane could hear the whole conversation from his room.

As if on cue, Martin glanced at Calvin's door. "Why you got your door closed? You never close it unless yer pissed off at me and yer sittin' in there sulking. Ya don't seem to be sulking right now."

Calvin cheeks warmed as he thought about his most recent activities behind that door. He cursed himself as he watched Martin's eyes narrow, head cocked as he looked at the door once more. "Let it go," Calvin warned him.

Letting things go was not Martin's style. He ran for the door. Calvin couldn't let his brother find Jane in there, so he tackled Martin to the ground.

"Damn it, Calvin, get offa me! What you got hidin' in there?" Martin kneed him in the gut.

Calvin grunted but didn't let go. He grasped Martin's belt and tried to haul him backwards. As he pulled, Martin's leg splayed out and kicked one of the kitchen chairs. It screeched as it slid across the floor. Martin twisted his arm around, grabbing Calvin's fingers and bending two of them back.

"Stop it, Martin!"

The door flew open. Jane stepped out, hands on her hips, and stared down at the two men wrestling on the floor. "Hello, Martin."

For possibly the first time in his life, Martin was struck speechless. He gaped at her, his mouth trying to form words but failing. Calvin pushed off of him and stood up.

"You were...he...he had you in there?" Martin stuttered out.

Neither of them answered. Martin lay there for a minute longer then chuckled. He picked himself up off the floor. "Well, welcome to our lovely abode You know, Calvin here put up the walls himself. Didn't like hearin' my snoring." He rapped on the wall next to Calvin's bedroom door. "I woulda been quieter comin' in if I'd known you and my brother were occupied." He said the last word with emphasis, smirking when Calvin blushed again before his focus returned to Jane. "I'm sure he hasn't been the best host." Martin guided her to a chair in the living room and plunked her down.

She laughed a little, awkwardly shifting on the chair.

"Let me get you a drink." Martin headed to the kitchen and poured a generous amount of pale liquid into a glass.

"Oh no, not the moonshine," Calvin muttered.

Both of them ignored him as Martin handed Jane a glass of his homemade brew. "Thank you, Martin." She smiled and took the cup. She gave Calvin a reassuring smile, then took a huge swig of moonshine.

Calvin gave her a lot of credit for not spitting it out. He watched as she struggled to swallow it and coughed.

"Wow, that's some strong stuff," she choked out.

Calvin sat down in the chair next to her and rubbed her back, his movements tentative and awkward.

Martin shook his head and, with a smile on his face, went back into the kitchen to return with drinks for Calvin and himself, which Calvin gratefully accepted.

CHAPTER 56

Jane awoke disoriented the next morning. With no curtains to block it, the sun streamed through the window, lighting up the small room brightly, making her eyes ache. Her head faintly throbbed.

It took a moment for her to recall where she was. Then she remembered and smiled. She was alone in Calvin's bed, remembering him tucking her in late last night. She hadn't drunk much more of the strong alcohol after the initial gulp, but it was enough to make her head cloudy. She wasn't sure where he'd slept, but she knew it wasn't with her. Even if it was improper, she wished he'd stayed.

She stretched languidly on the bed, breathing in deeply. His scent surrounded her. After a few minutes of just lounging and enjoying herself, she figured she really should get up. She dressed quickly from the clothes in her carpet bag and walked to the kitchen, planning on making breakfast. Martin snored behind his bedroom door on the other side of the kitchen. She wasn't the only one who'd slept in.

Then she spotted Calvin through the window. He was with Sky, and a smile spread across her lips as she watched him brush the horse. He looked so at peace doing the simple task. Sky munched on something, enjoying the brushing.

With the smile still on her lips, she proceeded to make a breakfast of eggs and biscuits with coffee. The smells emanating from the room must've been strong enough to awaken Martin, because he staggered out of his bedroom only wearing his shirt.

"Mmm, mmm." He pulled his pants on. "Ain't never smelled anything so good comin' outta this place."

Jane dished out three plates and handed the first one to Martin. "I had to thank you somehow for letting me stay here last night."

He took the plate over to the table and began scarfing breakfast down.

She walked to the table and sat across from him. "Listen, Martin. I wanted to ask if you'd be willing to work on the farm again."

Martin looked up with a crumb stuck at the corner of his mouth. "Yeah?"

"Yes. Now that Zeke's gone, I'm going to need help. You always seemed to get the jobs done he never did. I'd need you to work on the crops, too, because I know he'd been neglecting them. Do you know what he was doing out in those fields?"

Martin shook his head, mouth full of eggs.

"Me neither. He certainly wasn't working. Anyway, if you'd be willing to come back, I'd like you to run the place for me. You can even hire another farmhand once I get back on my feet financially. Shouldn't take too long now that most of the money won't be spent at the card table."

Martin smiled genuinely. "That's mighty kind of you. Best offer I've had in ages. I'll take that deal."

Jane laughed. "I'll even overlook the occasional nap in the hay loft."

Martin snorted at that.

Jane stuck her head out the back door and called Calvin, figuring it was a good idea since Martin was already eyeballing Calvin's plate. Calvin patted Sky on the side and headed to the rain bucket to wash his hands.

Jane jumped at a loud knock at the front door, and Martin strode over to open it. Alexander stepped into the house. Calvin came in through the back and nodded at the young man.

"Good morning folks." Alexander tipped his hat. "Glad you're here, Mrs. Lansing. I tried you at your house but was afraid I'd missed you."

Heat crept up Jane's cheeks. If it had been anyone else from town, it might have become a scandal finding her alone in the house of these two rough men.

Alexander carried on, "Sheriff Anderson sent me to alert everyone that there's going to be a town meeting this afternoon. He wants everyone there, and children can come too. Because we won't all fit in the inn, it's going to be held in the McKenzie's barn."

"What time?" Jane asked.

"Three o'clock, ma'am."

"We'll be there." She spoke for all three of them.

The men nodded. Strange things had been going on and it was high time they addressed them.

CHAPTER 57

The hot afternoon sun shone down as spring slowly moved towards summer. Sheriff Bill walked through town with his family to the McKenzie farm. It was rare that a town meeting was called, because things usually ran smoothly in Morley, but the past couple of weeks had been out of control with one problem after another. Murderers, maimed bodies, and demons bringing the dead back to life was more than enough to warrant a town-wide discussion.

Martha strolled by his side, her arm linked in his. After the horrific event the night before, Martha had refused to talk about it, only wanting to lay with his arms around her in their bed. In the darkest hours, for the first time in months, they'd made love. She seemed to crave his closeness, and the act was slow and tender. For a few hours, Bill slept peacefully.

Simon and Emily strode several yards ahead of them, whispering in each other's ear, resulting in a lot of giggling. He liked Emily a lot, found her to be a good influence on Simon, and was glad she had something to take her mind off the trauma of losing her father. Not that Zeke Lansing had been much of a father. He had a feeling the girl and her mother would be better off without the man.

"I envy them, being able to shove all this darkness aside and find something to laugh about. I wonder when we'll hear Tommy laugh again." Bill glanced back at his eldest son, shuffling along behind them, eyes fixed firmly on the road. After Cora went down and Victor took off, Tommy refused to talk. He'd locked himself in the room he shared with Simon and wouldn't let anyone in. Luckily, Emily and Simon were happy to camp out in the living room.

"He will. Last night was so traumatic for all of us, but him especially, knowing Cora sacrificed herself for him. What a horrific death! It'll take while for him to move past it." Martha laid her head on his shoulder.

"I wish Victor were here, backing me up." Bill swallowed. "Yesterday, after the whole town saw Warren change into a wendigo, I wanted to strangle him for exposing everyone to that terror. Why didn't he talk to me? I could've told him about my suspicion that he already had the demon inside him from eating infected deer meat." His body trembled, his words speeding up as he tried to keep his voice low. "But now he blames me for Cora's death! Couldn't he see she was already gone, that she was a monster?"

"Shhh, be calm, my husband. He'll come around again. He was drunk last night, and his eyes lied to him." She rubbed his arm. "At least you got to be the one to break the news to Cora's parents this morning. It was very kind of Alexander to volunteer for the job of alerting everyone about the town meeting so you could make the trip out to Cora's parents' farm."

Bill cleared his throat, getting control of his emotions. "Cora's parents were surprisingly stoic about the death of their daughter. Didn't seem right."

As they entered the massive barn set up with benches, Martha gave him a peck on the cheek and ushered the children over to an empty row. Simon and Emily waved enthusiastically to Clara McKenzie as she walked in behind her sister Rebecca and Daniel from the general store. They all sat in the row right behind his family so Clara could tickle the two kids. He couldn't help but chuckle at the outrageous laughs that drifted over to him. Even Tommy gave her a little smile, giving him hope.

Bill made his way up to the stage and saw Connor McKenzie and his son, Duncan, sitting on the side, watching the townspeople filing in. He waved as Lucy, George and Harold took their seats.

"Ye ready fur this, laddie?" the older Scot asked him, a twinkle in his eye.

"I don't think it'll be too bad," Bill responded. "If there were going to be a panic, I think it would've happened yesterday after the hanging."

Duncan spoke up, "T'was gruesome and unexpected but actually pretty fascinating, too."

Connor nodded in agreement. "Ye know, as gory as he tells me it was, ah wish ah could've bin there tae have seen heem change intae 'at wendigo thin'. I'm very curious about it."

Bill frowned. "Curiosity is fine, but these things are dangerous! That's why we have to have this meeting."

"Yoo're right, sonny." Connor shook his graying, blond head.

Bill glanced back out at the crowd. The room was almost full of everyone in town. Isaac Smith came in with his wife, and the blacksmith leaned against the doorway.

Connor squinted. "Is 'at Jane Lansin' comin' in wi' th' Drake boys?"

"I'll be damned, it is." Bill watched Martin break off from them and head right over to Lydia. Both her father and son seemed pleased to see him also, which just seemed odd to Bill. Usually Martin's boisterous attitude and crude mouth took some getting used to.

Duncan smiled. "Saw Calvin holdin' her hand yesterday after she got attacked."

Connor whistled. "Ye think something's gonnae on there? Calvin's rough around th' edges, but he's sure a step up from 'at no-good husband ay hers."

They watched Jane and Calvin walk to the seats in front of Bill's family. Before they sat down, Emily jumped up with a big smile to give her mother a hug. A small movement caught Bill's eye as Jane straightened up. Calvin's hand had brushed lightly across the small of her back and hesitantly hovered there until she sat down. Emily leaned forward from behind, resting one elbow on her mother's shoulder and the other on Calvin's shoulder. He couldn't hear what was being said but they all looked happy, even Calvin.

Bill rubbed his jaw. "Gee, it sure looks that way."

"Is that proper? She's only just widowed," Duncan pointed out.

Connor and Bill both glared at him.

"Ye moornin' fur Zeke Lansin'? Man was a wife beater an' belongs in hell. 'Hat woman could use someone tae watch out fur her fur once."

Bill nodded. The two of them had gone through a lot in their lives and if they could make each other happy, they both deserved it.

Stepping to the middle of the stage, he cleared his throat. All the chatter receded. Martha gave him a reassuring smile. He was grateful for that, as he didn't love public speaking.

"Good afternoon. You all know it's my job to make sure everything runs smoothly in Morley. Unfortunately, things have not run so smoothly as of late. Most of you have heard rumors about several incidents, and I'm here to inform you about exactly what's happening." Bill laid out the specifics of the mutilated traveler, the dead woman eating the bear, both of Jimmy's deaths, Warren's hanging and Zeke's attack. Gasps of horror rose from different sections of the room at different parts. People turned to those involved and gave supportive looks.

Bill took a deep breath. "Last night we lost another one of our own, Cora Wade."

All the heads snapped forward.

"My own son Tommy was walking home alone and was ambushed by these monsters." His voice cracked and he had to pause to swallow down the emotions. "Cora sacrificed herself for him. I'd appreciate a moment of silence for her bravery and for her loss." Bill hung his head, the awful memory of Cora's death playing in his head. The barn went eerily silent.

Bill motioned to Israel. "Now that you all know the details, I'm going to turn this over to Doc Silverstein. Doc?"

Israel took his place in the center of the stage, cleared his throat, and burst out in his faint Russian accent. "Hello, folks! I've done a thorrrough examination on each of the bodies and have deterrrmined all of them died and then came back to life."

Murmurs rippled through the crowd, people shaking their heads and some women crying.

Israel continued. "I know. It sounds crazy, even to me. But these are the facts. An Indian legend has been brought to my attention about a demon called the Vendigo. This demon inhabits a dead body and makes it come back to life with an insatiable hunger for flesh. I don't know if I believe the myth about a demon but something unknown to me is clearly causing the dead to rrrise again. Initially, it vas believed that the dead had to have been bitten or scrrratched to have the Vendigo taint them, but there has been a rrreport that neither of the crrriminals were injured. Yet they both ate meat from a downed deer that had been freshly mauled by an unknown crrreature. It's now believed that the deer vas carrying a Vendigo and the ingestion of that meat infected them. Be mindful, folks!" He crossed off the stage.

The sheriff faced his fellow townspeople again. "I need everyone to be extremely aware of their surroundings. It would be best if everyone stayed indoors at night and be with another person as much as possible. Keep yourselves armed, preferably with a gun, but at the very least a knife. Aim for the head on these things. Shooting the body makes no difference. If someone does get bit or scratched, seek help immediately. As most of you know, Victor Wade is no longer a lawman in this town, so I'm it. Therefore, I can't leave Morley. The nearest telegraph post is in Vigil, which is about a day's ride north. Alexander, the young man kidnapped by the outlaws, is from a ranch outside of Vigil. He's going to be making the journey there so we can send telegraphs to the authorities in both Denver and Santa Fe. I need a volunteer to accompany him."

The room fell silent. Someone coughed. A lot of people busied themselves studying their shoes. Bill understood, people didn't want to leave the safety of their homes or leave their families unprotected. Yet as sheriff and the only lawman in Morley, he couldn't leave his post.

"Damn it, I'll go with the kid!" Martin Drake stood up.

Bill was taken aback. Calvin's mouth gaped open as he stared at his brother.

Martin, ever the attention seeker, drew himself up proudly and smirked. "Hell, I gotta take out a few more of those things. My brother's killed three, and I've only gotten two. Gotta even up that score."

Calvin shook his head, frowning, but he didn't say anything. His reaction sharply contrasted with Lydia's, who smiled admiringly at Martin.

After a moment of silence, Bill spoke again. "Thank you, Martin. We all appreciate this. You can work out the details with Alexander afterwards on when you'd like to leave.

"In the meantime, we know these things will also eat our animals, as evidenced by the carnage at this very farm just a week ago. If possible, put as many of your animals in secure locations to keep them protected. School will be suspended until the town is safe for children. Does anyone have any questions?"

Worried faces stared back at him. Nobody spoke up.

"Good. This meeting is adjourned. Have a good day."

CHAPTER 58

People rose from their chairs, talking and milling about. It seemed like after all the excitement, no one really wanted to leave the security of the group. Only slowly did individuals trickle out of the barn to get back to their daily lives.

Jane took Emily's hand, commenting, "That was exciting, wasn't it?"

Emily dropped Simon's hand and gave him an apologetic smile. She really couldn't justify staying with him another night. She really needed to make sure her mom was doing okay after the attack by her dead father yesterday. Simon seemed to understand, nodding to her as the adults said their good-byes.

Calvin moved off towards his brother, and they followed behind him. Martin had a smug smile on his face, and one arm slung over Lydia's shoulders. Jacob looked up at him with wide eyes, like Martin was a hero.

"What the hell are you thinkin'?" Calvin questioned.

"Just helpin' out the town, lil' brother," Martin answered. "I won't be gone longer than two days. I know you'll miss me, but I'm sure you'll find somethin' to occupy yer time." His eyes flicked to Jane. Emily assumed he was making a lewd comment and decided to ignore it.

"I think it's very brave," Lydia stated.

Calvin clenched his jaw. "I think it's very stupid. When did you suddenly start caring about this town?"

Martin rubbed his chin. "Since it started carin' bout me." His eyes went to Jane again.

She gave him a small smile, and Emily narrowed her eyes, wondering what happened when she stayed at the Anderson's.

"'Sides, I didn't see nobody else speakin' up. I bet it'll be a boring trip, too, especially with only that kid along for entertainment." He glanced at Alexander talking with Bill. "Ain't no action when you're lookin' for it."

Calvin's shoulders slumped. "Ya better not die out there."

Martin belly laughed. "Wouldn't think of inconveniencing you like that, baby brother." Then he shouted over to Alexander. "Hey kid, we head out tomorrow mornin'. I got stuff to do tonight." He smiled at Lydia, then called out to no one in particular, "Who wants to buy me a drink?"

Lucy answered him. "For volunteering, it's on the house!"

Martin nodded, mumbling, "I could get used to this selfless shuff." With that, he and Lydia left.

Calvin fidgeted as Martin walked away.

Jane touched his shoulder. "You should go with them. Your brother seems like he's in a celebratory mood."

"Nah. Martin's in his element. Got everyone's attention focused right on him. I'll see him off tomorrow mornin'."

Emily piped up. "You should come for dinner! What are we having, Mom?"

Jane bit her bottom lip. "Fried chicken." She quickly added, "But you don't have to unless you want to."

His lips quirked up in a half smile, and his eyes seemed to sparkle. "Fried chicken sounds good."

"Oh, it is! Mom makes it the best," Emily boosted. That earned her a full smile from the quiet man. They walked out of the barn, waving to various friends, and made their way home.

As they passed the schoolhouse, Emily heard her mom sigh as she stared at the closed-up building. She frowned, thinking about why they couldn't go to school. Then Emily glanced at Calvin.

"Mama, maybe Calvin should stay over again tonight, just to make sure Father doesn't come back again."

"No, honey, we can't ask that. Calvin has done enough for us already; it wouldn't be fair. Besides, there's no way that your father is ever coming back again."

"Actually, the kid has a point. Maybe not her pa comin' back, but more of those things. I don't mind watchin' out," he said. "On the sofa." A light blush crept up his face.

Jane and Emily smiled. Having him there would make them both feel infinitely safer.

CHAPTER 59

Jane sat in her bed, picking idly at the blankets. It was completely dark save for the faint moonlight glowing outside. It didn't stop the chirping crickets, the sounds wafting through her window on the gentle breeze.

She didn't know the exact time, but she believed it to be well after midnight. She'd awakened from a dream she couldn't remember, but it had left her longing for the man sleeping on her sofa downstairs. A heavy sigh escaped her.

She wanted him. There was no denying it. She didn't quite know how to go about getting what she wanted, feeling he wouldn't initiate anything on his own. She remembered what Martin had said to him when she'd been hiding in his bedroom yesterday. She thought it sweet that he was so inexperienced with intimacy, yet willing to let her in. Her own experience with intimacy had been rocky at best. Zeke had never been gentle with her, but he had shown her some ways to please him. She'd used that knowledge on Calvin in his bedroom.

Taking a deep breath to screw up all her courage, she pulled the covers off and made her way out of the room. She briefly checked on Emily, who slept soundly in her bedroom. For years, Jane had been thankful that her little girl was a sound sleeper, giving her a tiny bit of reassurance that her daughter could sleep through most of Zeke's nighttime rampages. Jane closed the door carefully.

Pausing at the top of the stairs, she listened to the sound of Calvin's rhythmic breathing as he slept on the sofa. Silently, she made her way down the stairs. She knew just where to avoid the squeaky step. In the living room, she paused again, watching him. He slept peacefully on his back, his chest expanding with each deep breath. His boots and socks lay on the floor, half covered with the blanket she'd given him.

Her feet crept toward him slowly, and she winced when she hit one of the squeaky floorboards.

He reacted immediately, jerking upright. His eyes landed on her. "What's wrong?"

She didn't say anything, just shook her head and took his hand. He briefly resisted, but finally threw the blanket off and followed her willingly up the stairs. He paused again when she crossed the threshold of her bedroom, but she pulled a little more until he stepped through. She let go of him and shut the door.

Before she lost her nerve, she turned to him and pulled the ribbon holding her nightgown closed. It flowed open, and she stepped out of it, the cottony fabric crimpling to the floor behind her feet. She stood before him, naked and exposed.

She hoped she wasn't making a complete fool of herself. Her arms itched to cover her breasts, but she kept them in place. Zeke had used her body, never admired it. It had been about his wants. Now it was time for her wants. And she wanted Calvin.

He visibly gulped, his eyes roving over her body. His features appeared to be battling emotions of nervousness and lust. She took a step towards him, and saw his eyes widen.

"I want you, Calvin," she admitted to him.

He exhaled heavily, as if he'd been holding his breath. "Jane, I don't know how to do this." His eyes darted away from her.

She took another step toward him. "I can teach you." What was she saying? This was all new territory for her. "Do you want me too?"

His eyes locked on hers. He nodded.

She took another step forward, entering his space. "Kiss me."

He leaned down to touch his lips to hers, soft and sweet, like their first kiss. Was that just yesterday? It seemed so long ago after so much had happened. They broke apart, standing in front of each other without touching.

"Do you want to kiss me again?" she asked, her voice breathy.

He nodded once more. Hunger laced this kiss as his tongue traced her mouth, and he pulled her lower lip in between his. She opened her mouth for him, and their tongues slid against one another. His mouth tasted like the vanilla pudding they'd had for dessert.

He still hadn't touched her anywhere else, yet his hands hovered over her, like he wanted to hold her but wasn't sure how. Tenderly, she guided his one hand to her, laying it easily on her hip. He tensed, his hand trembling as his fingers moved across her smooth skin before tightening and pulling her closer into him.

Next, she took his other hand and placed it on her breast. He broke their kiss, redness burning his cheeks. He didn't move his hand away though. Instead, he caressed her ever so softly.

"Yes." She relished the sensation. Throbbing began to pound inside her.

He seemed to take this as encouragement. He brought the hand that had been resting on her hip up to cup the other breast. His rough thumbs rubbed over her nipples, and she couldn't help but moan. Her own fingers traveled to the buttons on his shirt, unfastening them and pushing the unwanted cloth down his shoulders. He detached himself from her long enough to pull the shirt off and toss it across the room.

She wasn't sure if it was lust or that he was now surer of himself, but his arms went around her waist, and he yanked her right up against him. The evidence of his want strained through his pants. His lips crushed against hers, his tongue exploring every aspect of her mouth. Her hands traced down his muscular back then unbuckled his belt.

Slowly, she walked him backwards toward the bed, and without breaking the kiss, she sat down on it. He stood over her, his mouth moving lusciously against hers. The throbbing intensified, and she needed him closer. She pulled away from him and scooted backward so that her whole body lay flat on the bed, her head resting on the pillows. He gazed, licking his lips.

"Take off your pants," she commanded.

He complied, leaving both the pants and his drawers in a pile on the floor. He stood naked before her, a beautiful specimen of masculinity.

"Come here." She patted the bed next to her.

He climbed on, settling his weight down.

She reached to take him like she had last night but he evaded her. "No," he said sharply. "I ain't gonna last long if you do that."

She withdrew her hand, unsure of what she should do next.

He made the next move instead. His mouth touched her neck, kissing and licking her tender flesh, his hand resting firmly on her stomach. His lips sucked her ear lobe into his mouth and a moan pushed past her lips.

"Show me what to do for ya," he whispered, his hot breath on her ear.

She hesitated, trying to think through the haze of excitement clouding her mind. Never had it been like this with Zeke. He took what he needed, usually hurting her in the process. Her mind skipped to last night, when she tried to please Calvin purely through intuition. Maybe? Her fingers slipped over the one on her stomach and guided it lower. His palm brushed against the center of her, and she spread her legs. He took over, his finger exploring her, hesitant at first but growing bolder as she spread her legs further.

Then he hit her bundle of nerves. Her hips bucked involuntarily as his fingers run over it. She hadn't expected that. He stopped, sensing this was significant. Experimentally, he ran his fingertip back and she bucked again, unable to keep a small whimper from escaping her.

His finger stroked her and she felt like jolts of electricity were radiating right through her, bombarding her brain with heat. Her back arched, and a delicious tension built up inside her. She writhed on the bed. He used his other hand to hold her still as he worked at her faster.

The tension hit a critical level, and waves of hot sensation washed over her. She cried out, grabbing a pillow to stifle the noise. As she came down off the high, she pulled the pillow off her face, feeling like she couldn't breathe. She whimpered, unable to speak. She marveled that this was his first time pleasing a women. His effort made her love him all the more.

Calvin rested his hand against her stomach once more, grinning. "Was that right?" he asked shyly.

Her hand touched his face lovingly. "Oh, yes! It was…it was perfect. I've never felt like that before."

His lips pursed. "Do you want to stop now?"

Her eyebrows shot up. "Stop? No." She leaned forward, kissing him deeply to show she wasn't finished with him yet. He kissed her back greedily.

Feeling that amount of pleasure made her grow bold. She pushed at him and managed to wiggle her body underneath him. He settled between her open legs, his hardness pressing against her. His mouth left hers, inching down to her breast and licking her nipple even harder. His tongue swirled around it.

"Please Calvin. I need you," she urged him, her mind swirling as the throbbing began anew.

He pulled back a little, took a steadying breath and moved forward, penetrating her. He was larger than Zeke and she stretched to accommodate his size, aching momentarily as he eased into her.

His breath exploded across her chest as he pushed all the way inside of her. He paused for a second and bit his lower lip, probably trying to keep himself under control. Then he moved.

The sensation was different from before, not quite as intense but deeper. She gasped as he pulled almost all the way out of her only to slam back into her body. Her head lolled back, and her fingernails dug into his shoulders. It had never been like this before. She wrapped her legs around his waist, urging him to move faster into her as the tension rebuilt, only centered deeper inside her now. Never had she felt this close to another human being, connected in way that transcended the physical.

His movements became jerky and irregular, as if he hung on by a thread. He panted heavily, sweat dripping off his body as he crashed into her harder. She bit his shoulder, conscious enough not to bite down too hard as her senses exploded with pleasure again. Her body clenched around him, and she tried not to scream like she had before, but a high-pitched keening sound still came from her.

It took him. He moaned as he experienced his own ecstasy, emptying himself into her. They both lay unmoving, and she reveled in the intense bliss. He kissed her ever so gently, his lips moving light as a feather over her closed eyes, her cheeks, her mouth, the complete opposite to the previous roughness but all very welcome to her. He still lay inside her, his movements causing delicious aftershocks. Then he pulled away and collapsed on the bed next to her.

"Was that right?" she mimicked him.

He smirked. "Yeah, that was right." He laughed and gathered her in his arms. Together, they fell into sleep.

CHAPTER 60

Calvin lay motionless in Jane's bed. He'd woken up some time before as the sun filtered through the curtains, but he refused to move. He savored the peacefulness. His eyes were glued to her, watching her sleeping.

She looked so serene and beautiful. Her long brown hair was out of its usual bun and fanned across her pillow. She always looked beautiful to him, but sometimes it seemed like she carried the weight of the world on her shoulders. He hoped now that he was with her instead of her damned husband, she'd have less of a load to worry about.

His hand twitched, wanting to touch her. He wanted to run his fingers through her hair and across her cheek. He wanted to trace the curve of her chest and abdomen down to where her hip flared out. He wanted to kiss her hand then her wrist then her arm and just keep kissing her everywhere. Unfortunately, he knew how clumsy he was, and he didn't want to wake her.

Instead, he eased out of bed and pulled on his clothes. As he headed downstairs, he thought about Martin leaving for Vigil. He wasn't concerned that he would miss his brother before he left. Judging by his mood the night before, Martin probably hadn't restricted his alcohol consumption, so Calvin doubted he'd leave at the crack of dawn. There was time.

He crossed into the kitchen, deciding to just grab some jerky and go tend to the animals. He knew Jane could do it, but he figured he'd get it all done for her.

"Morning!" said a small but cheerful voice.

He looked up and froze. Emily sat at the kitchen table, an open book and a bowl in front of her. He didn't know what to do. There was no way she hadn't noticed he wasn't sleeping on the sofa. Should he say something? Make up a story? Run out the door?

"Want some porridge?" She gestured to her bowl, her smile sweet and innocent.

All he could do was nod a little. She leapt out of the chair, grabbed another bowl, and spooned him out a generous portion from the large kettle hanging in the hearth. She poured some honey and cream over it and slide it across the table to him. He sat down stiffly and took the spoon she offered. They sat in silence for a few minutes, enjoying the sweet meal.

Emily put the spoon down and tapped the table to get his attention. "Hey Calvin, can I ask you a question?"

Just when he's started to relax. He sighed, sure it was about his sleeping location, and the warmth of a blush spread across his face at the thought of it. There was no way he could answer her, and he wished the ground would open and swallow him down. He didn't move a muscle, but she asked anyway.

"Do you think the Army's gonna come here and kill your Indian friends?" She looked down at her bowl.

Calvin frowned, not expecting this question. "Why do ya think that?"

"Nate at school said the Indians are killing folks for settling on their land. So the Army's coming to kill the Indians right back. Do you think means your Indian friends?"

He shook his head. "These Indians near here ain't killed nobody. But some white folks take land that ain't theirs. Mock the Indians too, callin' them savages. They really ain't savages. People gotta know their place ta keep the peace."

"Yeah, stealing and bullying isn't very nice. My pa was a bully."

He nodded in agreement and patted her shoulder. The gesture was ungainly, but she smiled brightly at him.

As they emptied their bowls, he stood up. "Tell ya what. You feed the chickens and I'll take care of the cow. Help your ma out and let her sleep a little longer."

She nodded enthusiastically before running out the back door to the chicken coop. She finished that chore before Calvin could even get to milking Bessie, who munched happily on the hay he had given her. Emily skipped into the barn and pulled the little milking stool over to the dairy cow.

"I know how to do it! My father never let me, because he thought I'd mess it up but I really do know how." She hesitated.

He sensed she waited for permission. "Well, stop staring at me and do it."

That elicited a giggle from the girl, who carefully cleaned the teats and got down to milking the cow. She was right; she knew what she was doing. He wondered how often she'd snuck behind her father's back to learn the skill. It made him smile thinking about her tenacity.

Jane walked into the barn just as Emily finished. "Good morning, you two. Doing all the hard work for me?" She winked at Calvin.

His brain froze, which instantly tongue-tied him.

Emily held up the half-full bucket of milk proudly and started to walk out of the barn towards the house. Then she turned and eyed her mother, a frown on her face. "Mama, were you sad last night?"

Jane blinked. "Why ever would you ask that?"

"Because I thought I heard you crying in the middle of the night. Then when I woke up this morning, I found Calvin wasn't sleeping downstairs, but his boots were still there. He couldn't have left without his boots, so I thought maybe he went upstairs to make you feel better. Did he?"

Calvin's stomach knotted, his heart thudding. How could Jane forgive him for causing this? His eyes swept to her. A blush had consumed her face, and her mouth hung open, as if words were stuck and wouldn't come out. Emily cleared her throat, her eyebrows still up, head cocked to the side, waiting for an answer.

Jane sucked in a breath, regaining her composure. "Yes honey, he did."

"Good." Emily smiled and walked out of the barn.

CHAPTER 61

"There's my baby brother, come to wish me off into the wild wilderness!" Martin shouted across the room, sitting at a table in front of a big plate of eggs.

Calvin led Jane and Emily through the doors of the inn and ducked his head away as all eyes turned toward him. They strolled over to Martin, who sat with Lydia, her son Jacob, and Alexander.

Martin leaned close to Calvin and whispered, "Here I was worried that you'd be too occupied to say good-bye."

"Stop talkin' like that," Calvin muttered under his breath.

Jane's steps faltered for a moment at Martin's words. Calvin glanced at her, his eyes wide.

Bill and Simon followed behind Jane into the inn, but if Bill heard anything, he kept his composure.

Martin got up from the table. "Join us. George gave us free breakfast for our brave sacrifice." He seemed to be loving every minute of attention. He winked and grinned, wrapping his arm around Calvin's shoulders. "So ya got any nice partin' words for me?"

Calvin snorted. "Don't get dead."

Martin laughed. "I think that's just about the kindest thing you've ever said to me, little brother!" He pulled Calvin into a big hug.

Calvin froze, his eyes darting from Martin wrapped around him to Jane and back again. The brothers didn't really have a hugging kind of relationship. Giggles erupted from Emily. Calvin frowned and pushed Martin away. "What the hell has gotten into you?"

"Can't a man hug his only brother before settin' out on a dangerous mission?" Martin jabbed his finger into Calvin's shoulder.

Calvin rolled his eyes. "You're only gonna be gone for two days."

Bill, an amused smile on his face, walked over to Alexander. The young man was just finishing his plate of eggs. He scrambled to his feet, saluting Bill.

The sheriff motioned for him to sit back down. "You ready for this?"

Alexander sat on the edge of his seat, his leg bouncing nervously. "Yes, sir."

Bill handed him an envelope. "This contains a letter explaining our situation as well as money for the telegrams. I expect you'll be wanting to go back home after that?"

"Thank you, sir. I do want to check in on my sister. I'm sure my eldest brother will be there by now, running the ranch. But, umm, sir…"

"What is it, son?"

"I'd like to come back to Morley with Martin after that. I can't bear to be in that house after seeing my ma and pa killed so ruthlessly."

Bill clamped his hand on Alexander's shoulder. "Morley would be lucky to have you, Alexander. Now, you got the weapon I gave you?"

Alexander pulled it out of the holster. "I cleaned it last night just in case."

Calvin assessed the boy who would be traveling with Martin. He'd been through a lot and seemed so serious about this mission. He hoped Alexander would gain some peace seeing his home again, even if he didn't intend to stay there. Then Calvin wondered if Martin would try teaching the boy his unique brand of bad behavior.

Bill tilted his head towards Martin and asked Alexander in a low voice, "You going to be good with him?"

Calvin chuckled. Was Bill reading his mind?

Alexander opened his mouth to respond, but Martin spoke up before any words came out. "Don't you worry, Sheriff!" He threw his arm around Alexander's shoulders and pulled him roughly against his side, almost knocking Alexander over. "I'm gonna take good care of the kid. Won't let nothin' happen ta him out there."

Bill nodded, then cleared his throat, summoning everyone's attention. "Before you two leave, I want to warn you about another wendigo attack that happened last night. Our reclusive guest who's been staying here the last few months, Roy Gaines, was out for one of his midnight jaunts and had a run-in near the Waller farm. No injuries, but those demon things are still out there. Be careful on your journey."

"Will do, Sheriff." Martin tilted his hat.

Bill and Alexander left for the stable to get his horse ready, Emily and Simon tagging along. Sky was already out there for Martin.

Martin turned and kissed Lydia on her hand. "You be a good girl while I'm gone."

She batted her eyelashes, smiling. "I'm always a good girl."

"Kill lots of wendigos!" Jacob spoke up.

Martin ruffled his hair. "You got it, little buddy." Then he turned to Jane. "You be a good girl, too. Make sure my brother stays out of trouble."

"Damn it, Martin. Will ya just leave already!" Calvin spat out in frustration.

Jane merely laughed and shook her head at Martin's comment. "Good-bye and good luck out there."

Martin nodded to her, gave Lydia one last appraising look then left for the stable.

Lucy came down the stairs, her eyes on Jane. When she reached the bottom, she pointed to George. "Get Calvin a free cup of coffee." Then she clutched Jane's hand and dragged her upstairs.

After a few minutes, Bill walked back into the inn while the kids stood outside the door, waving as the horses trotted away. George poured him some coffee. He sipped it, wincing a little at the bitterness of it. Even Calvin knew the coffee at the inn wasn't nearly as good as Isaac's across the street. Bill kept drinking it though, probably needing a boost to stay awake after the tragic events of the night before. There was no way to tell what might happen next in Morley.

Calvin shifted on the stool next to him, finishing up his own cup of coffee.

"So, you're helping Jane out?" Bill asked nonchalantly.

Calvin glared at him in silence. Was the sheriff trying to trap him into revealing his new-found relationship with Jane? Would Jane be ostracized for being with him so soon after the death of her husband? When Calvin saw no malice or amusement on Bill's face, he relaxed a little and nodded.

"Good. Jane needs a man like you helping her out. Zeke was a poor husband," Bill drank another gulp from his cup.

"He was an asshole."

The doors swung open across the room. Emily and Simon rushed in, straight for Bill and Calvin. They climbed up on stools next to them.

"Are they finally gone?" Calvin questioned.

"Yep," Simon answered. "We waved until they disappeared down the road."

"You don't think Martin will really die, do you, Calvin?" Emily's eyes looked up at him, eyebrows drawn together.

"Nah. He's a tough guy. Ain't no wendigo that could whip him. Don't ya worry, darlin'." Calvin poked her on the nose, eliciting a laugh. He caught Bill trying to hide a smile.

Calvin couldn't stop the smile that spread out on his face. He looked around at those surrounding him. The sheriff seemed to be enjoying drinking a cup of coffee with him after basically approving of his relationship with Jane. Simon and Emily giggled at each other's milk mustaches when George brought them full glasses. Emily glanced at him, her eyes filled with love for him. He'd never been so accepted by people in his life, and he couldn't believe how good it felt.

CHAPTER 62

Lucy slammed the apartment door shut and turned on Jane. "Spill it!"

Jane nodded, reaching into the pocket of her dress and withdrawing the money Lucy had given her. "Obviously now that Zeke's gone, I won't need to take this from you. Just know that it meant more to me than anything in the world that you'd be willing to give it."

Lucy's face softened, and she accepted the money back. "You know I would have given you more if I could have. I'm so glad you're staying though." She smiled warmly at her friend, but the smile quickly slipped off, and her brows drew together. "Now spill about Calvin Drake."

"Oh, is that what you meant?" Jane asked innocently.

Lucy groaned, putting her hand on Jane shoulders and gazing into her eyes. "Don't you play dumb with me, Jane. I saw him holding your hand the other day after you had to kill Zeke. Then I see you come in with him and Martin to the meeting yesterday. And again this morning you're with him! The last time we talked, you told me he hated you because you kissed him on the cheek. Now you're always together? What's going on between you two?"

Jane sighed, pulling Lucy's arms off her shoulders and slumping down on the sofa. "I don't know really. I guess you could say we're courting. We haven't talked about that. It all happened so fast. Some people are going to think I'm a strumpet for even being around him so soon after my husband's death."

"The dickens with them. Those people don't know you. They didn't know Zeke either. That man was no husband, and I truly believe he'd

213

have eventually killed you. But Calvin Drake, on the other hand, might make good husband material. I want details about him. Right now," Lucy demanded.

Jane couldn't help but grin at her friend's eagerness. "I was packing, getting ready to escape from Morley, when Calvin rushed into my bedroom. I almost split his head open with a fireplace poker because I thought he was Zeke. He told me Emily and I were coming with him, that he'd protect us. Then he…kissed me."

Lucy cocked her head to one side. "Calvin Drake kissed you." She said the words slowly, as if she needed more time to process that information. Then it clicked, and her eyebrows shot up. "Oh my, I was right after all! What changed?"

Frowning, Jane tried to think of something specific. She shrugged her shoulders. "Nothing I know of."

"Doesn't matter," Lucy said quickly. "So tell me about the kiss. Was it wonderful?"

"Oh, Lucy. Being with him is everything I was missing with Zeke."

Lucy's eyes widened. "You took him to your bed, didn't you?"

Jane's mouth gaped open. "How can you possibly know that?"

Lucy's smile became smug. "I can tell. You glow when you talk about being with him. Who would have ever thought shy Jane was such a shameless vixen!"

Lucy's body sagged into the sofa. "I'm jealous. Harold and I have been dancing around each other ever since he came to town. He's been so sweet and attentive but now that Abigail's better, I just want him to admit if he has feelings for me. I'm not sure if he's ever going to have the stomach to do it though. What if he just leaves to go back to New York and I never see him again?"

Jane patted her hand. "You've just got to make clear how you feel. Although maybe don't be quite as forward as I was. Harold is a very proper man. But if he has interest in courting you, him going back to New York will not be the end."

Lucy nodded then smiled. "You know, I've never been to New York City before. I think I might have to buy another dress!"

Both women dissolved in giggles, echoing the giggles from the children downstairs.

CHAPTER 63

George cursed under his breath as Victor walked in the door. Well, it wasn't so much a walk as a lopsided stagger. The man barely made it to the stool at the end of the bar and swayed slightly as he used both hands on the bar to steady himself. Alcohol fumes wafted off him.

The place was already starting to fill up, as it usually did in the evenings. People came in earlier the last few weeks, because they wanted to leave before it got too dark. Strange things came out in the dark around Morley, but that didn't mean folks didn't want to be social. Over two dozen people crowded the place, listening to the sweet melody Connor played at the piano. Lydia and her family dined at the table closest to the door, and they eyed Victor warily as he came in.

Victor slapped his hand down on the bar. "Soup," he slurred.

Abigail rested on a stool behind the counter. She'd just come down from a nap, and even though she said she felt fine, George knew she was rushing the healing process. She didn't need Victor's attitude right now.

"Let me deal with him," George said quietly. "I think Isaac needs a refill of his tea," he redirected her. Normally, she'd argue with him, always wanting to be able to handle anything, and he was thankful when she relented.

As she turned away, Victor spoke up, his tone cocky. "Glad to see you up and about, Miss Abigail. You can thank me for getting rid of your attacker."

Abigail stopped and turned back.

Eyes around the inn focused on them.

"Thank you, Mr. Wade. Wish I could've seen it."

Victor leaned back, his lips cocked in a lopsided yet somehow arrogant smile, which faded as Abigail continued.

"We're all so sorry about Cora, too."

Victor's lips thinned. "Just get me some goddamned soup."

George waved Abigail away, not liking how black Victor's mood had become with the mention of Cora. George grabbed a bowl and ladled a small amount of chicken soup into it, wondering if the drunk man's stomach would hold it down. The moment George put it in front of Victor, he turned the bowl up and slurped it down.

"More," he demanded.

"Are you sure that's wise, considering how much you've had to drink? You might not keep it down." George picked up the now empty bowl.

"More. Now!" he bellowed in George's face.

George shook his head. "I think you need to leave."

Victor's eyes narrowed on him. Then he reached back and pulled his gun out of the holster. He placed it on the counter, his hand on the handle but his finger off the trigger. "I ain't gonna ask again."

George read the imminent threat and fetched a bowl with more soup. He looked on as Victor slipped his gun back in the holster then slurped it up.

Lydia's father whispered to her, and she nodded, pulling Jacob up as she stood. They headed for the door.

Before they could get to the exit, Victor spun around on his seat and aimed the gun at them. "Sit back down!" He stood up, wobbling a little and waved the gun around. "Nobody's going anywhere!" he yelled at the crowd in the room.

The piano stopped playing, and he had everyone's attention. Then the gun discharged, firing a round right up into the ceiling above him.

For a split second, even Victor looked surprised, his eyebrows raising and his mouth dropping open, but he recovered quickly. He spun around toward George and Abigail. "Hands up! Get away from that shotgun," he commanded them.

217

Seeing the wild look in his eye, George led Abigail to a table on the other side of the room with the rest of the crowd. Everyone seemed to cringe back away from the moving pistol.

Lucy and Harold appeared at the top of the stairs.

Victor pointed the gun at them. "Stay right there!"

"Victor, what are you doing? You put that pistol down right now before you hurt someone!" Lucy yelled at him.

"Shut up, Lucy! This is my town and I'm taking it back," he declared.

The tinkling sound of happy laughter floated through the front door and the gun swung in that direction. Rebecca McKenzie stopped short halfway through the door, the smile on her face instantly dropping. Daniel's face paled, but his back straightened as he placed himself between Rebecca and the gun.

"McKenzie girl, get over there with your papa and brother."

Rebecca blinked and looked at Daniel. He nodded at her, and she dashed over to her family.

Victor watched but kept the gun trained straight at Daniel. "Hey, shop clerk, I've got a job for you."

CHAPTER 64

Bill struggled to keep his eyes open, his head nodding forward uncontrollably. He snapped his head back, opening his eyes wide and shaking himself to stave off total exhaustion. The coffee from that morning was long gone. Without a deputy, all the responsibilities of protecting Morley had fallen on his shoulders, leaving him at the office almost around the clock. When he was able to grab a few hours of sleep, his head filled with nightmares of people he knew turning into wendigos and trying to bite him.

The worst nightmare had been just last night. Illogical and disjointed, like any dream, it had started right with a memory of when he put Cora down, her arm still stiff and reaching for him. Her body became overrun by insects as if the invisible bugs she'd always feared had taken her away in the end. He'd been disgusted by the swarming mass and turned away.

That was when Tommy tried to attack him. In the dream, his son hadn't gotten away unscathed. A bloody scratch ran across his handsome face, now twisted by the demon, his eyes blank. He'd dodged away in fear, but it was difficult to run as the perceived loss of his eldest boy overwhelmed him.

The dream hadn't let him go yet. He tried to run home on heavy legs, but the scene changed to the schoolhouse, and he stood at the back of the room. All the desks had been occupied by children facing forward. He'd recognized Simon's back and had called out to his middle son. All the children's heads slowly turned toward him, their white eyes almost glowing.

219

From the front of the room came a piercing scream. With absolute horror, he'd watched as his baby son, Harry, crawled unnaturally fast towards him. The infant had also changed. Bill's feet seemed glued to the floor, and the scream that wanted to rip from his chest wouldn't come as his monster son clawed up his leg and sank his now-sharpened teeth right into his flesh.

He'd awakened with a cry, cold sweat covering his body. Martha had awakened with him, but he refused to tell her what the nightmare had been about. Since then, he couldn't stop just looking at his boys. They were so alive and vibrant, he appreciated their mere existence. They hadn't been taken from him, hadn't been turned into undead monsters. It made him more determined to ensure that his nightmare never came true.

"Dinner won't be ready for another half hour." Martha broke into his thoughts. "Why don't you take a nap? You look so tired. Tommy's upstairs. The other two are playing in the backyard and know not to take a step farther than that."

He nodded, and she stepped back into the kitchen. He'd come home for a home-cooked dinner, planning on heading back to the office afterwards for evening rounds. He settled his long, lean body into the corner of the sofa, allowing his muscles to relax. Before he could even close his eyes, a frenzied knocking sounded on his front door.

"Sheriff!" shouted a frantic voice.

Bill wrenched the door open, revealing Daniel, drenched in sweat and panting.

"Daniel?"

The thin man gulped thickly. "It's Victor."

"Victor?" Martha scurried up behind him, drying her hands on a towel, her full focus on Daniel.

Daniel nodded. "He's gone crazy! Taken everyone at the inn hostage! Half the town's there, including my Rebecca. Says you two have to come to him, or else he's going to start shooting."

Martha gasped, "Victor wouldn't do that." It didn't sound like she was completely convinced by her own statement.

"I'm not lying, I swear. He put a gun in my face. Made Rebecca go inside with her father and brother to ensure I came back with you. He's out of his mind!"

Bill's mind worked in overtime. "Daniel."

The younger man stared off towards the center of town as if he might bolt at any moment.

"Daniel!" Bill reached out and shook him. "You got your gun on you?"

He shook his head. "Don't have one. I've been saving up to get one, especially since dangerous things keep happening. I want to protect my girl, you know? I don't have enough money yet."

"Well, today's your lucky day. You're getting one from the sheriff. We'll sneak into the office from the back. Martha, you stay here with the children. Get them inside."

"No!" Daniel interrupted him. "Victor specifically said Martha had to come, too. He was adamant she be there. I think he might kill people if she doesn't come." His hand shook as he gripped the sheriff's arm.

"Absolutely not." Bill shook his head.

"Bill." Martha's voice was calm. "It's not worth someone else getting shot. I've got the protection you gave me." From her pocket, she drew out her small pistol.

Bill looked from the gun in his wife's hand up to her face. He gritted his teeth, his gut churning. "Okay. But you're staying right behind me. You are not going inside that inn."

Martha nodded. "Let me get the kids inside."

The two men waited on the porch as Martha turned toward the stairs. "Tommy!" Get down here now!"

Bill watched Tommy descend, his footsteps slow despite the desperate note in his mother's voice. However, she didn't wait for him, but ran through the house and jerked open the back door. "Simon! Emily!"

Tommy glanced at Bill, his eyes were red rimmed. Bill's heart clenched at the thought of his son crying alone in his room. "What happened?" Tommy asked.

Bill raised his forefinger, waiting to tell the story until everyone stood together. Daniel fidgeted beside him, rubbing his arms and glaring back at the inn.

Simon and Emily ran in the house, tracking dirt in on their shoes.

"What took you so long? You better not have been in that old root cellar," Martha yelled. "The whole structure's unstable and could fall on your heads. Simon, I'll tan your hide if I catch you in there."

Bill gathered the three children close. "We have to go out. You two must stay inside. Do you hear me? You're not to leave this house for any reason. I mean it, Simon. Tommy's in charge. Tommy, Harry's sleeping upstairs. Do you all understand?"

The kids stood wide-eyed, nodding their heads.

"What happened?" Emily asked.

"I promise we'll tell you when we come back." Bill mussed Simon's curly hair and patted Tommy on the back before turning to the door. He wanted Tommy and Simon to know his love for them before he headed into this unknown threat.

Martha kissed Tommy lovingly on the forehead, gave Simon a matching kiss on the top of his head, and gave another to Emily.

Bill's stomach twisted in knots, and he could taste bile at the back of his throat as he snuck into the jailhouse. He quietly removed a pistol for Daniel out of the safe. His mind raced thinking that Victor blamed him for Cora's death, but it wasn't right. She'd been dead when Bill shot her! Yet that wasn't all that pushed Victor over the edge. His envy of Bill's life had also contributed, and he wondered why Martha needed to be involved. If something happened to her, he'd be devastated. Bill took her hand and they walked across the street to the inn.

Outside, the inn looked peaceful, although eerily quiet. Several people could be seen through the windows. It was strange how still they were, not talking, drinking or eating. The only one moving was Victor. He must have been pacing, because he would come into view through one of the windows and move out of sight again. His pattern repeated over and over again. Sometimes it looked like he was swinging the gun around haphazardly.

"Daniel," Bill whispered.

The thin man held his new gun firmly as he crept up beside the sheriff.

"I want you to go around back. If it looks like he's going to shoot anyone, I want you to shoot him first."

"Bill!" Martha breathed out in shock.

"No, Martha. This is how it must be. The man's gone crazy and he's endangering the lives of everyone. If I can't talk reason into him, and he tries to kill someone, we've got to take him down." Bill reached out and gently caressed her cheek.

Tears leaked out of Martha's eyes, her hand on her throat, but she nodded silently.

Bill faced Daniel again. "Think you can handle that?"

"Yes, sir." Daniel slipped silently off into the growing shadows.

"You stay right behind me," Bill reiterated to Martha, and they moved outside the door. "Victor!"

The dangerous man paused in his back and forth motion. He smiled, his feral grin like a wolf about to catch its prey. "Bill."

"Victor, you need to let these people go. They haven't done anything to you. It's me you want. Isn't that right?" Bill's voice was steady, although there was a touch of pleading underlying it.

Victor's face reddened with rage. "I want you gone! That's what I want! Everything that was supposed to be good in my life's been taken by you. I should be sheriff; I'm smarter and stronger than you. I can make the hard decisions. You can't! And you took Cora from me! It was your boy's fault those monsters attacked her. Then you shot her in the head!" Tears ran down his face, and the gun shook in his hand. "You didn't even give me the chance to make sure she was actually one of those demons." He wiped the tears away with his gun hand and sobered, his nostrils flaring and eyes narrowing. "It's your fault, and now you're gonna give me Martha in payment. Besides, she wants to be with me more than you. She said that if you weren't here, she'd be mine!"

"That's not what I meant! Bill, please believe me. I'd never leave you for him!" Martha clutched at his shoulder, her voice high-pitched.

223

Bill put his hand on hers and squeezed gently before turning back to Victor. She seemed to sag behind him. He'd deal with that information later, but right now he needed to get Victor out of the inn.

Victor whirled to the back window, the gun discharging loudly. The upper pane shattered, the shards of glass crashing to the ground outside.

"I know you're out there, shop clerk! You'd better drop that gun and get your ass in here before I put a bullet into your girl." He swung his pistol toward Rebecca.

Rebecca cringed back. Connor tried shielding his daughter with his body. Not that it would have made much difference against Victor's gun. They all heard the dull sound of the metal hitting the dirt, and Daniel slowly opened the back door. His wide eyes held both fear and anger at being discovered.

"You stay right there, clerk," Victor threatened him.

Bill cursed under his breath. There went his back-up plan. "Victor! What do you want?"

"A draw. You and me. In the street with all these nice people watching right now."

"You sure about that? It's starting to get dark out here. Don't you want to sober up first? We could do this in the morning."

"Shut up! I said now!" Victor pulled the trigger again, the bullet hitting the wall just over Isaac's head.

Most of the people ducked under the tables, and a quiet sobbing came from the back of the room.

Bill put his empty hand up in surrender. "Okay, Victor. You want a draw now? Fine. Let all the people stay in there. They can watch from the windows. You come out, and we'll draw."

Victor smiled again and walked to the door. He paused, addressing the townspeople once more. "Remember, when I'm done with him, this town is mine, so you people had better be respectful when I come back in here." He strutted outside.

As Victor talked, Bill guided Martha behind a large water barrel, giving her at least partial coverage. He moved out into the middle of the road. His revolver rested in the holster at his hip, as were the rules of a draw. Victor moved out into the road as well, a good twenty paces away from Bill. His gun was also back in his holster.

For a moment, they surveyed each other. Their shadows grew long as the sun began its descent. Bill stood calm and steady, even though his heartbeat pounded in his ears and sweat gathered under his hat. Victor, however, didn't look as good. His eyes were glassy and his skin a feverish red, and even in the dim light of the fading day, Bill saw sweat soaking his shirt and little rivers of it flowing down his face. Victor quickly swiped his arm across his forehead.

"We don't have to do this. We can find another way," Bill offered once more. He wasn't afraid for his life, although maybe he should have been. He knew Victor was a faster draw, but he was drunk. Bill was more concerned about the innocent bystanders.

"There's no other way," Victor responded, his tone hard. His eyes steadied, piercing into Bill.

"On the count of three." Bill's hand hovered over his pistol, body tense. "One…two…"

The loud bang of a gunshot echoed around the buildings, yet both Bill and Victor still had their guns holstered. Bill blinked, confused.

Victor looked down at his chest. A hole ringed with red appeared in his shirt. The red stain grew, enveloping more of the fabric and dripping down. Victor looked back up at Bill, and the sheriff thought he saw some regret in the ex-deputy's eyes. Then the man groaned and collapsed forward.

Bill's head whipped around, searching for the shooter. Behind him, Martha stared at Victor's unmoving form, her gun clutched in her hand. She gasped for breath, her body trembling with the effort.

"Martha?"

Her eyes snapped to his, tears overflowing. Then she fainted dead away, her body collapsing to the ground.

Bill ran to her side, his fingers going to her neck. As her pulse pounded against his fingertip, he released a huge breath. He cradled her head and stroked her cheek. She did for him what he was prepared to do, but what he never wanted to do.

A few of the braver souls ventured out from the inn.

Connor checked Victor for a pulse then shook his head. He motioned to Duncan and Daniel. "Will ye two fetch Doc Silverstein tae pick up poor Victor here?"

His son nodded, and the two of them ran down the road.

Bill looked up at the Scottish farmer, who seemed to be evaluating the unconscious Martha.

"Brave woman," Connor murmured.

CHAPTER 65

Dinner was a quiet affair at the Lansing farm. Jane's mind whirled, going over the recent events relayed to her by Bill when they'd picked Emily. The shocking story about Victor's death had stunned them all. Jane's heart broke for Martha, who'd frantically tried to convey to them that Victor was going to kill her husband and it was her fault. The she'd sobbed uncontrollably until Tommy lead her upstairs.

Emily ate in silence, seeming to also be pondering the story she'd just heard about Deputy Victor Wade. Victor had mostly ignored Emily, his interest more so on Simon. However, he'd supposedly been one of the good guys, a lawman. How could a lawman do such a bad thing as take half the town hostage? Jane had a difficult time explaining that even lawmen were people with flaws, just like everyone else.

Once Emily settled to sleep in her bed, Jane walked back downstairs to find Calvin. She found him laying out the blankets on the sofa, his boots already off. He gave her his quirky half smile.

She smiled back at him, thinking of their afternoon activities together. They'd spent the day examining the turnip field, trying to figure out what Zeke had been doing with the crops. Plants grew in random locations with no indication of rows or any other such pattern. It appeared that half the seeds hadn't taken either. It was hard work, and neither of them was an expert on farming.

Near the end of the day, both of them tired, sweating and hungry, Jane's foot had landed in a rabbit hole. She'd fallen forward with a cry, but he'd caught her before she'd hit the ground. He'd laid her gently down and checked to make sure her ankle wasn't broken, despite her protests that she was fine, only her ego bruised. With her sitting on the ground and him leaning over her, his hand had drifted up from her ankle to her bent knee. He couldn't stop himself from crushing his lips to hers, and they'd rolled around on the edge of the field until Jane noticed how late it was getting.

Watching him settle on the sofa, she put her hand out to him". "You don't have to sleep down here."

"It's okay. We're both tired, and I don't want nobody sayin' any nasty things aboutcha." He swung his legs up on the sofa.

"I don't care about them!"

His eyebrows shot up.

"I want you with me, even if all we do is sleep."

He frowned. "Don't want no people callin' ya a strumpet. Cause then I'd have ta beat them. You know in them people's eyes, I ain't good enough for you."

"Not good enough for me?" She sat down on the sofa next to him, her fingertips tracing down his cheek. "Calvin, have you looked at yourself? You're like a Greek god. Women would fawn over you if you'd let them."

"I don't want none of those women, only you."

"Why? I'm old, used up." She blinked rapidly and looked away from him. In a strangled voice, she told him, "I'm not even sure I could give you children."

He put his arm around her shoulder, hugging her into his side. "Who says I need any children? Wouldn't know what ta do with a baby anyways. 'Sides, there's a darlin' little girl lackin' a father already."

Jane's eyes met his. "You mean that."

"Yeah."

She took his hand and led him upstairs. She closed her bedroom door behind them. They curled up in each other's arms, gently kissing each other good night. Then the two of them fell asleep.

CHAPTER 66

Martin couldn't wait to get into Vigil. Dusk was descending and his ass hurt from riding all day. The telegraph office would probably be closed, so the first thing they'd do is find the boarding house, then something to drink. Hell, he'd even buy the kid a drink. He'd earned it for not talking his ear off during the ride. Tomorrow morning they'd send those telegrams and head back out.

Maybe they had a brothel in this town, he mused. He could use a little action. He frowned, remembering Lydia back in Morley. Was he actually courting someone? He chuckled at the thought. All the more reason for them to finish up and get back home. He was too old for the trash in the brothels anyway.

During the ride, they'd run into two wendigos. Martin was disappointed. He wanted to exceed his brother's number of kills of these demons, but he'd only caught up so far, especially since Alexander had taken out the first one. Granted, it had apparently been an old man before death, moving slowly and missing an eye, but there'd still been the deadly hunger driving it steadily toward them.

They'd stopped their horses but didn't get off. Martin had taken the first shot and cursed when the bullet struck the elderly monster in the jaw. Bone exploded with teeth fragments spraying outward, but not enough to stop its forward shuffling. Before Martin could try again, Alexander had shot the thing in the head. The kid had looked so pleased with himself, right until Martin grumbled about the sun in his eyes and spat on the ground.

The second wendigo had been more disturbing. It looked like it had been a little boy in life, about eight or nine years old. As slow as the elderly man-thing was, the child-monster was fast. A huge chunk of its shoulder had been ripped off, but that didn't slow it down. It ran at them from out of the woods, making a menacing growling noise. Alexander froze, shocked at the creature's youth and speed. Martin had leapt off Sky, who'd spooked by the little wendigo coming at her and had danced backwards. It had gotten almost to him before he'd accurately lined up the shot with its uncoordinated movements. Luckily, the shot had hit true. Martin would never admit how disturbing it actually was to kill what looked like a child, even if it was trying to eat him.

"I think we're getting close," Alexander commented as they rode past a large farmhouse.

It was the second one they'd come across, this one nicer than the last. There was no sign of movement other than the billowing of laundry in the breeze on the side of the property. Martin frowned at the silence around them but decided that was ridiculous. It was close to supper time, and people were probably all eating inside. Of course, there wasn't even the bark of a dog or the crow of a chicken to break up the quiet.

Alexander shifted in his saddle and peered around. "Never seen it this quiet here. See that house there. That's the Macey house. They've got eleven children. There's always a few of them running around outside."

Martin waved his concerns away. "Bah. They're probably all eatin' supper together inside."

They fell silent again. The horses trudged along, and buildings appeared down the road.

"Oh, yeah. I can't wait to get off this horse." Martin focused on the whiskey he'd order as soon as they got to the saloon. "No offense, Sky." He scratched the horse behind the ear. Leaning over to Alexander, he poked him in the arm. "Ya ever had a real drink, kid?"

The young man rolled his eye. "My mama used to let me drink a little wine when I was young. My father was a fan of brandy, which he gave me a taste of once. Can't say I liked it though." Alexander wrinkled his nose and stuck out his tongue.

"Ya ever been drunk?"

"No, sir. Not sure this is the right time for it now though. You know, with us being on a mission and all." Alexander tightened his grip on the reins and straightened in his saddle.

"Aww, yer a stick in the mud, kid," Martin mocked him, but there was no real venom in his voice. He smirked. "You lookin' to take over the deputy position? That why you tryin' so hard to make a good impression on our good sheriff?"

Alexander's face colored, and he refused to meet Martin's eyes. Martin snickered, knowing he'd hit a touchy subject. Those were his favorites, made life more entertaining to exploit them.

The horses clomped onto Vigil's main throughway. Although bigger than Morley, that hardly made it a sprawling metropolis. Yet, Martin frowned at the apparent lack of activity. The hairs on the back of his neck rose up. He examined the first structure on his left, the smithy. It stood empty, the tools scattered about haphazardly and the forge cold.

Twisting his head to the building on their right, the sign advertised it as a post office. That's where the telegraph would be. Martin slid off Sky and checked the door. Locked tight with the shades drawn. Martin knocked. Surely it would be okay to disturb people with their emergency situation. No answer. Shadows stretched further as darkness descended. Where the hell was everyone? A tight knot of fear settled in his stomach, and he pounded on the door.

"Martin?" Alexander asked him from on top of his gelding, a slight waver in his voice. "This is all wrong."

Martin ignored him, cursing at the lack of response. He jumped back on Sky and waved for them to move farther into town.

After passing a couple more buildings, the stench hit, and Martin choked back a retch. Alexander put a hand up to his nose. A noise rose against the silence, the buzzing of hungry flies coming out of the half open door of the general store ahead of them. Martin slowed Sky to a stop, glad he couldn't see whatever was hidden inside and equally glad the kid knew to keep his mouth shut as Alexander pulled up next to him. Silence was definitely better.

A movement caught his eye at the other end of the street. The last bit of sun shone in his eyes, silhouetting a figure. It stumbled toward them, and Martin thought he saw the flash of a sheriff's badge.

"Sheriff Burton?" Alexander shouted at the figure.

"Hey, where the blazes is everybody in this god-forsaken town?" Martin called out to the lawman. When there was no reply other than the quickening of the man's awkward pace, Martin knew what had happened in Vigil. The pit of fear in his stomach grew, making his heart pound.

"Um, Martin?" Alexander's voice squeaked out.

Martin ignored him again, pulling his pistol out of the holster. He assumed that Alexander realized that the man coming towards them was not the sheriff he once knew. Martin's eyes never left the oncoming wendigo as it ran full speed at them. The sun flashed off the badge again. The horses fidgeted nervously.

"Martin!" Alexander's panicked tone disrupted his concentration for a moment. A curse slipped past his lips as he turned to quiet the kid but froze as he looked past the boy.

The Vigil saloon was far larger than Morley's inn with its little restaurant. It must have been completely full of people when the wendigos attacked, and not many had been able to escape.

Body after body poured out of the saloon, focused intently on them. The half open door to the general store a few buildings down the street squealed all the way open as more creatures filled the open space in front of them. Some had been pretty torn up, but others had just a few scratches or looked like nothing had touched them. All of them had the same white eyes, which could clearly track them.

Martin whirled Sky around. They had to get out of town fast. Alexander followed his lead, spurring the large gelding with his heels. Before they could get past the smithy, another pack of wendigos appeared around the building, drawn by the commotion on the street.

They cut off their path of escape out into the countryside, trapping them in the middle of two converging, bloodthirsty groups.

"Damn!" Martin spat and leapt back off Sky, guns blazing. He smacked her hard on the rump, sending her sprinting away. If he'd stayed on her, both of them would have been goners. On his feet, Martin had a better chance of making his bullets count and she had a better chance of escaping. He knew how much his little brother loved that horse, and he grudgingly admitted a fondness for the beast himself.

Alexander mimicked his actions, stumbling as he landed on the ground, trying to clear himself away from the frightened animal. The big gelding bolted after Sky without any prompting. Martin knew he should turn and run but his breath caught in his throat as he watched several of the undead break off from the approaching group to go after Sky. She reared up, trampling the closest one under her front hooves and then slamming one away behind her with a strong kick of her back legs. Then she took off back in the direction of Morley. He silently cheered her on.

Though she escaped unscathed, the wendigos turned their efforts on Alexander's horse, a closer target. The gelding fought valiantly, but he was no match for the pack of undead. His kicks and bites tore at their dead flesh and broke their bones, but his efforts were ineffectual. The creatures were relentless in their pursuit for live meat.

Martin only stared at the gruesome scene long enough to see the horse pulled down on the ground and the creatures swarm over it. A peek over his shoulder revealed that the dead mob coming from the saloon and general store was almost upon them. It looked like there was over a hundred of them, and more emerged from other doorways and around far corners. He grabbed Alexander, who stood frozen watching the death of his horse. Martin spun him around, and Alexander snapped out of it and pulled his gun out.

"Get up against me, back to back!" Martin hissed at him.

Martin growled in frustration. He wouldn't leave this earth without a fight. No, he would take as many of these bastards down with him as possible. He shot his revolver, his aim perfect in his battle for survival. Heads exploded around him, and bodies hit the dirt. Alexander did the same, missing some but picking off several of the closest monsters. They kept coming.

The sound of the dull clicking of his empty gun sent a chill through Martin. There was no way to reload, the majority of the spare ammo in the saddle bags of their horses. Even the few spare bullets he'd slipped into his pocket would've taken too much time to load. With a snarl of anger, he pulled his knife out.

Alexander whimpered when his gun ran out. Martin knew the kid had a knife, but his body shook so badly against Martin's back, he wasn't surprised when he heard the thunk of the knife hitting the ground. Martin shoved his knife through the face of an oncoming dead woman. Her face had been painted thickly with make-up, as if she might've been one of the whores at the brothel. If he survived this, he'd never be able to enjoy a prostitute again. This woman's face would invade his mind, poisoning anything else.

As he wrenched the knife out of the women and plunged it into a fat man still wearing a black hat on his head, he felt Alexander push against him. Martin hoped he was holding his own. Martin pulled at his knife, but it seemed stuck inside the dead man's skull. In the blink of an eye, he saw the teeth of a dead girl opening to sink into the flesh of his arm. He couldn't move. He would be torn apart while still alive.

The girl creature's head exploded. Several of the monsters fell from head shots.

"Get to the post office!" a deep voice screamed at them from the roof, a shot gun protruding off the edge. It fired several more times, felling demons in front of them, opening a path to the nearby building. Martin grabbed Alexander and dragged the kid along. Please let the door be easy to break in. There wouldn't be much time for a lengthy effort, not with the horde behind him.

As they approached, a living, Hispanic woman with dark curly hair swung the door open for them.

Alexander gasped. "Anna!"

The woman startled. "Dios mio! Alexander!" She glanced behind him. "Hurry!"

The two men flew through the door, and she slammed it shut behind them. Wooden slats blocked the shaded windows. The woman shifted a very heavy bookshelf in front of the door as it creaked from the pressure of dead bodies crashing into it. Alexander quickly helped her with the barricade.

A large Hispanic man rushed down the back stairs. "We've got to hide, right now! I've never seen such a frenzy!" He motioned them to run behind him through the building then heaved open a trap door under the stairs. They all scrambled down the dark, tight stairs. He jumped down afterwards, pulling the door closed over them. Darkness assaulted them on all sides.

CHAPTER 67

Sky ran.

She wasn't a young horse, but she had a lot of life still in her, and she didn't want to die.

She'd always loved humans. They'd taken good care of her throughout her life, never starving or abusing her. That was especially true of her two current human companions, with the smaller one her favorite human ever. Not only did he give yummy treats and brush her until her coat shone, but his quiet manner relaxed her.

Yet she knew what followed behind her were not humans. They looked like humans and moved like humans on two legs, but they were not. She could smell death and decay rolling off them in waves. Her brain screamed to run from the danger.

She galloped away fast, pumping her legs with all her might. She managed to put several miles between her and the not-humans. Once her sides heaved and her legs ached with exhaustion, she stopped at a tiny stream for a drink. She nibbled at the green grass growing there and slipped into a light sleep on her feet as night fell. She didn't dare lay down in the soft meadow.

A scraping noise woke her from dozing. It was them, pursuing her even in darkness. Were there more of them now, shuffling along trying to get her? She ran from the rotten ones, pushing past her fatigue, getting far ahead again.

A familiar sight in the distance caught her eye. The Jicarilla Apache camp beckoned her, and she knew there'd be real humans there. She slowed to a trot as she approached the fire and found the human who petted her and slipped her bits of fruit during their meetings.

He leapt up at the sight of her. His wide eyes appraised her as he spoke words in his human language to his people. His hand brushed gently over her shaking, sweaty shoulder. He led her to a pen with other horses and gave her some water. She felt safe in the pen.

Within minutes, the Apache camp exploded with movement all around her.

CHAPTER 68

Martin sat in the utter darkness in the basement under the Vigil post office, barely able to see the others around him. They didn't dare talk or even move considering what hunted them above. For a long time, they stared up at the ceiling, listening to the shuffling and groaning of the undead on the wooden planks over their head. Not long after they'd taken refuge, the front door had collapsed in. The monsters seemed to know they hid somewhere in their vicinity but didn't have the mental capacity to understand the trapdoor.

As the night wore on and the adrenalin wore off, Martin's attention waivered. The scent of mold lingered in Martin's nostrils, making the room stuffy. At least being underground kept it cool. The heat would've tormented him even worse.

His mind meandered through thoughts about how much his life had changed since moving to Morley. When he thought back on his life, it now seemed so trivial. He simply followed his impulses, seeking women, gambling, excitement. He never considered the future or settling down the way his brother had. Now in Morley, he lived in his own house, had a good job and the townsfolk seemed to grudgingly accept him. And he liked it.

Martin couldn't help but grin, even in this desperate situation, when he thought about Lydia. She hadn't let him take her to bed, and he surprised himself that he was willing to wait. With women before, that was the only goal and once achieved, he was done with them. Not Lydia. Something about her was different. Or maybe he was different.

Even her having a child didn't bother him the way it used to. Jacob seemed like a good kid.

The image of his Calvin clutching Jane's hand rolled into his head. He couldn't believe what had transpired between the two of them right under his nose. When had his brother grown the balls to be with a woman? Last time he'd checked, Calvin hadn't spoken a word to Jane and was a fidgety mess in her presence. Not that his behavior wasn't like that around all women. Martin had once wondered if his brother even liked females, or if he was a Mary.

Then Calvin trying to hide her in his bedroom? Holy shit! Martin had been speechless at that. Never would have expected such a move from his brother. He'd almost jumped for joy at the idea of his brother becoming a real man. Plus, Jane had been a lot of fun that night, drinking moonshine and laughing at his jokes. She'd always been kind to him but quiet, constantly cringing under the shadow of her stupid husband. This new side of her was interesting. He wondered how she was in bed and smiled, thinking his brother would kick his ass for such thoughts.

A loud crash hit the ceiling on the other side of the room, bolting Martin out of his head. No one made a noise but glanced at each other wide-eyed. Martin feared Alexander would panic, but the kid seemed to be toughing it out. Heavy footsteps pounded toward the crash.

"Post office scale," the other man whispered very quietly.

Martin shuddered. One of the flesh-eaters must've pushed it off the counter and those things were solid. The racket probably attracted a fair number of wendigos. They sat with nerves on edge as the moaning intensified, but as the minutes ticked by, the wendigos must've realized there was no real meat there so moved on. Silence settled above.

Martin wondered about the time, knowing they'd been down there a few hours already. Alexander shifted beside him in sleep. His head rested on Anna's lap and his breathing rhythmically slowed as she gently rubbed his back. It was obvious he knew their rescuers but they couldn't discuss it at the moment. Martin briefly contemplated tackling Alexander just to scare him for a laugh. Probably be quite entertaining.

However, Martin knew the young man would scream like a girl and bring the wendigos right down on them.

Martin closed his eyes. Wouldn't hurt to rest them a moment. But after the long day of travel followed by the almost-fatal encounter in Vigil, his body forced him into a sleep of utter exhaustion, which lasted several hours.

A boot kicked his shin sharply. He awoke with a growl, ready to do battle with whatever roused him. Faint light filtered through the slats of the ceiling. Morning had come. He glanced down at the man's boot, the one close to his leg.

"You were snoring," the man whispered. "Loudly."

No sounds of movement could be heard from above. Alexander still slept, no snoring coming from the kid. The Anna also slept, her head her head hunched over Alexander, her arm draped around his shoulder. She looked like a child in sleep, not the fierce woman who'd saved their lives the night before.

"Not that I ain't grateful for your helpin' us out, but who in tarnation are you people? Ya seemed to come outta nowhere like a couple of angels." Martin whispered.

"We're not angels. Call me Edgar, and this is my sister Anna."

"Name's Martin, and ya obviously already know Alexander. Came ta use the telegraph ta send a message bout these wendigos, but looks like them monsters got here first. How'd you two keep from getting chewed on, unlike the rest of this damned town?"

"I'm a cattle wrangler for the big ranch on the other side of town, the one owned by Alexander's family. We were running a herd, and a few of the head broke off. Anna rode with me after them. Took several more days than we planned, but when we got back to the ranch, it was complete chaos. We've just been trying to survive since then." Edgar's voice held an edge of bitterness and exhaustion.

"You stay up the whole night?" Martin noted the bags under Edgar's eyes and his drooping eyelids.

He nodded. "Si," slipped out along with a yawn. "I think a lot of them have been drawn off. I've been watching the shadows since the

240

sun came up, and there hasn't been any activity. This may be our chance to get out."

"Amen! Screw this hell-hole," Martin answered, keeping his voice low but forceful.

Edgar gently shook Anna awake, who in turn woke Alexander.

The young man woke with a snort. "Anna? Edgar? What happened?"

Anna smoothed his hair down with her fingers. "We had to collect some run-away cattle. When we got back, everyone in the whole town had turned into these demons! We found your sister, and then your brother, like this. They tried to attack us. No, they tried to eat us! We assumed you and your parents had suffered the same fate. How did you survive?" She clutched him in a tight hug.

"Got kidnapped by outlaws." His voice cracked. "They killed my ma and pa."

"Pobrecito!"

"What do we do now?" Alexander asked as they pulled apart.

"We're getting outta here, kid."

Only Edgar and Martin had any ammo left to reload their guns. Edgar cracked open the trapdoor just enough to see out. The bookshelf lay on the floor, the broken door trampled on top of it and papers strewn around the room, but no wendigos moved. As silent as possible, they left the safety of the post office basement.

"Out the back." Anna pointed to a small door hidden behind the main counter.

"Wait!" Alexander hissed. He ran to the front, despite everyone trying to stop him.

When they followed, his face had fallen, and Martin could swear his bottom lip quivered as he held up the ruined remains of the telegraph machine. It wouldn't be sending any more messages.

"Drat," he muttered, setting it on the counter.

Creeping with weapons raised, they eased around the building and found the street empty of undead, but numerous rotting bodies from their encounter created a stench even worse than before.

"We need to get to Denver. There will be help there," Anna said.

"Hell no! I'm gettin' back to Morley. Those things could be headed right for my town, and we ain't gonna make it back in time if we go to Denver. You with me boy?" Martin elbowed Alexander.

Alexander hesitated, his brow scrunched. "The sheriff said we've got to get a message to the authorities."

"Come on, kid! Won't matter if we get the authorities if there ain't nothin' left of Morley," he said in a fierce whisper.

Alexander nodded. "You're right. I'm with you, Martin!"

All of them cringed at the loud sound of his agreement, even him. He covered his mouth, and Martin prayed the monsters hadn't heard.

In a whisper, Alexander said to Edgar and Anna, "Come with us. There's nothing left here for any of us."

The two of the nodded.

Their weapons ready and their eyes open wide, they started the long march back to Morley.

CHAPTER 69

Anxiety rose in Nantan's gut the more he thought about the white man's horse that had appeared in their camp. She'd been sweating and packed like she was on a journey, but she'd run in alone. He feared Calvin Drake, the first white man he'd ever respected, was dead.

He thought about the wendigo, once a myth but no longer. The wendigos had plagued the northern Algonquian tribes, never the Apache. He only knew of the demon because the Chief's great-grandfather had left for a time and heard the stories on his travels. Chief Taza used to tell the myth to little children on dark nights, but none of them believed those monsters would curse them. Children in these parts feared Big Owl eating them much more than wendigos.

They hadn't had an encounter with a wendigo in three days, so people breathed easier, hoping the plight ended. The horse arriving seemed to be a bad omen. Her path suggested she traveled from the north, where Vigil lay. Something must have transpired there or on the road. He'd awakened several more men to add to their usual sentries. That also woke a number of the women, who hustled about packing essentials in case of evacuation.

He couldn't stand the tension any longer. Without a word to the men around him, he marched to the Chief's abode and pushed his way inside. Nantan was not surprised to find the Chief's daughter and medicine woman to the village, awake. She seemed to have the uncanny ability to know exactly what happened in the village around her. She looked up at him, pausing from gathering important herbs along with bandages, salves and liquids into a large carrying bag.

243

Without a word, Nantan pressed his lips together and pointed to the Chief Taza, sleeping bundled snugly in his blankets to the side.

She woke her father gently.

The old man seemed confused at first, rubbing his eyes and glancing around. His eyes fell on Nantan and his features tightened. "Is it time?"

Nantan frowned, unsure what to make of the question.

"Is it time to escape the wendigos?" Taza clarified.

Nantan sighed loudly, squatting down. "I think so, great elder. The horse of the white trader has come here. She was alone but packed for a journey. I fear the wendigos have possessed her master and possibly even destroyed one of the white man's towns. The horse may have set them on a path here. I need your wisdom to guide me on what to do next."

The old man pondered his words while the medicine woman continued to pack. It seemed she'd already made up her mind on what the next course of action should be.

"A bird will abandon its nest if danger is perceived, whether that danger is real or not. If it did not listen to that instinct and the danger was present, it would be doom for the bird. What does your instinct tell you? Is there danger?" Taza stood up, stretching.

"I sense great danger."

"A good leader would heed his instincts. Better for his people to be scared and inconvenienced for no reason than to be attacked and killed in their sleep."

Nantan nodded, standing up. "We must escape. Move into the foothills. It must be done now." He feared they may already be too late.

CHAPTER 70

The sun shone brightly through the wispy curtains of the bedroom. Calvin woke up to the pleasant feeling of having Jane asleep in his arms, curled around him. He watched with a small grin as she breathed rhythmically in and out. His thoughts naturally went to what happened a few hours before, when they'd both woken during the night and wordlessly gave themselves to the other. The lovemaking had been unexpected but wildly passionate. She was incredible. He briefly considered waking her now for another round, but then he thought of the child down the hall.

Jane shifted, her cheek rubbing against his chest as she roused into wakefulness. She breathed out a moan of satisfaction. "I could get used to waking up like this." She tilted her head to rest her chin on his sternum and smiled at him, her eyes twinkling.

His fingers wound through her long brown hair, only let loose for sleep. "Yeah, guess it ain't so bad."

She giggled and sat up, still naked. "You going to get up, or do I have to drag you out of bed?" She swatted at his feet, then she sighed. "I can't get Martha out of my head. I might offer to take Simon off her hands for the day, maybe let him sleep over tonight. They've been so generous taking Emily for two nights in a row. I owe them that."

Calvin shift uncomfortably, unable to keep his eyes off her as she dressed. "Ya think it's alright with them sleepin' together? Ya know, like in the same room and all?"

She tilted her head. "Well, Emily's ten and Simon just turned eleven. Emily knows about the facts of life. I've already had to explain where

245

babies come from when Harry was born. I believe Simon does as well. Both of them act like they're being stabbed in the eye when they've seen adults being romantic, so I'm not too worried they've engaged in any inappropriate behavior yet."

"Yet? I swear the second that boy hits thirteen, he ain't stayin' here no more. If he does, he's on the sofa," Calvin grumbled.

Jane laughed, poking him in the foot. "Why, Calvin Drake, you sure sound an awful lot like an overprotective father."

His eyes widened for a moment. She was right. He narrowed them and he glared at her. "That boy just better keep his hands to himself."

Jane giggled as she left the room. "Very overprotective," she said as she closed the door.

He threw a pillow at the closed door.

Emily was already digging into her breakfasts when Calvin came downstairs. She didn't act fazed that he was still there.

"Good morning, Calvin!" Emily chirped, her mouth full of eggs and toast. Jane brought him a plate and sat it down on the table for him.

"Don't talk with yer mouth full, kid. Yer gonna spit on me."

Emily took a big swallow. "Eww. Sorry."

Once Jane finished her own breakfast, they got to work on the field of beets that had been so neglected. She gave Emily a choice: join them working in the field or stay in the house. She decided to stay in the house, complaining it was too hot outside, preferring to do inside chores. Jane emphasized the part about staying in the house.

In the field, the sun beat down on them, making them sweat. After a couple hours, both of them had their sleeves rolled up and were frequently wiping their brows.

"You should take off your shirt," Jane teased, growing bold around him.

He grunted. "You should take off yours."

She tried to hide a smile. "You'd like that, wouldn't you?"

He smirked. "Maybe."

Then he paused, his eyes on the ground in front of him. They were almost at the edge of the field. Jane walked up behind him, peeking over his shoulder. Her breath caught in her throat.

Several plants had been bent and broken, the dirt around them disturbed. A shallow hole in the ground contained a small open box, an amber bottle open inside. Large splotches of dark, dried liquid had sunk into the dirt around the area.

Calvin leaned down and sifted a small amount of the discolored dirt through his fingers. "Blood." Jane didn't say anything as he went to the box and lifted out the bottle. Examining the little bit of fluid left in it, he smelled it and then tasted the tiniest bit. "Opium."

"Opium?" Jane's voice squeaked.

Calvin dropped the bottle back down into the box. He faced her, his eyes piercing into hers. "I think this is where Zeke died. His blood. His snake oil." He kicked the box, which flipped closed.

Jane nodded, her eyes just staring at the closed box. "This is what he's been doing out here all these months. This is what he wasted our money on, letting the farm my parents built waste away. This was why he made our lives a living hell!" Her voice climbed an octave and her fists clenched tight as she stared at the box.

"Hey, stop." Calvin stepped up to her. His arm slid around her waist, drawing her into him.

Her body shook, every muscle tense. He could tell she tried desperately to keep control. He held her, his awkwardness at comforting her melting as he rubbed her back gently. "He's dead and ain't never comin' back. He can't hurt ya anymore."

She breathed deeply, wiping tears from her eyes, and drew back. "I'm glad he's gone. I'm glad you're here with me instead." She kissed him on the lips then turned away. "Think we should show this to the Sheriff? It means there were wendigos tramping through my fields."

Calvin nodded. "How 'bout you fix some lunch fer us and I'll take this over ta the sheriff?" He picked up the box, took her hand and led her back to the house.

CHAPTER 71

Bill sat in the office, nothing but quiet surrounding him. He needed to write his report. Needed to get down on paper how his ex-Deputy had taken half the town hostage and how his wife shot him dead. The pen hovered over the empty paper.

His mind churned as he tried to work out the events of the last few days. Did Victor really think he'd be able to simply walk into Bill's role after murdering him in a shoot-out? Perhaps he was more delusional and power-hungry than Bill originally assumed. Cora might've been the mentally unstable, but Victor had become insane right behind her.

The fact that he hadn't actually been the one to kill Victor should have been a weight lifted off his shoulders, but Martha's actions only added to it. Martha had realized Victor had become a danger and no amount of talking would've brought his sanity back long enough to stop him from shooting his gun, killing Bill or an innocent bystander. She blamed herself and took the responsibility off Bill.

He wondered briefly if Martha would've accepted Victor into her life if it had happened differently. Perhaps if the wendigo in Cora had killed him. Victor had blurted out that she'd said something to that effect, but when he'd guided her home in hysterics afterwards, she'd chokingly told him she never would have left him. He believed her, and Victor's words didn't matter now. An idea came into his mind. He wanted another child. Tommy was growing up so fast, and Simon wasn't far behind him. Harry would need someone to play with. It would be a happy event to help off-set all the recent bloodshed. Maybe it would be a girl this time.

The door behind him swung open, and Calvin Drake strolled in, stopping in front of the desk. Calvin tossed a small, wooden box at him. It clunked heavily on top of his blank report. Then Calvin put both hands on the edge and leaned in.

"Found Zeke's hidden snake oil in the middle of his field. Also looked like he'd been eaten up there too," Calvin stated matter-of-factly.

Bill blinked. "What?"

"Ya heard me. Bastard was drugging himself on opium out in the fields. Then that wendigo Indian woman ate him out there. Those wendigos are still wanderin' around in our town."

Bill examined the little amber bottle. "No wonder his farm was going to hell." He looked up at Calvin. "Take me to the murder site."

The two men hurried out of the sheriff's office. They slowed down as something odd emerged from around the bend. A horse walked slowly down the road, nearing the center of town. Bill squinted and realized with horror what they were seeing.

"Sky!" Calvin took off in a hard run towards his horse with Bill close behind.

A figure hunched over Sky's back. Her saddle and other riding gear were missing. The figure, obviously weakened, slid off her back, no longer able to keep himself upright.

"Martin!" Calvin screamed. His knees hit the dirt as he rolled the figure over on his back.

Bill skidded to a halt behind Calvin, breathing hard.

But it wasn't Martin.

It was Nantan. The Apache was in bad shape. A jagged bite wound lay open on his thigh and long scratches ran down his arm. His clothing hung in tatters. Nantan burned with fever, his face flushed red.

"Nantan, where's Martin?" Calvin patted the Indian gently on the face.

Nantan's voice sounded like it was being hauled over gravel as he spoke. "Horse came alone."

Bill filed that information away to be processed later. If Martin were dead, he'd deal with that fact when he didn't have a man dying right in front of him. "What happened to you?"

"Wendigos...attacked village. Horse warned us." Nantan feebly raised his hand to Sky. Then he gripped the front of Calvin's shirt, his hold strong. "Demons coming. Follow behind me..."

This warning captured Bill's full attention, snapping him into protector mode. "Wendigos are coming here? How many?"

Nantan seemed to struggle to find the correct word to convey the figure. He squeezed his eyes shut, his mouth working fruitlessly. Then he blurted out "Huge."

"A huge number of them?"

He nodded and gasped, his hand flying to his throat. "Kill me!" Blood droplets sprayed out his mouth, making them recoil.

Calvin gripped Nantan's shoulder in comfort. Then he stood up and pulled out his pistol.

Nantan nodded, eyes on the weapon.

"Thank you, friend." Calvin pulled the trigger.

CHAPTER 72

Bill and Calvin stood over the unmoving body of Nantan, concerned by both the condition he was in at the end as well as the warning he conveyed. Then Calvin looked out towards the horizon in the direction Nantan had come. He grabbed Sky's reins, whirled away from his friend's corpse and stalked off toward the Lansing farm.

Bill's head whipped up to Calvin's retreating back. "Hey!" He jogged to catch up.

Calvin whirled around, eyebrows drawn together and teeth clenched. "What? I can't just stand here gapin' at a dead body like an idiot. Once this is over, I'll come back and give him the respect he deserves. But not now. I probably lost my brother today to these goddamned wendigos, and I ain't gonna lose anyone else." He spun back around.

Bill matched his pace as he walked along the road with Sky. "Calvin, I'm sorry about Martin and the Indian. Martin turned out to be a better person than I ever realized. But there isn't anything we can do to help him right now. We need you, Calvin. This town isn't going to make it through this without you. Help me." Bill gripped Calvin's shoulder, halting the man's forward progress.

Calvin wrenched his shoulder away but did stop and eyeball the sheriff.

"Please," Bill implored him.

Calvin sighed heavily, his body seeming to relax slightly. "Damn it. Jane's gonna wanna help. She's all carin' like that. Okay, I'm in. But if she's in trouble, I'm ditchin' ya'll. Ya got that?"

Bill nodded. "Of course." He scanned the horizon like Calvin had done before, squinted his eyes, trying to detect any visible threat. "How long do you think we have?"

Calvin shrugged. "He was on horseback so movin' faster than most of the wendigos. Maybe two hours, little more if he got a good head start. What do ya want me to do?"

"We need figure out a plan and get everyone on board with it. Are you with me?"

Calvin nodded.

"We're going to need firepower. Get everyone you can gathered in the inn to put our heads together. I'll meet you there."

Calvin dashed across the street, ripping the door to the restaurant open.

Bill rushed home. Martha heeded his warning and gathered all the weapons in the house they had. They then locked the house tight and went to the sheriff's office, gathering every gun and all the ammunition stored there.

The whole town would soon be ready to do battle.

CHAPTER 73

Calvin rode past the schoolhouse. Panic threatened him, but he consciously willed it back down into his gut. It was like he couldn't move fast enough to get back to the farm. He wished he could push Sky into a full run, but she needed this little time for rest from her travels with Nantan. She'd be pushed to her limits soon enough and he didn't want to exhaust her more now. After all this was over, she would get a much-deserved rest and lots of sweet treats.

He reached the farm, ran to Jane's door and bolted inside, knowing Sky wouldn't wander far. "Jane! Emily!" For a second, he had this horrible sense that they weren't there. They'd left or been killed or turned into demons. His heart wanted to explode out of his chest, his mouth dry.

"Hey." Jane walked down the hallway from the kitchen. "The Sheriff didn't want to see all the blood in the field?" Then she examined his face and frowned. "What's wrong?"

Calvin swallowed. "They're comin'."

"Who?"

"The wendigos. A whole damned army of them. There ain't much time so we gotta get ready. Now." He seized her hand and pulled her into the kitchen. Emily sat eating lunch. Before she could open her mouth, Calvin blurted out. "Let's go, both of ya. A mass of wendigos is headed this way. Jane, get yer gun."

CHAPTER 74

It took only half an hour to get the entire town ready. After a very fast brainstorming session at the inn, they had a plan. Harold had come up with the idea and Bill couldn't help but be impressed by the city dweller's ingenuity. When they'd spread the word to the rest of the townsfolk, not one person had argued about the urgency of the situation. They all seemed scared, but none of them panicked. It made Bill proud that in a time of emergency, he could count on Morley to stand up for itself.

Now he stood with a large group of parents outside the McKenzie's farmhouse. Even though he knew there was precious little time before the wendigos came through, he decided to take just a moment to encourage his people.

"Listen, all of you. I've known most of you for years, and I trust that you'll all do your very best to help save this town. I don't know what's happening out there in the rest of the world right now, but it doesn't matter. What matters is us, here and now. We will survive this. I'm so proud of you all."

Some people smiled at him, others had tears in their eyes, while yet others nodded seriously at his words.

A swell of satisfaction rose in his chest. He'd rather have these people by his side than the entire Unites States Army. "Let's go kill these rotting demon spawn!"

With a cheer of concurrence, the townsfolk leapt into action. The children said farewell to their parents as they hustled into the house.

Jane hugged Emily fiercely. "You listen to what the adults say and stay as quiet as you can. We're going to get through this and I'll see you when it's all over. I love you, baby." Tears flowed freely down her face.

"I love you too, Mama." Emily wiped away her mother's tears, and she turned and latched onto Calvin in a tight hug.

The man tensed up, as if unsure what to do. Then he relaxed, actually wrapping his arms around her protectively. He chewed at his bottom lip but his gaze down at her blond head was more like a father's than Zeke had ever looked at her. Jane turned away, more tears gushing down her face.

Bill stepped aside as Tommy arrived with Simon and Harry. He took Emily's hand. She waved solemnly as the older boy lead her away. Bill nodded to his eldest son, almost a man now. Tommy would help protect the younger children to the end.

Bill passed guns out to anyone that didn't have one, along with boxes of ammunition. He'd raided the whole Morley stockpile of weapons. He hoped their plan would work and no shooting would be needed. But if events didn't go as planned, they'd need every chance possible. How would they survive if they ran out of bullets?

CHAPTER 75

Calvin left at a run to scout ahead for any signs the wendigos were already upon them. Jane walked quickly but silently back towards the center of town.

As she passed the inn, Lucy rushed outside and grabbed Jane's arm. "I'm coming with you!"

Jane tilted her head, glancing at Abigail and Isaac standing in the doorway. Abigail, standing upright and smiling, nodded to her.

"This army of wendigos is hitting your farm first. Calvin won't be there to help and you can't defend it yourself. I'm coming to help." Lucy stood up straight, dropping Jane's arm.

"Don't they need you here? What about the horses in the stable?"

"Bill and George took two of them so there's only three left. Besides, the stable's behind the main street, hidden from direct view. If Calvin does this right, the wendigos should go right by. Abigail can handle a gun and she and Isaac are going to keep feeding them to keep them quiet." Lucy pointed at Abigail, who held up a revolver.

"What about Harold?"

Lucy bit her lip and twisted her fingers together. "There was an incident with Roy Gaines."

"The man who never shows his face and only comes out at night?" Jane questioned.

Lucy nodded. "The sheriff said we don't have time to deal with him right now and there's too much risk of him making noise in the jail. So we've got him bound and gagged in the root cellar. Harold's down there to keep him quiet. But I think you need me more than he does."

Jane sighed. "I could use another hand. Let's go. There's not much time. But you've got to tell me everything once this is over."

Lucy grinned and nodded. Then she ran back to the door. She hugged Isaac first then gripped her little sister in a fierce embrace. "Just stay quiet," she advised them. Then she ran off with Jane.

As they came upon the farm, Calvin walked back toward them. "Way's all clear, for now at least. Gonna help y'all set up and then I gotta go," He led them to the barn.

They moved efficiently as a group, securing Bessie inside the stall farthest from the entrance. Unfortunately, there was no way to dismantle the chicken coop in order to get it in the barn. The chickens would have to go in another stall. Even though she nailed a blanket over the top of the stall, it didn't cover the entire opening. The chickens could flap out and roam free inside the barn. Jane desperately hoped they wouldn't attract too much attention from the wendigos. After the ravaging of the McKenzie's flock, there were only three chicken coops left in Morley, and no one knew how soon, if ever, supplies would come again.

Then the three of them raided the house, carrying chairs, tables, a coat stand, whatever they could manage. They propped everything outside the barn door, which had been nailed shut. With any luck, the barrier would hold.

With their guns loaded and every tool that could be used as a weapon piled in the front hall, the two women headed into the house. They would be stationed in the Jane's bedroom, which had a window with a perfect view of the barn. If the creatures did try to break into the barn to get the animals, they could shoot them from up there.

At the front door, Jane turned to Calvin. He needed to go. She knew that, even though it hurt her to think of what he must do. He, Bill and George had the most dangerous job of all of them, luring the wendigos into their trap. She studied his face, trying to memorize every line and every curve in case she never saw him again.

Unable to stop herself, she leaned in for a kiss, needing to feel his lips on hers one more time. She saw his eyes flick nervously to Lucy waiting on the stairs. Lucy smiled at them. Jane didn't want to embarrass him so she backed off, giving him a smile instead.

As she moved away, not wanting to prolong things, his hand snapped out and wrapped around her wrist. "Get back here," he growled and pulled her into his arms. His other hand pressed on the back of her neck as his mouth captured hers in a passionate kiss. He seemed to pour all his emotions for her into that kiss, leaving her breathless and lightheaded as he pulled away.

"Be careful," he told her in low, concerned voice.

"Been through worse," she assured him.

He nodded and left the doorway, whistling sharply.

Sky trotted over and he climbed on. She appeared somewhat more rested than before, no longer sweating and breathing hard.

Giggles burst out of Lucy. "Damn, that was something."

"Shut up," muttered Jane, who couldn't keep the smile off her face.

Together, the women marched up the stairs and waited for the show to start.

CHAPTER 76

The first one came into sight almost exactly two hours after Nantan's warning, just a black shape against the blue sky. A quick glance wouldn't have garnered much notice from a casual observer but even at this distance, Calvin could make out the creature's uncanny movements. He sat on Sky, the reins loose until now. Another one came into view, smaller than the first one, but followed by more and more. Waves of them cresting over the horizon, headed in his direction, seeking out the prey that had escaped them earlier.

While he'd only been waiting about ten minutes, he'd fidgeted, picking at a rough spot on his trousers. He'd never been good at just killing time. His mind drifted back to the kiss. He'd been so nervous when she'd leaned in like that, although he wasn't even sure what he'd been afraid of. She'd seen his panic and backed off, but when she'd turned away from him, he couldn't bear the thought of never touching her again. If he died, he wanted her to be the very last pleasant thing in his life.

Shaking his head to dispel the sweet but distracting memory, he centered his attention back on the situation at hand. He'd positioned himself on the road in between his house and the Lansing farm, wanting to make sure none of the undead wandered in her direction. They should all be focused on him and Sky. It was the most dangerous part of the plan, but he'd volunteered for it, not trusting anyone else with the role. If his timing was off, he'd be a dead man.

The monsters ambled closer. He wondered how many there were as more came into sight. Most of them were white. A small number of them were Indians and he feared they might've been from the Apache village. Children were mixed in also, a disturbing sight, but he ignored such feelings. He had to remember they were all murderous creatures, even the little ones.

The ones leading the group saw him. They picked up the pace, their arms now stretching to reach for him, growling and hissing more clearly. They were so desperate to grab him, but they just couldn't force their broken bodies to respond quicker. However, he noticed some of the outlying ones veering away, as if not realizing he was there.

"Hey, hellspawn! Come and get it!" he shouted at the top of his lungs.

That got their attention. Now every one he could see headed for him. Good.

Sky grunted and pranced on her feet, shaking her mane as the first rotting odor wafted over them. Calvin put a calming hand on her neck, gently rubbing her. The undead moved closer still, but Calvin waited. He counted slowly to five. He might not have been able to read, but he could at least count.

The wendigo in front had been a pretty woman in life. It was tall and thin with long, blonde hair and wearing a stylish red dress. Now as a demon-possessed monster, the skin on its face had become desiccated, pulling back off its mouth to reveal a grim smile of brown, blood-stained teeth. This one had been feeding. As it got within ten feet of him, Calvin pulled Sky's rein to spin her around. He dug his heels into her sides, and she took off at a gallop away from the approaching monsters.

He spared a glance at the house as he flew by. Then he raced headlong down the dirt road with Sky, drawing the wendigos after him. The flight of their prey spurned them on even faster as they poured down the road.

Calvin adjusted Sky slightly over to the side of the road as he approached Nantan's body still lying in the road where he died. There hadn't been time to move him, but someone had covered him with a sheet as a sign of respect. The creatures wouldn't bother him; he was beyond where they could hurt him. He murmured an apology to his friend as he hurtled past.

Morley's main street sat empty, as it should have been. Everyone needed to be out of sight in safe locations for this plan to work. He passed the blacksmith, the embers fully extinguished, and the Doc's place. He rode through the McKenzie farm, quiet as a coffin. He knew several people hid around him, watching for stragglers. The vacant fields still smelled of cattle, but all the animals had been corralled much farther out by the farmhands. Even one loose chicken could destroy the plan.

CHAPTER 77

Jane watched the road as Calvin sped by on Sky. She'd been waiting up in the bedroom, but they couldn't see anything in that direction. The tension had been killing her, and finally she'd gone downstairs. Lucy had protested because it left her much more exposed if anything came through the door, but Jane refused to listen.

She peered through a very narrow crack in the front door. They all knew Calvin had put himself in between them and the coming danger. It was a task he felt only he could do being the best rider in town, but she worried something would go wrong. Tremors of fear ran through her body, and her muscles already ached.

As Calvin rode by, she couldn't help but admire him. He was so strong and brave. From this distance, he really did look like the Greek god she'd called him. The bright sun shone down on his blonde hair and tanned skin, a fierce expression set on his face. If the situation hadn't been so dire, she might've swooned a little at the image of him. His head turned for one moment toward the house. There was no way he could see her, but she gave him an encouraging smile anyway, hoping he knew just how she felt about him. She loved him. He'd saved her and her child from a life on the road. He'd saved her from that Indian wendigo. If they both made it through this together, she resolved to tell him.

He flew out of sight down the road. Seconds later, the dead army chasing him came into view. He was in so much danger! A whimper escaped her lips at their frenzied hunt. She fisted her hand, and bit down on it to keep herself quiet. The mass of them surged after him.

"Jane! What's going on?" Lucy hissed from upstairs.

She looked up at her best friend. "There's so many of them. They're following him."

Lucy nodded. They both knew it was all part of the plan.

Jane turned back to the crack in the door. The mass still moved down the road after him, a testament to just how many of the monsters there were.

"Jane, get up here! Right now!" Lucy hissed again.

Jane glanced up, surprised that Lucy no longer stood at the top of the stairs. She raced up and found her looking out the window towards the barn.

"They must've come through the fields," Lucy murmured.

Frowning, Jane saw about twenty wendigos shuffling around her farm. A few more trickled in from the field even as she watched. Two of them seemed quite interested in the barn, examining the blockaded door. One tilted its head, like a dog that heard a sound. Jane held her breath, willing it to move on. Unfortunately, one of the animals inside must have made noise, because suddenly the thing desperately clawed at the barrier. Another followed suit and then another.

"Damn it!" Lucy spat out and pushed open the small window. Her gun fired, blasting away those demons closest to the barn. Several of the creatures spotted them, changed course, and banged against the wall of the house in an effort to catch them. However, the gun noise must have further disturbed the animals because quite a few more attempted to get into the barn.

Lucy's gun clicked with an empty sound as it ran out of ammo. Jane quickly took her place. She had little experience firing guns and was disappointed when she missed on her first shot. Her second and third shots hit true though, dropping two of the undead threatening her farm. Lucy hurried to reload behind her.

The gun in Jane's hand clicked empty. She was about to move out of the way for Lucy when her eye caught a disturbing sight. On the side of the barn, one of the boards must've been loose or rotten because she saw it starting to give as one of the small undead pushed persistently at it. If that thing got inside, her animals were dead. A number of others seemed to realize that this little one was onto something and crowded around it, pushing at the barn wall. Most of the ones in front had been dispatched but a few more came out of the field, joining the growing group on the side.

"Lucy, aim for the crowd right there!" Jane yelled. Lucy got in front of her and started shooting again. Jane reloaded as quickly as she could with shaking hands. Taking a fleeting look over Lucy's shoulder, she cursed. She couldn't see the little one anymore. Was it still in the crowd or had it slipped inside? She needed to know, right now.

Lucy's gun emptied, and Jane passed her the fully loaded one instead of stepping up to the window herself. Then she turned and practically jumped down the stairs.

"Jane, no!" Lucy screamed at her but didn't follow.

"I have to save my animals! I can't let them eat Bessie!" Jane wrenched the wicked-looking scythe out of the pile of tools on the floor. It was usually used for reaping the crops, but now she was going to be reaping monsters.

CHAPTER 78

Emily, Simon and Jacob stared out the front window. Emily's muscles cramped from being so tense, but she refused to move. Sweat trickled down her neck. They hid in the small, second floor sitting room in the McKenzie's farmhouse, the room eerily quiet despite the number of children crammed inside.

Emily glanced back at Clara, who attempted to distract some of the younger children with her old dolls. The children knew something bad was happening, but they didn't really understand what. Luckily, most put on brave faces and allowed themselves to be entertained. Twin girls took turns braiding each other's hair. A few of the older boys, who better understood the situation, sat on the floor in the corner playing the card game War. A young girl rocked a tiny baby boy, soothing him into sleep. Tommy played little Harry's favorite game with him, stacking wooden blocks. He laid on the floor, blocking the doorway, a rifle within reach.

Calvin rode fast down the road. Emily almost jumped up and down at her excitement to see him. Within a minute, the hungry mass of the undead followed behind him. Emily gasped and quickly covered her mouth. There were so many of them!

"Shit," Jacob breathed out softly.

Only the two next to him heard the curse, but Emily glared at the older boy. He spent too much time around Martin, starting to sounding like the abrasive man.

They seemed to be holding their collective breaths as they watched the creatures move down the road. Emily gripped Simon's hand and he gave her a squeeze back. However, his voice held a note of panic.

"They aren't all going to the ravine," he whispered.

As if the creatures below could hear him, some broke off from the hungry mass of undead pursuing Calvin. They shuffled towards the house and barns, just a few at first. By the end, over fifty had disengaged from the marching army and searched for fresh meat on the McKenzie farm.

CHAPTER 79

For the next several miles, Sky tried to pull farther ahead of the army of wendigos following them. Calvin had to loop back twice to make sure he stayed in their sight. Finally, the Purgatory River ravine with the rickety old bridge emerged into view. The project had been abandoned after Jane's brother had tragically fallen to his death eighteen years earlier. Calvin had heard whispers the young man had been trying to impress a girl.

Sweat ran down his face as Sky neared it. At this section of the river, the ravine plummeted down deep into rushing waters with no escape on either side. Surviving a fall was unlikely. The bridge showed its age with splintered and uneven wood planks rotting in the sun. Several open spaces indicated where some boards had already fallen.

"Come on, Calvin!" Bill and George waited for him across the chasm. They'd rode hard to go the long way around the ravine in order to get there in time. Bill waved frantically. Calvin noticed the little barrel on the bridge.

This had been a bad idea. The bridge would never support Sky's weight, even if he got off her back. In his head, the ravine had seemed narrower, but now it appeared as a great abyss, mocking him. He glanced back. The wendigos progressed towards him, a death more certain than the risky path ahead. He refused to entertain the thought of leaving Sky behind or veering off the other way. That would ruin their plan.

He whistled under his breath. He glimpsed the wendigos pressing forward. Not much time. Taking several deep breaths, he turned Sky around and rode towards the monsters several feet. They lunged at him in an even more frenzied pace, even though he remained out of range.

Turning back to the bridge, Calvin squeeze his legs tight around Sky and made a click with his tongue. She took off at a full gallop, dirt and stones thrown up in her wake. He leaned far forward in the saddle as she approached the bridge.

"Jump!" he shouted, urging her on with the reins.

Sky flung her head back and skidded to a stop just before hitting the bridge. She squealed then planted her feet, her body tense as iron.

"They're coming, Calvin!"

Calvin swallowed, his mouth dry and his heart racing. He stroked his horse's mane, scratching behind her ears. He ignored Bill's warning.

"I know this is scary," he whispered to her. "I know we could die on this bridge. But we're gonna die anyway if we stay put. I'd rather die tryin' ta save this town then get ripped apart. I believe in you, Sky."

The horse nickered, relaxing some.

Looking back, Calvin estimated there was barely enough clearance to get Sky back up to full speed. Grimacing, he rode her to within inches of the deadly creatures, turning her quickly. One wendigo reached out, trying to grab her tail. Its fingers whispered through the brown hair but couldn't get purchase as she reared up on her back legs.

Jumping forward, Sky ran for the bridge. Calvin had never seen her gallop so fast, as if she put her entire being into her speed. This time, she didn't hesitate. Calvin clutched at her mane, squeezing his eyes shut as they sailed through the air.

Half expecting to plunge down the ravine into the turbulent waters below, Calvin's was caught off-guard by the sudden, hard landing. His body launched out of the saddle. He only opened his eyes for a split second before he hit the rocky ground. The air whooshed out of his lungs.

He could hear his horse screaming. He forced his head to turn, scraping his cheek on the dirt.

"Sky!"

Sky had jumped an amazing distance, spanning most of the bridge.

She lay with her body on solid ground, but her back right leg was stuck between two of the boards. She tried desperately to lift herself up with her front legs. Behind her, the wendigos reached the bridge. Sky's eyes widened.

Bill had gripped Sky's halter, yanking with all his might, but it wasn't enough.

"Help her!" Calvin yelled at George, who sprinted in his direction.

George skidded to a stop and rushed to Sky. He grabbed the halter on the other side, pulling hard.

The wendigos surged forward, hungry for the incapacitated beast. Most of them fell off the edge of the ravine, but some successfully shuffled onto the bridge.

A loud snap sounded through the air. The broken board trapping Sky's leg detached from the bridge, falling away. Sky screamed again, fighting with renewed vigor.

Calvin struggled to get to his feet. He rolled to his side, aching and bruised. He leaned on his left arm as he heaved his body up. Red hot fire shot up his arm, and he writhed in pain, crashing back to the ground. Sparkles covered his vision right before it all went black.

CHAPTER 80

Duncan McKenzie threw open the barn loft door high above the wendigos milling around his property. Balancing on the edge, he pulled out his rifle, picking off the ones closest to the barn. Daniel joined him, shooting with a pistol.

The wendigos found their quarry, crowding in front of the barn, smashing into the large, locked doors. Emily could see the walls shaking from the force of their blows. A loud, creaking noise filled the air as one door cracked.

Duncan wobbled on the edge of the hayloft window as he tried to reload his rifle. He frantically grasped the wood frame, his rifle slipping out of his hands and falling into the group of monsters. Daniel reached out to grip Duncan's shirt, but he was too late. Duncan's weight threw him over as the barn shook from the door below collapsing inward. Duncan fell to the ground. The man hit hard then lay still. While most of the wendigos traveled into the barn, some backtracked, heading towards Duncan, now helpless.

Daniel desperately shot down at the demons surrounding Duncan until the bullets ran out. He didn't dare take the time to reload. He shouted at the wendigos below, catching their attention. Then he gripped the rope dangling from the pulley system to haul the hay into the loft and swung himself down to land right by his friend. He scooped up Duncan's rifle in time to slam the butt of the gun into the head of the wendigo descending with open mouth towards Duncan's face.

At that moment, Connor ran around the corner of the barn. He jerked as he took in the scene then ran to his unconscious son. He kicked the nearest monster starting to lean over Duncan with a savagery that crushed the thing's skull in. Then he pulled out two pistols and fired them simultaneously at the wendigos now attacking him.

Daniel crouched by Duncan's prone body. He fumbled to reload the pistol as Connor defended them. A wendigo emerged out of the darkness of the barn behind Daniel. It didn't look like Daniel saw it. and Emily crushed Simon's hand in fear for the clerk. Jacob made a choking sound, like he wanted to call out a warning to Daniel, but there was no way the man could hear him.

Daniel must have spotted the thing out of the corner of his eye because he ducked just as it reached out to grab him. Its arm swiped through the air over his head. On his knees, he brought the gun up to the thing's face and pulled the trigger.

Nothing happened.

CHAPTER 81

Jane sprinted outside and around to the barn, jumping over the bodies of the dead they'd already shot. Rather than pushing through the cluster of undead attempting to break into the barn on the side closest to the house, Jane headed straight for the barricade at the front. Squeezing between two tables, she shoved a chair out of the way and was able to get the door open just enough to let her slip through.

Jane surveyed the damage in the barn. The little one, a dead boy probably younger than Emily, was devouring one of the chickens. Another one had also broken in, a little bigger than the boy, possibly a young girl. It, too, was destroying one of her chickens. Bessie the cow was on the other side, in her stall. Even though Jane could hear the frightened movements of the animal, the two hadn't yet noticed the cow, too engrossed in their chicken dinner.

A quick glance at the small opening almost made her smile. Lucy had managed to kill a large wendigo that must've been in front of the crowd. Unable to understand the difference between pushing and pulling, the creatures behind the downed one had firmly wedged the body into the hole. They'd inadvertently cut off their entrance.

She gripped the scythe firmly, having only used it a few times before. With a deep breath, she swung at the nearest one, which had its back to her. The head bounced away, the mouth still opening and closing but harmless for the moment.

The larger one become aware of her and dropped the chicken carcass to launch itself at her. Jane brought the blade around barely in time before it hit her, but she managed to cut into the head, and the thing fell into her. Dead, black blood splash out and covered the front of her dress. With a sharp cry, she pushed against the rotting flesh and got herself clear of it.

CHAPTER 82

Bill pulled with everything in him on Sky's halter. It was like trying to move an elephant as he avoided getting kicked by her thrashing front legs. Large numbers of wendigos fell off the side of the cliff. Yet, Bill warily watched wendigos attempting to cross the bridge. He tensed as he watched a wendigo almost tip the small barrel he put on the bridge.

George joined the effort a moment later. The giant, black man far outweighed him, and Bill hoped George's brute strength would make the difference. But when board trapping Sky's leg shattered, the horse finally broke free. She stumbled as she regained her footing, shaking her head as she trotted away to the two other horses several yards away.

"Sheriff, the wendigos!" George pointed at the bridge.

Bill spun around, his gun out. More and more monsters plunged into the ravine but two of the putrid creatures managed to cross the bridge. They reached out for him, their blank, white eyes bulged and their jaws snapped open and shut. He shot both through the forehead.

A few more made it across the bridge, driven by their hunger. George used Lucy's trusty shotgun bestowed upon him for this occasion to dispatch them.

"Get him!" Bill pointed at Calvin. "We've got to finish the plan."

George raced to the unconscious Calvin, throwing him over his broad shoulder, and hurried away from the bridge. "Do it now, Sheriff!"

Bill dashed a few paces back. A long fuse stretched to him from the barrel on the bridge. With a sense of urgency, he whipped a box of matches out of his pocket and slipped one out. Before he could strike it, he caught sight of another wendigo crossing the bridge. He watched in horror as it tripped over the fuse line.

Only by sheer miracle did the barrel jostle but not tip off over the side. Unfortunately, the fuse line pulled out from its anchoring point. As the wendigo tumbled down into the ravine, the fuse line tangled around its foot, snatching it out of Bill's hand as it fell. Bill's stomach dropped as his plan crumbled.

Shots rang out as George fired on the oncoming wendigos. His eyes widened as he looked between Bill and barrel. Calvin lay at his feet, his skin deathly pale.

There was no choice now. Bill pulled his badge off his shirt and pushed it into George's hand. "Give this to my family. Get as far away as you can!" He shoved at George and turned back to the bridge.

George's big hand tangled in his shirt, halting his forward progress. "No, Sheriff! Let me do it."

There was no time to argue. With all his strength, Bill punched George in the face. The man stumbled backwards, going down to one knee. As Bill ran back to the bridge, he yelled. "I can't lose anyone else! I'm the sheriff, and it's my job to protect the townsfolk of Morley!"

Bill kneeled down by the barrel, glancing at the seemingly never-ending stream of wendigos reaching for him but falling instead. However, several wendigos stumbled across the bridge out of sheer luck and attacked him. Their sharp fingernails scratched trails of blood through his sleeves as he shoved them out of his way. He yanked the matches out again.

Closing his eyes, he drew in a slow breath. Teeth bit into his shoulder, tearing his flesh, but he ignored the pain. His mind focused on a picture of his family. Tommy, Simon, little Harry. Martha.

Then he struck the match. The tiny flame blazed, capturing his attention with its beauty. Then he shoved it into the barrel full of black powder.

The enormous explosion enveloped his body, the wendigos surrounding him and the old Purgatory River bridge.

CHAPTER 83

Daniel looked at the gun, dumbfounded. He couldn't tell if it was empty or jammed, but it didn't matter. It wasn't working. The dead thing lunged for him, and Daniel scrambled backwards in a crab crawl, leaving Duncan unprotected. Daniel swept his leg around, knocking the creature to the ground. It grabbed his foot, and he tried to shake it off, his eyes wide and mouth open in a silent scream as he retreated.

Duncan sat up, his eyes squeezed tightly closed. His hand held his head, a few drops of blood leaking between his fingers. He was too dazed to realize the mayhem occurring around him.

One of Connor's pistols ran out while three wendigos converged on his position. His second pistol took out two before it emptied, and he whipped out a knife as the last one reached for him. He tried to grip it with arthritic fingers, but it slipped out of his hand. Connor threw his body at the monster, sending the wendigo sprawling into the dirt as he recovered his knife. He urgently tried to get to his unprotected son, slamming his knife into the forehead of the wendigo in front of him, but another hit him from behind.

"Oh, no. No!" Connor screamed, his eyes on his only son.

Half a dozen wendigos descended on Duncan. His eyes opened just as the first one bit into his arm. Then they just overwhelmed him, biting and clawing. His screams echoed across the farm, drawing more demons to him.

Shots fired out of the windows of the house. They knocked down several of the wendigos enveloping Duncan. But it was too late. One of

Duncan's legs stuck out of the bodies piled on him, and it jerked wildly. After few moments, it stilled. He was beyond any help.

Rebecca ran out of the house, firing a rifle at the creatures devouring her brother. Tears streamed down her face, bullets flying wild. A few hit the wendigos in their heads, but several hit Duncan's body and ricocheted off the barn.

Daniel gasped then sprinted towards Rebecca, ducking a bullet whizzing by. The wendigo he'd been grappling with lay motionless, its head stomped flat. He tackled his love, pushing the firing gun into the air and saving her from the clutches of the creature creeping behind her.

CHAPTER 84

Jane recovered the surviving chickens and threw them back into the stall next to Bessie. She hoped they'd say there. Then she slipped back out the door, encountering several more wendigos. Jane lopped off the head of one of them but when she swung at the next one, her blade lodged in its shoulder. It reached for her with grasping fingers, and Jane was forced to release her hold on the weapon. There were no more sounds of gunfire, and Jane knew they'd run out of bullets. Even though there weren't that many undead left, there were enough to overwhelm the women without more weapons.

From the field she was being driven toward, four more wendigos emerged. There'd be no way to avoid them any more than she could avoid the three that pursued her. This could be the end of her life. Now, when she'd finally found happiness. Her heart squeezed. Emily. Surely Calvin would take care of her. Her hands shook as she pulled out her small knife, desperate to survive, to be there to watch her daughter grow up, to tell Calvin she loved him.

Unexpectedly, the four wendigos from the field passed her and attacked the three in front of her. Jane blinked in shock as she watched the new figures using knives to dispatch them. Despite being covered in gore and smelling like rot, it was obvious they were human. And two of them she knew! With a breath of overwhelming relief, her knees gave out and she dropped to the ground.

Martin drove his knife through the eye of the one closest to her. As Alexander and the other two people took care of the stragglers, Martin smiled down at her.

"Damn, woman. Yer a mess. Looks like ya'll had a bit of action here, didn't ya?" He laughed and offered her his hand.

She gratefully accepted.

CHAPTER 85

Emily whirled around, face red and teeth clenched. She'd just watched Duncan McKenzie torn apart by wendigos. Daniel, Rebecca and Connor still faced great danger. She couldn't just watch anymore. "We have to do something!" she cried.

Tommy hustled to the window beside them and saw the carnage. Clara got up to follow, but he immediately motioned her back. Tommy pulled out the gun his father had entrusted to him and threw open the window in front of him. "Maybe we can help them." He took careful aim and fired. One of the wendigos shambling after Connor hit the ground. None of the others seemed to notice. He did it again, missing the second time and hitting the side of the barn. He groaned loudly. With only a few remaining, he picked off all the rest, then closed the window.

Connor kneeled beside Duncan's mangled body, crying. He touched his son's face, gray and streaked with blood. Daniel and Rebecca lugged the dead wendigos off him, then stood by Connor. The old farmer stood, wiping his nose absentmindedly on his sleeve. Rebecca let out a wail and clutched her father in the tight hug. Together they wept as Daniel guided them back in the house.

Doc Silverstein emerged from the house, stopping at Duncan's prone form. He touched Duncan's unscathed shoulder then his lips moved with unheard words. He stood and looked up at them watching him from the window. He motioned them to back away.

"Come on, let's not watch this." Tommy closed the window and steered Emily, Simon and Jacob in the corner. Then he gathered Clara in his arms and held her close.

A gunshot echoed through the air.

CHAPTER 86

The clomping of the horse's hooves underneath him gradually brought Calvin back to awareness. He rested in a void of blackness, only the gentle sway of his body allowing him the luxury of knowing he still survived. Then he frowned as he realized the pattern was uneven, a little hiccup with every other step. Sky was limping.

The nagging sensation of burning tickled over the skin of his face, neck and arms, which grew more uncomfortable as consciousness dawned. His eyes struggled to open, the lids glued shut with dried tears. He forced them open, everything blurry. His body had been draped over Sky, and he dared not move yet. A faint hint of burned fur wafted over his nose.

"Almost there. Almost there. Almost there." The mumbling seemed like a chant, the chant of a desperate man reassuring himself he would reach his destination.

Calvin blinked, clearing the ocular residue from his vision, and stared at George's back. It appeared as if his shirt had been burned off from the bottom of his shoulder blades down. Blistered of various sizes covered his back, and despite his dark skin, redness radiated from him. He also limped as he led Sky along.

Too disoriented to know exactly where they were, he could hear the river to his right. George had traveled many miles, away from the ravine, down to the shallowest area to crossover, and now headed back to Morley. Calvin had been unconscious for hours.

Picking up his head, he shifted his body to sit up. Air exploded from his lungs and nausea rolled through his stomach as the pain in his left arm reemerged. It didn't knock him out again though. He groaned loudly.

Stopping in his tracks, his mantra pausing, George slowly turned to look at Calvin. Tears coursed down his cheeks, his eyes were red. "Almost there," he stated once more.

Calvin gently slid off Sky, not putting any pressure on his left arm. His legs almost collapsed under him, but he gripped the saddle awkwardly with his right hand and managed to stay standing. He glanced around and realized they truly were almost there, only a few miles from Morley. "What happened?" Calvin's voice sounded like sand had been shoved down his throat.

George swallowed. "Couldn't get the black powder to go up. Had to do it himself." He swallowed again and sucked in a large breath. "Tried to cover you, to protect you. Bill…" He shook his head and more tears ran from his eyes.

Calvin grimaced. The sheriff had sacrificed himself. Brave man.

"Where are the other horses?" Calvin glanced around for them.

"Ran off with the blast. I could only stop Sky from running."

"Come on, we're almost there." Calvin took the reins from George. Together, they slowly trudged along.

As they reached the edge of Morley, he found about half the town ready to set out as a search party for them. His family. It was the most welcome sight Calvin could imagine.

Emily sprinted ahead, whooping with joy as she crashed into him, almost knocking him off his feet. She bumped into his left arm.

He screamed, his right arm circling his body to cradle the injury.

Emily leapt back. "I'm sorry, Calvin! I've hurt you."

Jane appeared at his side, her hands caressing his left arm softly. "Oh, Calvin, it's broken."

Seeing her, totally covered with gore and her dress shredded, shocked him. He'd left her safe in the house. That meant she'd left it, gone outside to fight. It made him want to punch something to know she was forced to face that kind of danger.

Lucy must've seen the rage on his face. "You should've seen her with that scythe, Calvin. A real banshee slaughtering those wendigos. She saved her own farm."

Jane's face colored red, but she met his eyes.

Emily stared at her mother with wonder. "Really, Mama? You saved the farm?"

Jane bit her lip, nodding.

Calvin's chest filled with pride, melting his heart. Despite her being splattered with dead, black blood, he slid his hand behind her neck and pressed her forehead into his. "Prouda you. Don't do it again. And the Doc'll fix my arm." Shifting his body, he pulled Jane and Emily into a warm embrace, never wanting to let them go. Then his eyes widened as a smirking Martin strolled over.

"Damn, baby brother! You got some serious sunburn!" He poked Calvin's burned cheek.

"I thought you was dead. Nantan rode in on Sky, not you."

"Wendigos tried. Boy, did they try! Thought I was a goner, but I found me some help in Virgil."

Calvin snorted. He should've figured nothing, not even a plague of flesh-eating demons, could kill his big brother.

Tommy emerged from the group, Simon and Martha behind him. His eyes scanned the immediate area. "Where's my Pa?"

George fell to his knees, blubbering sobs shaking his huge body. Lucy stepped to his side, touching his shoulders, but he barely noticed. "He...he wouldn't let me do it." He sobbed harder. "Said it was his job to protect the townsfolk of Morley." George broke completely, leaning over to put his head in the dirt.

Lucy gasped when she saw the damage done to George's back from the explosion.

Martha turned white. Her fingers climbed up to her neck, gripping the lace there. Her mouth moved, but no sound emerged. Empty eyes stared out at the horizon. She didn't seem to register the wailing of her middle son.

Tommy caught her as she swooned. His grim face set as stone as he laid her down, cradling her head. "It was his duty. He never shied away from his duties." The monotone quality of his voice betrayed the emotional turmoil underneath.

Emily disengaged herself from Calvin, her arms encircling Simon.

Martin stepped over, laying a hand on the boy's shoulder. "Yer papa was a decent man and fair sheriff." Martin took off his hat.

Everyone there followed suit, heads bowed.

"Your father was a hero."

CHAPTER 87

Calvin nodded his thanks to the Doc and his assistant as they finished tying the leather straps to Sky's saddle, then departed. Calvin looked down at the body of his friend, carefully wrapped in a white sheet and securely bound to a makeshift wooden stretcher. He alone would take Nantan back home. Both Jane and Martin had offered to join him, but this was something only he could do.

Nantan had saved all their lives, just like Bill. If he hadn't come to warn them, they would've been wiped out by the mass of wendigos. Calvin had only just begun to realize what kind of life he could have with Jane and Emily, and it might've been lost before it even really started. Calvin didn't know how he would ever repay his friend for his sacrifice, but he knew the Apache brave would rest more peacefully back with his people.

As he neared the Indian camp. he noted a lot of activity, people moving around on various errands. That was good. He'd been worried that the entire tribe had been destroyed. It looked like the majority of them had been unharmed.

Several braves standing watch confronted him before he could draw closer. Almost all of them brandished spears and arrows already notched in bows pointed in his direction. He even noticed that two of them held rifles. This was a new occurrence he hadn't seen previously when dealing with the native people.

The leading man jogged ahead, his rifle gripped tightly. Calvin held up his hands. The brave paused and blinked at him. His eyes shifted over the horse, and his grip on the gun loosened. He barked out a command to the men behind him, causing them to stop and relax their own weapons.

To Calvin, he spoke "Sky." He stepped forward and delicately touched her soft nose. "Sky," he said again with reverence.

Calvin nodded and indicated the stretcher she dragged. "Nantan," he said, his voice also filled with reverence. Stooping down, he gently moved the sheet away. The body had been prepared with care, the blood washed off and the hole in his head covered with hair.

The brave stood up. He waved the other men forward, speaking softly to them. One younger man broke off in a run back to the camp while the others carefully untied the stretcher from Sky's saddle. As they lifted it on their shoulders and carried the body of his friend away, Chief Taza returned with the young brave. The old man panted as he rushed towards Calvin, taking in the scene.

Taza stopped inches from Calvin, and he had to fight the urge to take a step backwards. The Chief examined him from head to toe His expression was unreadable, and for one moment, Calvin feared that he would be blamed for Nantan's death. While it was true that the brave had been bitten, it was Calvin's own gun that had officially ended the man's life.

Taza pursued his lips and Calvin waited on edge for the man to speak. He was caught off-guard by the words.

"Thank you for sending your spirit animal to warn us of danger and bringing our brother home," Taza stated, saying each word clearly and distinctly. Then he did something even more unexpected. The Chief of this Apache tribe bowed to Calvin. He watched in amazement as all the Apache people around him bowed as well. Tears pushed from the backs of Calvin's eyes, and his throat closed. He sucked in a few deep breaths as everyone straightened back up and went back to their normal activities.

The Chief laid his hand on Calvin's shoulder, and looked him directly in the eyes. "Nantan would be proud." Then he walked away, leaving Calvin and his horse alone on the edge of the village.

EPILOGUE

Jane lay on her back, her shoes strewn haphazardly on the ground beside her, staring up at the fluffy clouds gliding across the bright blue sky. She'd brought out a big blanket from the house and spread it across the ground, intending not do anything productive that day. She decided they'd all earned a rest day. Because of their efforts yesterday, the town had been saved from the awful wendigos. The sad exceptions had been poor Bill and Duncan.

The cloud directly overhead had looked like a little house with smoke coming out of the chimney, but it slowly mutated into a big fish as it moved lazily. A breeze swept over her, cooling her skin under the warm sun. She buried her bare feet in the lush grass of her front yard.

She'd almost drifted into unconsciousness when his body plopped down on the blanket next to her. Her eyes opened and squinted at him in the sunlight, meeting his warm gaze watching her. He twitched his lips up at her in a crooked smile.

She rolled on her side to face him. "How did it go with Nantan's people?"

"Good."

She leaned in slowly and kissed him sweetly on the mouth. That brought on a full grin from him. She pulled back and laid a hand on his chest to halt him from trying to claim another kiss from her.

"Calvin, I have to say something. When I was facing down those wendigos, thinking it was the end for me, I promised myself that if I ever saw you again, I would tell you everything inside of me." She paused, took a deep breath and then plunged right in. "I love you, Calvin Drake."

He stared at her, as if having difficulty comprehending her language. He swallowed thickly, his throat seeming to be working but no noise coming out.

She cupped his face to calm him. "It's okay. I don't need to hear the words. I just needed to say them. I just needed you to know."

Calvin nodded, then wrapped his arm around her shoulder and pulled her into him. His mouth captured hers in a passionate kiss.

"Hey, stop kissing on the lawn!" came an indignant voice from above.

They broke apart and looked up at Emily, who seemed impossibly tall standing over them. Then the girl smiled and dropped down on the blanket next to her mother, giggling.

Jane looking up at the sky again, joy filling her heart. Her hands clasped the two people she loved best in the world lying on either side of her. Together they watched the big fluffy clouds move across the beautiful sky.

"I love you, too, Jane Lansing," Calvin whispered.

THE END

ABOUT THE AUTHOR

Robin Goldblum is an award-winning writer and veterinarian. She lives in Montgomery County, Pennsylvania with a wonderful husband and their three beautiful but rambunctious children. When she's not healing small animals (if you can call Irish Wolfhounds and Great Danes small) she sneaks time to write. Her first book was inspired by a family trip to the ghost town of Morely, Colorado.

Visit Robin's website at www.robingoldblum.com to further explore Robin's writings!

A TASTE OF LUCY AND HAROLD'S STORY...

Lucy knew it was now or never. He had finished eating, was probably ready to get back to work, and if she didn't act quickly, it would become awkward. Before he could fully comprehend what she was doing, she crossed the room and sat down in his lap.

He instantly went rigid. His eyes wide as saucers behind his glasses. She kissed him, pressing her mouth to his.

He didn't respond, just sat there stiffly except for his hands curling around the arms of the desk chair. She moved her lips against his, hoping to elicit a response but none came.

She was making herself look like an idiot at best, or a whore at worst. She broke the kiss.

"Sorry, this was a mistake." She jumped off his lap and made for the door, trying not to cry at her own stupidity. Before she'd taken two steps, he caught her hand and pulled her back onto his lap. She landed on him hard, but he didn't flinch.

"I don't think that was a mistake," he said softly. "I've wanted to kiss you since I met you. I just wasn't prepared for it. You're such a beautiful, lively, intelligent woman, and I can be such a bore. Can we try again?"

Lucy pressed her lips together and nodded, still trying to hold back tears. She leaned forward and kissed him again. This time he responded, his lips meeting hers. His hands came off the arms of the desk chair, one curling around her waist and the other brushing through her hair.

It was nice and sweet, just kissing him. His fingers tightened a tiny bit on her waist, which she liked. He deepened the kiss.

Out of nowhere, a deafening bang splintered through the room. The two of them leapt out of the chair, knocking into the desk. A stack of papers shifted and fell. Some of the pages caught a draft and wafted across the room, but neither of them noticed.

Their attention focused solely on the small hole in the floor. A tiny wisp of smoke curled up from it. Lucy's eyes moved to the ceiling. A matching hole sat directly above the one in the floor.

Bile rose in Lucy's stomach as her anger soared. "Who the blazes is shooting up my inn?" She ran for the stairs with Harold right behind her.

Made in the USA
Middletown, DE
05 September 2019